1

Wastelanders: Part 1

"An exciting new voice in the Young Adult Genre. The Wastelanders **is** the new Hunger Games!"

Stewart MacKay. Author of ' The Angel of Charleston'

"From the opening page The Wastelanders grips tight and refuses to let go."

Robert Campbell. Author of 'The Gold Rim Perspective'

"Never mind The Hunger Games. The Wastelanders is the one. Great book. Great Writing. Bring me more Nicholas Grey."

Dr DDS MacKay. Author of 'The Net and The Fish'

The Wastelanders: Part 1

Nicholas Grey

The Wastelanders: Part 1

GableHouse. Ltd

For Katharine:

Couldn't have done it without you!

"Battle not with monsters, lest ye become a monster, and if you gaze into the abyss, the abyss also gazes into you."

Friedrich Nietzsche.

"Three things cannot be long hidden: the sun, the moon, and the truth."

Buddha.

Prologue

The air is cooler at the top of the metal ladder and she gratefully fills her lungs before turning and squinting back into the gloom of the tunnel below. The space has narrowed but the knowledge that she's almost made it gives her a sense of renewed hope.

Slowing her breathing she tries to remain as silent as possible, tries to listen out for any tell-tale signs that someone has followed. But there is nothing. Only the sound of blood rushing in her ears as she grips on to the metal.

Stretching a hand out above her head she feels for the wheel she knows will be there and tries to squash the fear that is threatening to return, threatening to overwhelm everything. If it turns then the air vent will open and she can get out. But if it doesn't…

Her head snaps back as a sound reaches her from below. Something is scraping along the rungs of the metal ladder.

It can't have found me already!

Turning back to the wheel, both hands gripping the cold metal, she focuses all her strength on turning it just a few more inches.

"Come on. COME ON!"

Nothing.

The noise sounds again as she strains against the metal, pain shooting across her shoulders as she struggles to maintain her footing on the ladder.

"Please! Please…" Images begin to flood her mind, images of teeth and claws and it's all she can do not to scream out in panic.

Gripping harder on the wheel she strains until the veins in her temples throb, ready to burst, the scratching sound moving nearer and nearer.

And then the smell hits her. The smell she's been forced to live with for as long as she can remember. Rotting meat.

The stench fills the air as her whole body burns with effort.

And then it moves.

It's no more than a fraction of a centimetre but it gives her hope and she redoubles her efforts, pushing against the metal until the wheel moves again, this time a little easier.

Each time it turns she can hear the air vent above creak open a little more and adrenalin keeps her going as she ignores the shooting pains in her arms, the stench of filth that is all around.

The scraping sound on the ladder below.

A rush of fresh air tells her that the vent is almost fully open but despite her eagerness to squeeze through she turns the wheel a few more times because if she gets stuck, if she is unable to get above ground…

Letting go of the wheel she pivots her body to the left until her face is fully exposed to the cold night air. Reaching across to the lip of the vent she presses her foot down hard on the next rung up and pushes out until her arms and head are through and into the open.

For a split second her legs dangle in empty space and she closes her eyes against the images of what might be reaching for her out of the dark. Digging her fingers into the ground, she hauls the rest of her body out until she is left lying on her back, gasping for air.

Shut the vent.

Pushing up on her elbows she scrabbles across the dirt and slams her weight against the lid until it begins to give way under the pressure, a clanging sound as it hits the metal rim telling her that she is safe, for now.

Looking up the moon is full in the sky and as she gets her bearings she looks to her right, to where the Great Wall should be, five hundred yards or so, looming up at her like some giant's play thing. She's got to get there, she's got to let them know what's happening, but where is it? Why can't she see it?

And then the realisation hits.

She can't see the Wall because it's shrouded in mist.

For a moment the knowledge doesn't sink in as she lies there in the dark, and then the panic of earlier begins to return, holding her throat in its vice like grip. The Mist shouldn't be there, not *tonight*. It's not meant to return for days yet.

The thought turns in her mind as she begins to crawl away from the vent, the first wisps of the mist crawling along the ground towards her like so many bony fingers.

I've got to warn them! I've got to warn them!

But it's not the Mist she's afraid of and it isn't the Mist that stops her in her tracks as the smoky fingers begin curling around her ankles.

It's what the Mist contains that fills her mind with fear. The shadows she can see moving around.

The gnashing of teeth and the scraping of claws.

And the stench of rotting meat that accompanies them.

Chapter 1

My eyes begin watering as I look up at the sky, squinting against the sun's glare. There's not a cloud anywhere, nothing, except the bird that I'm following as it swoops and rolls high above my head. I can't remember the last time I saw one this close up and my heart beat quickens as adrenalin begins to build.

Steadying myself on the rooftop, I shift my weight from leg to leg as it dips its wings and begins to drop like a stone until I think it's going to hit the ground for sure. My right foot stretches towards the edge of the roof as I lose sight of it in among the slums of Sanctum.

The place I call home.

I scan the top of the broken down roofs, the scattered and rotten remnants of people's homes, desperate to catch another glimpse and then my head pivots to the right as I see the bird burst from nowhere and streak upwards like a rocket, a black dot against the vastness of the sky.

The bird slows before beginning a wide circle directly above me, as if it knows I'm here watching it, *willing* it to pick me up in its talons and lift me high in the air, far beyond Sanctum and its damned walls, to whatever lies out there on the horizon.

Beyond the Wasteland.

I smile as the idea takes hold, to be beyond the city's great walls, to be out *there*, and extend my arm, reaching my hand out, willing the bird to come closer, my skin tingling as I imagine Sanctum disappearing below.

Thwump.

The noise jolts me from my daydream and I don't even realise it's an arrow until it knocks the bird sideways, embedding itself in its chest, a shower of feathers as it drops like a stone towards the streets below.

Moving to the edge of the roof I crouch down before peering over to the mass of people below like so many ants, desperate to scrounge whatever they can before the sun goes down. Before the curfew sounds.

I guess the arrow must have come from one of the other streets beyond because I can't see anyone fighting over it; not yet anyway. For a brief moment anger rears up, but it soon gives way to reality as the hollowness of my stomach begins to gnaw away at me, and then all I feel is shame.

Nothing lasts long in this damn place! Not peace, not quiet and certainly not anything edible and a picture begins to form in my mind, a picture of the bird being plucked and cleaned, roasted on a makeshift spit, a small meal but a meal nonetheless. All other thoughts of the graceful flight, of soaring high above the great walls, disappear.

My mouth fills with saliva and before I can stop myself I slip from the roof and twist as my hands grip the edge so I'm hanging from the tips, my face flat against the wall below. Shimmying along the edge I let desire spur me on and feel with my right foot for the piece of wood that's jutting out a few inches.

Shelters are so hastily put up in the slums that people use whatever materials they can and don't care what the end product looks like. It makes the place look like an endless row of broken teeth but it also provides a million and one things to climb over and as I balance on my left foot I'm able to take the pressure off my arms and my fingers thank me as I wriggle life back into them.

Crouching down on the piece of wood, I spread my arms out against the wall for balance and turn my head towards the bird that is still lying on the floor no more than thirty yards from where I now hang.

Sliding my hands over the wall until I find a crack big enough for my whole right hand to fit into I look around for a foothold, moving my left leg as far as it will reach until I'm almost horizontal. Stepping away from the wood my fingers and toes do the rest as they search out cracks and holes and I zig zag down the wall until dropping the last five feet or so, landing with a thud in the dirt below.

Then I'm back on my feet eager to reach the prize on the other side of the lane, but down here at ground level there's too many people and as I weave my way through I'm careful not to push into anyone. Confrontation is never far from the surface, especially when the sun begins to go down.

All I am to these people is just another of Sanctum's unwanted, another orphan in rags looking to steal whatever I can find. Well that's fine with me because it happens to be true, and I just happen to be pretty good at it! I guess I have to.

What other choice is there?

As I near the other side of the lane I can see a small group gathering and my heart sinks because I can't see the bird anymore and a feeling of anger wells up as I picture someone else tucking into its flesh. There's tension in the air, like something is about to happen, as if there's about to be a fight. The atmosphere can change in an instant down here and you soon learn how to tune into it. You have to.

Stepping to my right I circle the group as voices begin to rise.

"…saw it first!"

"…over my dead body…"

I count at least five people, but can sense that more are beginning to get interested. And then the tension explodes in a whirl of fists and arms and I'm practically swallowed up by the mayhem as the mass of bodies threatens to drag me into its orbit.

Dodging to my left a flying elbow catches me on the shoulder and I half stumble to the ground as more and more get involved.

I know I should go but the hollow feeling in my stomach drives me on as a kind of excitement begins to grip. This is what hunger does to you. This is what living in *Sanctum* does to you. It forces you to crawl through the dirt and filth for the promise of a morsel of food that you'll probably never get.

It strips you of your humanity and dignity.

It makes you behave like an animal.

Crawling to my left trying to dodge the bodies I see the face of a man looming over me, scarred from eye to chin. I know what he's trying to do, he's trying to escape the others, trying to get to the food but his left arm is caught by someone and he starts to resist being pulled back.

"Get that bird for me boy!" I scramble back as he leers at me, pulling at the crowd, trying to tear himself away. I can smell his breath as he pushes forward until our noses are practically touching. It smells like disease and I try not to gag. I see the scar, a deep angry slash of red. "Bring it here boy or I swear…"

And then he's dragged back into the crowd and I scramble backwards pushing at the ground with my feet, feeling behind me in the dirt with my hands. I should never have come down here, not on my own and certainly not this late in the day, this close to curfew. What if the Guards come along?

The thought fills me with renewed panic and I push again against the dirt, the flying fists and arms getting larger now as more people join, people who have gone the whole day with no food or water, who are on their way to wherever it is they sleep with no hope of a full stomach. People who've got nothing left to lose.

At least the fighting and yelling is *something*. At least the cuts and bruises are *real*. Better than just being left alone with the thoughts in your own head.

As I push back I feel a cold hard surface against my back and figure I must have made it to the far wall. I begin to gather myself, pushing harder, rising onto my feet when a murmur sounds like a ripple of electricity. I know what it is; it's the feeling that always accompanies *them*, like a charge that pushes at people before they've even arrived.

It's the Guards.

I look to my left, beyond the elbows and fists in front to the crowd that's formed in the rest of the lane, haggard faces of Sanctum's unwanted, Sanctum's outcasts and I can read the same fear in their eyes as they begin to move aside, flashes of red appearing from every direction.

"DON'T MOVE! EVERYONE STAY WHERE YOU ARE!" But the command is not obeyed as people start to scatter in all directions. The Guards swarm through the lane, batons raised, crashing down on anyone in their way as the fight breaks up and I remain frozen to the spot, unable to move, barely able to breath.

"Get your hands off me!"

Looking to my immediate right I see the man with the scar looking up at me from the ground, blood trickling from a wound on the side of his head, the black boot of a guard pressing down on his back. I can't draw my eyes away as he struggles and yells.

"GIVE US FOOD! GIVE US WATER!"

Murmurs of agreement fill the air from those that have backed off but remain in the lane watching on, the whole place a tinderbox ready to explode. Clever. He's trying to whip up the crowd, trying to get them going.

I look at him closely, to his one good eye as it looks past me to my right, fixed on something in the distance and then my mind clears a little and I follow his gaze to the floor next to me, although I already know what he's looking at.

He's looking at the dead bird that's right next to me.

My heart beats loudly in my ear as I stare at the clump of feathers no more than ten yards from where I crouch. Although part of the arrow snapped off I can still see its triangular head glistening, feathers stuck to its side.

I need to move quickly. I need to grab it and run.

As the idea takes hold my stomach intrudes, rumbling its own agreement and I look back around to the Guards who are beginning to pacify the crowd. If I don't go now it'll be too late and I won't be able to use the mayhem as a cover. But if I get caught, if they see what I'm doing.

Every day the choice; life or death. And then an image pushes its way to the front of my mind and I ready myself to move.

Ellie and Doughnut. It's not just me I'm looking out for, it's them too.

I picture their faces and my body twitches. Gathering myself I look at the man with the scar as the Guard begins to pick him up off the ground. I can see the panic in his face, his one good eye darting around as he tries to make sense of what's happening. He fixes his glare on me and I instinctively shrink back against the wall because I can see his mouth opening. I know what he's going to do.

"Please! It was *him* who started it!" His arms are pinned behind his back but he begins to nod furiously in my direction, his voice weaker than before, without the defiance of earlier. "He stole my food! He stole my food!"

I can hear whispers from those still here watching, and suddenly I'm aware of eyes turning towards me. I need to get out of here so I begin to move, pushing my back up against the wall, fingers scrabbling in the dirt curling around the cold body of the bird.

MOVE. NOW!

The man with the scar struggles to free himself, "LOOK. He's got it!" But the baton of the Guard silences him and, pushing away from the wall, I hold the bird close and disappear among the bodies in the lane.

Hands grab at me but they're half-hearted at best, the threat posed by the red uniforms more than enough to keep everyone subdued.

I want to run as fast as I can but at the same time I'm scared of any more eyes falling upon me so my body settles into an uncomfortable half jog, the bird stuffed under my ripped shirt.

My feet fall into a steady rhythm. I know the Lanes like the back of my hand and I begin to settle into auto pilot, the last few minutes seeming like a lifetime, nervous energy still coursing through my body.

As the Lane splits off into three different directions I take the second avenue on the left, trying to ignore the traders and sellers desperate to make anything they can before the sun goes down.

My breath catches in my throat as I look up to the sky, at the gloom that is beginning to spread from the west. Darkness will begin to set in before too long and that means the curfew will begin to sound.

The thought makes me speed up because I need to find Ellie and Doughnut before the darkness arrives.

I need to find them before the Wastelanders come.

Chapter 2

The thought of what lies out there beyond the Wall fills me with dread and I pick up speed, wheeling in and out of people as they make their way to wherever it is they call home.

I picture Ellie and Doughnut waiting for me; Ellie's face in particular frowning, her foot tapping the earth as she ticks down the time until the curfew sounds, furious at me for making them worry like this.

She's like the mother of our weird little family even though we're nearly the same age.

"Sorry, I didn't…" The words come automatically as I spin away from the shoulder I've slammed into. I don't even turn around to check what's happened because there's no time. There never is.

Up ahead I can see the lane narrowing, more people that I've got to fight my way through so I slow down and begin looking for a way to get me higher, to get me above the bodies. The roof is where I can really move, where I can really put some distance between me and everyone else.

Looking up I see a low wall ahead of me about ten yards that leads to a crumbling brick building, part of which looks like it's under reconstruction. It's rare to see any thing made of brick this far into the Lanes as bricks have to be made in a fire and that costs money but the good thing is that it should be enough to take my weight.

As I get nearer I look around for my way up onto the roof. There's enough wooden scaffolding to support my weight, and stretching the last few steps I swing my free arm and grab one of the wooden poles, pivoting my body onto the low wall. The momentum I've gained is enough to propel me towards the building and as I reach the brick I crouch and spring from my right foot back onto the wooden framework.

From there it's easy, even with only one arm, to negotiate my way up the structure until I'm standing on its crumbling edge looking back down at where I've just come from.

It wasn't the best of climbs and if Doughnut had been here to see it I'm sure he would have had one or two words to say about my style, but a least I'm free to move about a lot quicker, as long as I watch my footing.

As I begin to speed up again my body relaxing into the moment, I'm aware of where I am and begin to look out for footholds, assessing my next move and how best to get there. The roofs are notoriously weak and unbalanced and it's madness to take their sturdiness for granted but I've been doing this sort of stuff for as long as I can remember; it's second nature to kids like me, Ellie and Doughnut. We've been doing it all our lives.

Running.

As I settle into a rhythm my mind begins to play over what happened before, the man with the scar, the tiny little bird clutched to my chest, and I can't help the anger begin to rise again from the pit of my stomach. I guess it's never really that far away.

How on earth did we ever end up like this? Scavenging for scraps in the filthy street. Ignoring other peoples suffering. Just trying to stay alive.

I wasn't born when the *'Great Light'* appeared, I guess not many of us were, but we've heard the stories millions of times, it sometimes seems like it's all the adults ever have to talk about.

The way they tell it the world had been fighting for a long time over everything; land, ideas, resources; you name it. In the end we forgot why we were fighting in the first place; we got too greedy, we had all that we could ever need and we wanted more, until someone, somewhere pressed the button that started the beginning of the end. The button that released the bombs.

At least that's what we're told.

For a time people lived underground or in caves, trying to escape the wind that brought with it death and disease, that burnt people from the inside out. Millions died all over the world.

When I was younger, and always late at night, I had to cover my ears to stop the screaming when I pictured all those people dying. I still do. Sometimes it works, sometimes it doesn't.

At first, so the story goes, we were the lucky ones. Most of the bombs flew over us hitting other areas. It was only after the initial dust had settled that what became known as *The Terror* began. Those who couldn't get under ground fast enough, the ones who didn't die in the flames and the poison, survived but at a cost.

We grow up hearing these stories. After a while they become a part of who we are. Those that were exposed, their bodies became deformed, their minds diseased as the chemicals took their toll, poisoning the land and the sea, killing all the creatures with it. There was nothing to eat and no clean water to drink. In the end, after months of starving, people had no choice. They had to do what humans were never meant to.

They had to feed on each other.

Before my father died and I had to fend for myself on the streets, when he used to tell this part of the story it was as if he aged before my eyes, like he did so quickly when the Cancer set in. He said it had nothing to do with the Great Light, but I know different. Sometimes, when I went to bed, I could hear him in the next room to me. Crying.

Something at the back of my mind disturbs my thoughts and I feel brick crumble under my hand as I jump from one section of roof to another. My body instinctively pushes me away from the weak area and before I can stop myself I'm spinning to my right as momentum takes me to the far edge of the roof. I'm at least thirty yards from the ground and seeing a metal pole I jump, raising my left foot, using it as a fulcrum to spin my weight back to the centre.

Although this time I'm on my own, Ellie and Doughnut love it up here just as much as I do, even though Ellie in particular is always worrying about how dangerous it is and how much damage we could do to ourselves if we slip or fall through a weak patch.

We're not supposed to be up here but we always are, especially in the late afternoon when the sun's strength is waning. People shout at us and some throw things but every now and again I catch a glimpse of a smile as if they're remembering their own childhood when they did the same, urging us on to run harder.

Using my free hand I pivot over a series of small walls, rolling over on my shoulder as I leap onto lower levels, careful to keep the bird safe. My heart's racing, blood roaring in my ears as I gain speed once again. Up ahead there's a gap between the buildings but I can't remember how far it is, even though I've been up here a million times before. I could slow down and try and get my bearings a little more. In fact that's exactly what I should do but where would be the fun in that?

Speeding up I count down my stride.

3-2-1

And then I'm off, my legs and arms still working like I'm running on thin air.

Time stands still.

The roar of air against my skin,

I'm free.

My mind flashes up Ellie's face scowling at me with that look of hers and the image puts me off and I begin to wobble. The ledge is nearing but I'm not sure I can make it; my concentration is shot. Feeling for the edge of the roof my foot comes down hard, the pain sharp as it sends me sprawling until I come skidding to a halt. Not my smoothest landing.

I lie there coming to my senses, waiting for any pain to arrive telling me I've busted my ankle or leg.

Nothing.

So I'm up and heading off again but this time fear begins to spread over me from head to toe because I can hear the faintest sound in the distance, like a high pitch whistle and I don't need anyone telling me what it is or what it means.

It's the sound of the curfew and it's telling me I'm in danger

Chapter 3

The curfew.

It starts as a high pitched whistle but then soon changes to a kind of low rumble as if something heavy is running far off in the distance, making the ground shake underneath your feet. It goes on for what seems like an age until the pitch finally changes, winding itself up like its now climbing a steep hill or like a baby that wants its mother.

When it hits the highest pitch, when your ears are hurting and it feels like your brain is going to explode, it suddenly stops and for a split second you're left with a wailing echo before the whole process starts over again.

And then the fear begins to creep over you.

No matter how many Guards Our Leader sends, *they* still manage to get beyond the Wall and in the last few months more and more pictures of the missing have been placed on boards at the crossroads into the Lanes. It breaks your heart to read the messages and despite the constant reassurances from Our Leader and the increased presence of the Guards, if anything their threat is getting worse.

My dad used to say that in the early years when people began to band together against attacks, for safety in numbers, they had grand ideas of taking the best of the old world and creating something new, something better where everybody was free and had an equal say in everything that happened.

In the beginning it worked and as they dug in and began to build what is now Sanctum, everyone sharing in the work *and* the rewards. But the way dad told it two main things happened to upset the progress; Sanctum grew at a rate that no one could have predicted with more and more people making it through the Wastelands, poisoned by the fallout from the Great Light, asking for protection.

But they had not been there at the beginning and didn't understand the founding principles. People began to fight for resources, for the precious water that was buried deep in the ground and for the last remaining areas of land that could grow edible food. The very same problems that caused the Great Light in the first place.

And then the Wastelanders came.

As I jump down from the rooftops to ground level I can see from the faces still making their way home that they too are picturing *them*; that they too are filled with the same fear as I am and I'm just grateful that at least I've got somewhere to go and somebody waiting for me when I get there.

I try to focus on Ellie and Doughnut sitting underground in the place that has been our home for the last few weeks. Nothing more than a crack in the earth, hollowed out and long since abandoned, enough for three people. But it's no good because the siren intrudes in on my thoughts and I begin to hear my dad's voice in my mind as clearly as if he was right here next to me.

"It was as if they could smell that something was happening on the air son, and just as we were trying to build a new future so they began to come, somehow changed by the Great Light, by what they'd had to do to survive. The forsaken. Those of us who couldn't get below ground quick enough.

The damned.

First one at a time, scratching at the doorways, sniffing the earth, trying to find where the best meat was and then more and more, raiding homes and stealing the little ones; barely human at all. After a while we retreated behind the walls you see around us today but by then it was too late, the rot had already begun, people praying on the fear of others, offering protection for payment, fear making us obedient.

Around this time, before you were born, Our Leader appeared and began to take control; reinforcing the walls, ensuring patrols of citizens to guard against a mostly unseen enemy. The people were too frightened, too desperate to see what was happening and with each successful patrol, with each Wastelander raid repelled his strength grew.

He began to demand more and more taxes to pay for defence, used the guards against the people when they had nothing to give. In time we were herded together, the Neutral Zone created to separate us from him. We were just as trapped inside as we would have been out there. We hadn't learnt anything from the Wars.

We hadn't learnt anything at all."

I've heard from others like me who lost parents young that over time the memories begin to fade until they have a hard time remembering them at all. I imagine that for some this is a good thing because it stops them from reliving painful memories of loss and separation but it's never been an issue for me.

My dad's voice has never faded, not once. In fact as the years go by it grows stronger, as if he's always there when I need him with words of advice or a stern look. It's like he's never really gone away.

As the Lanes begin to thin out, I look around me before heading for the huge fencing that marks the start of the Neutral Zone. If you want to survive in Sanctum as an orphan and not be captured by the Guards and put to work then you need to have your wits about you and you need to constantly change where you sleep.

A week or two is the most you can afford to stay in one place because a pattern in your movements will have started to develop and patterns get seen by people. The Guards have quotas they have to fill and are willing to pay for any information. Trust no one.

You don't even have to be an orphan to get grabbed. We've all heard of people taken from the streets if they're stupid enough to be out after the curfew. Our Leader protects us from what's out *there* but if you break the rules…

At first, when Ellie showed me the new place she had found for us to sleep I practically laughed in her face.

"You expect me to sleep here? Near the Neutral Zone fence? The Guards patrol here more than they do in the Lanes. What's so wrong with the roofs? A least we've got a chance of escape up there if we get discovered. We'll be sitting ducks out here!"

"Quack, quack. I like sitting ducks."

"Shut up Doughnut you idiot."

"Quack quack. Quack quack."

I smile at the image of Doughnut, hands folded under his armpits shuffling about with his elbows stuck out at right angles, Ellie tapping the ground with her foot, arms folded.

"You've never even seen a duck."

"Have too!"

"Where? In your dreams?"

I shuffle on towards the fence, the bird still somehow safely tucked under my arm as if it's the most precious cargo I've ever had, my mind a whirr of images.

The Neutral Zone.

Funny how they call it that since everyone knows it's anything but. It's to keep us away from the inner city, where Our Leader's lives along with his Senators, or to stop them having to see us.

Dad used to say that it circles the inner city and that hundreds of years ago it would have been called a moat and filled with water but I never believed him. How could anyone have that much water to waste? They say that water flows in the Inner Sanctum and you can eat whatever you want. But *they* say lots of things.

This is what it does to you, living in this place. One minute you're flying over the rooftops the next you're worried the alarms will sound and a net fired over you. It makes you live in fear. It makes you weak.

Shaking my head clear I take a deep breath and move on. The Lanes are now behind me, hardly anyone daring to venture this far, but now that I'm on my own I can't help but want to get back there.

The fence is higher, much higher than I seem to remember, coils of razor sharp barbed wire at the top. It stretches off into the distance far beyond the horizon on both sides and as I step a little closer I can't help but stare at the stubby trees and shrubs that provide a second thick barrier to the centre of Sanctum. They too seem to stretch on forever. Sometimes I wonder if there's anything at the heart of Sanctum at all. No one I know's ever seen it.

A noise to my left takes my attention, probably a rat or something but it reminds me of the danger I'm facing just being this close to the fence. It reminds me that the Guards could be here at any time.

The Guards.

Who are they anyway? Nothing more than hired thugs, people who can no longer bear to fend for themselves. People who, for the promise of food and shelter, have given up their freedom, have turned on their own kind.

I need to calm down. I need to calm down and look for the markers, the piles of rocks we placed as a kind of map to tell us where to go but I can't see them. Panic rises again as my mind changes the image from the Guards to *them* and all of a sudden the siren sounds as if it's getting louder and I picture the blur of red as the Guards spot me.

"HEY YOU! DON'T MOVE. STAY WHERE YOU ARE!"

But there's something behind them, something darker, something fiercer, hunched over, desperate to get at me.

I close my eyes against the images and then I have to force them open, to move my head along the fence line as my feet start to work again. Is that one of them? That pile of stones up ahead, is that one of the markers?

There's another pile about twenty yards away and a surge of excitement rushes through my body as I force my feet to move and I follow the signs along the dusty ground until I can make out the first dry bush of the Neutral Zone.

How many do I have to find? Is it three or four? The sun is now fading fast as I stir up the dust with my feet, my eyes darting around, looking for danger of any kind.

And then I see it.

The foliage that we carefully picked to cover the entrance. It looks like any of the other dry, spindly bushes out here save for the stones in front that tell me what it really is. I feel a weight beginning to lift almost immediately as I carefully push through the foliage and begin to worm my way in.

The sides to the entrance are smooth and as I lie on my front with only my feet sticking out I crawl forward using my elbows and knees. With one last effort I drop down onto my hands into the main chamber before rolling onto my back.

"Holy crap!"

"Doughnut!"

"Sorry Ellie, but I thought he was, you know…"

"I know exactly what you thought and if *he* doesn't tell us why he's been out beyond the curfew he's going straight back out the way he came!"

As I sit upright and shake my head clear I see them both at the back of the chamber, faces lit by the small glow from a fire to their left; Doughnut trying his best to look at the floor and not laugh and Ellie piercing me with her eyes that tell me I've scared her by being out so long and she's going to let me know about it.

She's got a look on her face I know very well and for a split second I wonder if facing the Guards above ground would be the easier option.

Chapter 4

"I...I lost track of time!" My voice drifts off into nothing as I try to avoid Ellie's stare. If we were outside she'd be tapping her foot on the floor, arms folded, but down here in this cave she's only able to draw her knees up to her chest, hands linked in front, a study in teenage self-righteousness.

Frightening.

I think she's just about the only person who has this effect on me, who can make me feel about a millimetre small.

Looking up I see Doughnut grinning at me, that stupid goofy smile he puts on when he knows someone's in trouble and it's not him. My initial response is to want to grab him and rabbit punch his arms until he can't move them, or sit on his chest until he gives up but that would be a bad idea. I need to make it right with Ellie first. I've scared her and I need to find the right words, the right gesture.

The cave is about twenty feet wide and about the same again long and the two of them are at the far end where our beds are. *Beds*! I mean what are they? Stuff we've scavenged; blankets, bits of cardboard, anything that gives a little bit of comfort. To the left is a little fire that we keep going to give us some warmth.

I was sceptical at first because I didn't want any smoke to give us away but there are enough cracks in the rock all around us to absorb what little smoke there is and besides, I've looked above ground for any tell-tale signs and it's barely noticeable at all. Underground is like a network of honeycomb, like a bunch of gaps all separated by different sizes of rock.

I swear that if you look through some of the cracks in our little hovel then you can see shards of light far off in the gloom. Not much has changed I guess in all these years. People still forced to find shelter underground.

Shuffling forward Ellie makes a big deal out of turning her head towards the fire and again I see Doughnut with his big, wonky teeth grinning at me. "Jakey's in trouble! Jakey's in trouble!"

"Shut up you little rodent!" I know it's not exactly the way to win her round again but I can't help it. He's the little brother I never had and he's bloody irritating.

Keeping close to Ellie he moves a little from out of the shadows, the light from the fire illuminating the left hand side of his face and I can tell he's spotted something because his eyes have narrowed.

"Watcha got there?" He nods towards my right arm.

"Oh yeh, right." I lift my arm up and remove the bird from under my shirt and I can't help but notice that although she's still giving me the silent treatment, Ellie's now looking over here again.

"This is why I'm late." Why didn't I just show them the bird straight away? Why has she got to be so, so annoying? "I saw the bird get shot with an arrow and, well, took my chance I guess!"

"Woah, let's have a look then!"

Doughnut shuffles forward and I push the bird towards him. It's not much now that I look at it; scrawny thing really that'll look even smaller when plucked but it's food nonetheless and what's more, it's different to the normal scraps we scavenge and God knows we can do with something out of the ordinary. Just this once.

"Look Ellie!" Doughnut picks it up and turns it in his skinny fingers examining the arrow head that's sticking out of its chest. "Arrow's still inside it!" And then he holds the bird in one arm and pretends it's flying while the fingers of his other hand narrow to make a point.

"Neeeooowww…thwump!" Then he pretends the arrow's got him too and rolls onto his back with his legs in the air. "Uh. Oh. It got me! It got me!"

"Will you stop being such an idiot!" Ellie's voice is stern but I can see the ghost of a smile on her lips and I offer a silent thank you to Doughnut for his play acting. Sometimes he's too annoying, always talking and jumping around but he always seems to know when the atmosphere needs changing. He always seems to know how to make us laugh.

I grab his arm and start to turn it over. "Not much meat on this one!"

"Oi! Get off me you big douche bag!" And this time Ellie snorts a laugh that even she can't hold back any more.

"Douche bag! I suppose you are a bit aren't you!" I look from Doughnut to Ellie and back again, at how they are both laughing, and although I can't help but laugh as well I try to keep up the pretence of being angry.

"What did you call me you little weasel?" I bend his hand forward until it's nearly touches his wrist and he starts to yell.

"Owww. Get off!" But he's still laughing and crucially so is Ellie who has shuffled forward away from the wall and is now next to the bird.

"Let's get this little thing on the fire shall we?"

"What this little thing?" And I press Doughnut's hand again and then throw his arm back towards his chest.

"Aargh, that hurts you dick!" Doughnut inspects his hand as Ellie starts to prepare the bird.

I lie back on my elbows grateful that the atmosphere has lifted and this time I give myself up to the laughter, and for a brief moment it feels good, like we're almost a normal family. Almost.

I was right when I thought that there wouldn't be much meat on the bird but as it cooks away over the fire in the corner, Ellie turning it over on the wooden spit, I tell them the story of what happened. I guess I'm mostly telling Doughnut who's sitting next to me living every moment as I describe the fight that broke out and how the Guards were there in a second to beat them off each other.

Doughnut swings his fists as if he's there in the midst of it and I see Ellie out of the corner of my eye, smiling at the scene I'm describing. I can tell that she's still worried though because every time I mention the Guards she winces a little bending her head forward some more so her hair covers most of her face.

It's the memories. I know because I've got them too.

When dad died there was no one else to look after me, no one to look after the house and when he knew the Cancer was too much, when he knew he didn't have long left he made me promise that I would go to one of the 'Orphanages' that Sanctum has, work house by any other name. I've heard some call them Houses of Death because it's relatively easy to get into them, it's getting out alive that's the hard part.

He even had me go along for an appointment and I did, for him, because I knew it would give him some sort of comfort at the end but there was no way I was going into one of those places, not after everything I'd heard about what goes on.

I remember the man that sat across from me, behind the big desk, big fat man with a few strands of greasy hair stuck down across his bald head. I remember how he kept looking at me from the corner of his eye as he told me about where I'd stay and the work I'd have to do.

"You want to be a good boy for Our Leader don't you? You want to be a good boy?"

But his eyes were telling me something different. His eyes were telling me what really went on.

I shiver at the memory and re focus on Doughnut who's still trying to act out parts of the story I've just told.

When Ellie tells the story of how we met, and boy does she like to tell it, she says that she saw me on the far side of one of the Lanes, a skinny little boy, barely old enough to make my way in the world, staring up at a broken table full of rotten apples. She says that she normally wouldn't have been anywhere near there unless it was time for one of Our Leader's speeches in the Square by the Peoples Court.

"Dunno why I was there really, just walking around in a daze I guess. Anyway, I could practically see the drool running down your chin, making a puddle on the floor!"

I maintain to this day that I would have gotten away with it in any case, and *that* I definitely do correct her on, but she still insists that if she hadn't come over in time, if she hadn't have pretended I was her brother and scolded me to put the apple back then it was more than likely a Guard would have seized me after the vendor made such a fuss and I probably would have ended up in the damn Orphanage anyway!

After that I suppose she couldn't really get rid of me. In fact, when I really think about it, I guess I owe everything to Ellie. She showed me where you can sleep up against the wall of a bakery for warmth if you were lucky. She showed me how, if one person makes a diversion then it's far easier for the other one to steal food.

"It's not stealing, it's liberating! And in any case, they don't need that much – they're just being greedy!"

Her story's similar to lots you hear; her parents died when she young, killed in the frequent raids by the Wastelanders before the Wall had been finished. She doesn't talk about her mother much; guess it's just too hard to remember what it was like before. I often wonder what it would have been like, to lose my dad to the Wastelanders instead of watching him waste away like he did.

"It's cancer, son. Damn virus won' let go of your ol' man."

Would I feel different? Would I *be* different?

Sometimes I think that's what happened to Doughnut and that's why he never speaks about his life before we found him, or more accurately before Ellie took pity on this skinny little kid following us around all day.

We never really even said anything to him, just kind of let him hang out with us until he became part of the family. Couldn't get rid of him so I guess we sort of adopted him. I reckon Ellie would try to take care of every little street rat if she could.

Ellie divides up the bird as best she can, laying the bits out on a piece of wood in the middle of the floor. Despite being ravenous with hunger both Doughnut and I know better than to dive in straight away, at least when Ellie's around. That's what she does I guess! She makes us remember our manners, she forces us to try and behave ourselves and I think, for the most part at least, we do her proud.

The siren is still sounding outside but it's now fainter than it was and as the light from the fire flickers all around our little makeshift home I can't help but think of the absurdity of what we're about to do, but Ellie won't let us eat until we do it so with a sigh from Doughnut we move around the food and join hands so we're all linked.

"We give thanks to Our Leader for this food and hope that his wisdom and strength will guide us through these terrible times. Our Leader!"

"Leader."

Doughnut's voice and mine are barely above a whisper because as far as I am concerned, cowering under ground, living in constant fear of the danger that exists both inside and outside of the walls is nothing to be grateful for. But I guess she does it because she needs to have faith in something.

We eat in silence, each of us trying to savour for as long as possible the meat as it melts on our tongues and slips down our throats. I can't remember the last time I had something warm like this and as it reaches my stomach a low rumble echoes throughout the cave.

"Oops." I take a breath to calm by digestion. "Guess I'm not used to such fine dining!" Doughnut grins and I can see bits of meat stuck between his teeth. Somehow, despite the meal being tiny, he's managed to get most of it on his chin and around his mouth.

"Can you not feed yourself properly?" Ellie makes to wipe his face with her sleeve but he backs off still grinning.

"What are you doing? Are you crazy? I'm saving that for later!"

As the fire spits its fractured light, laughter echoes off the walls and we struggle to keep it down because noise travels fast and we don't want to give ourselves away to the Guards.

But it feels so damn good to laugh with food in our bellies and for the moment at least the worry of where the next meal is coming from is forgotten.

For the moment.

After the meal sleep isn't difficult to find for any of us, the warmth from the embers coupled with the fresh food in our bellies making us sluggish and sleepy. The difficulty is staying asleep. The difficulty is keeping the nightmares at bay.

I sleep, as I always do, between the entrance and the others, forming a sort of barrier, much good it would do if we were suddenly discovered but I've found that I can't go to sleep any other way. I guess I need to feel like I'm protecting them or something.

But as fast as sleep comes it soon disappears as I lie there, listening to the breathing of the others. I can't sleep because I can't calm my brain down, too many thoughts are whizzing around all at once, bumping into one another. But there's another reason and even though I don't want to think about it I'm powerless to stop myself.

It's the dream I've been having for as long as I remember. Sometimes it goes away for weeks on end. Sometimes I can almost forget about it. But it always comes back.

Always.

The dream started, as many of our dreams do, with the great Wall at my back and the Wastelands stretching out in front of me. For the longest time, that was it. I would wake up soon after with the image of the ground beneath my feet stretching out towards the endless horizon. Always waking up at the same place in the dream, never advancing from the Wall.

Until recently.

Until I began to see the mist in the distance creeping along the ground like so many withered fingers searching for something.

Until I began to see the figure within, the outline of a single person illuminated by the moonlight.

It's the same dream I always have. The shadow moving with the mist, inching towards me. Only recently it's been accompanied by the smell that I wake up with still clinging to my nostrils. The smell of rotting flesh.

And it's this that has me scared to fall asleep at night, that has me making any excuse to stay up, to stay awake, because I don't know who the figure is.

Chapter 5

When I wake my body feels sluggish and at first I'm a little confused until I realise that I've probably had just about the best night's sleep that I can remember. The sun has only just begun to rise as I worm my way out of the hole, pushing aside the foliage with my hands. Ellie's already up and as I pull my legs through and roll on to my side I see her sitting on the dusty ground looking out through the fence.

"Shouldn't we get away from here?" I look around as if expecting to see a flash of a Guard's red uniform, baton in hand, "They'll already be on the lookout won't they?" Silence meets my words as Ellie continues to stare out into the Neutral Zone.

I shuffle along until I'm almost beside her and try to see what she's looking at but in all honesty it's nothing more than skinny trees and bushes that seem to extend on for as long as the eye can see.

"What do you think it's like?" Ellie's voice sounds flat and distant.

"Huh? What do you mean?" I look back at the side of her face and my eyes are drawn to the dark circles under her eyes. She always manages to make herself look presentable, even in the rags that we sit in, she always looks somehow *clean*. But recently I've noticed that she seems more tired than usual, as if she's having trouble sleeping, as if she's got something on her mind that won't allow her to rest properly. She coughs a little and I hear, deep down in her chest, a faint rattle, like something's come loose.

"The Inner Sanctum. Our Leader's home." She turns slightly and her hair falls away from the side of her face. "What do you think it looks like? Do you think it's true that they have running water whenever they want and houses so big you can walk for hours without having to step outside?"

I look at the ground and trace patterns in the dust with my finger. "Dunno." I've never been comfortable talking about this kind of stuff. Maybe it's paranoia? Maybe something else. "But you can bet anything you like that he's not living in a hole in the ground, like us!"

"They need it right? I mean the Senators and him. They need to live differently to protect us, don't they? To keep their strength up?"

I know there's something else she wants to say. I can tell from the way her cheeks have flushed red and I start to get even more uncomfortable. I've been feeling like this a lot recently when I'm around her, like I can't sit still, like I can't look her in the eyes as I used too. It's fine when Doughnut's with us because he takes the focus but when we're on our own I've started to get a bit tongue tied. I've started to get nervous.

"Don't you think?"

"W…what?" I look up expecting her to be laughing at me as if my thoughts were being broadcast to the world like the siren is every evening, and she *is* laughing, well, smiling a least.

"You haven't been listening to a word I've been saying have you?"

"No, no. I was, I mean, you were talking about Our Leader and what kind of house he lives in!" I still can't shake the feeling that I've given something away, that she knows more than I want her to.

"That's exactly why I love speaking to you, Jake." She gets up from the dusty ground and ruffles my hair. I hate having my hair ruffled. "You never listen so I can say what I like and I know you won't remember!"

Now it's my turn to blush.

"Did we, did we save any of that bird from last night?" Doughnut's voice comes from the foliage and for a moment I sit in the dirt watching Ellie as she skips a few feet away from me. He emerges from the undergrowth like he's seeing the sun for the first time, all scrunched up eyes and stretchy arms, and I smile and begin to stand.

"There was barely enough for dinner!" Dusting myself down I look up at Ellie who's folding her arms like she means it. "But, but what there was, well…" I pretend to lick the tips of each finger as if I'm savouring the taste again and Doughnut starts to laugh and copy.

"Mmm! Delicious!"

Ellie just stands there unamused until finally turning and walking back along the fence towards the Lanes. Doughnut's too busy licking his fingers, eyes closed for maximum effect, to notice so I follow trying not to laugh because when he opens his eyes again he'll have no idea what's going on.

Four. Three. Two…

"What the, hey! Wait up! Wait for me!"

"Do we have to go?" Usually it's Doughnut bleating from behind us about being hungry or tired but this time it's me who's dragging my feet in the dust. I thought we were going to scavenge food as we always do, maybe search for somewhere else to stay, see what the day brings.

I'd completely forgotten about the meeting. The bloody meeting in the Square by the Peoples Court. The same damn thing we've had every single month since I can remember.

"It's gonna be a load of the same old crap as before."

"Same old crap!" Ellie shoots a look at Doughnut that tells him to watch his mouth. But I'm not in the mood because I'm hungry and for some reason anger is forcing its way from the pit of my stomach.

"I mean all we ever hear is how great *he* is and how dangerous the Wastelanders are."

"Keep your voice down, Jake!" She practically hisses from the side of her mouth as we make our way across the boulders and stones towards the Lanes. "You know they can hear us!"

"Yeh, whatever!" But I lower my voice all the same. We've all heard the stories of people being taken in the streets; Guards suddenly appearing from nowhere. It's all part and parcel of the mystery, of the mystique. "Why can't we just hide away until it's all over for another month? It's not like he's going to say anything new to us, is it?"

But I know what her response is going to be and she knows mine. I'm going to go – of course I'm going to go. I know it, she knows it, the whole of Sanctum knows it. We go when and where he calls us. We all do. It doesn't matter how many times I moan about it. I haven't got the strength to defy him.

None of us have.

It doesn't take us long to get back from the fence into the hustle and bustle of the Lanes and even though it's only sun up people are beginning to make their way to the Square in raggedy lines. It's funny but you can always tell when it's this time of the month because things are quieter than usual. There's lots of people shuffling about as there always are but the conversation is usually less about how to make some money for food and water and more about what is going to be said to us when we get there.

I've no idea why though. It's always the same old rubbish about how amazing he is and how lucky we are to have his protection against the Wastelanders. Sometimes I wonder if it wouldn't be easier to try and sign up as a damn Guard. Get it all over and done with.

I've seen enough of them, broken down people with that look in their eyes as if they've got nothing left to give. I've seen them go into the recruitment centres after standing outside for what seems like hours as if they've somehow got a choice. But when they come out they seem *different*, as if whatever light they had left has gone from their eyes.

Maybe it's the shame at what they've given up; their freedom.

As I look down at the torn and filthy rags that pass for clothes hanging loosely from my body I wonder just exactly where this much fabled protection actually is.

"Don't even think about it!" I look up at Ellie but she's got her eagle eye on Doughnut and for a moment I'm puzzled, her voice breaking the awkward silence that has fallen over us, until I smell the fresh baking and see where he's looking.

Up ahead there's a bunch of Guards, uniforms bright red and freshly laundered for the day's events, and they're huddled around a rickety old table underneath an old, ripped tent as what smells like fresh bowls of stew are carried out to them by the owner.

As we walk past, stomachs growling, my mouth fills with saliva and I fantasise about going over there and grabbing one of the bowls right out from under their noses.

"Bet they got some fresh meat! How do they always get the fresh stuff when the rest of us have to make do with the dust off the damn ground?"

"Keep your voice down for God's sake!" Ellie hisses again out of the corner of her mouth and I know I've got to get all our minds off food because it's the easiest way to get in trouble out here, when you're hungry and you've got next to nothing to lose.

"The amount of farting you did last night I'm surprised you need anything to eat at all!" I push Doughnut with my shoulder and pretend I'm wafting away a bad smell and he looks up at me, big grin spreading over his face.

"I sat on your face while you were asleep! Did one right in your mouth!" and then we're both off, exploding into fits of giggles and it's all Ellie can do to push us through the increasing throng of people so the Guards don't take notice of us.

"There's something badly wrong with both of you!" She tries to sound as stern as possible but can't help but join in until all three of us are leaning on each other for support.

We walk the rest of the way in relative silence following the crowds as they get larger. It's the only thing about these so called meetings that I know we all enjoy; people watching. I'm struck as always by how shabby everyone looks but I think it's because of the contrast with the uniforms of the Guards. In comparison we must look like a bunch of dirty, unwashed refugees fresh from the Wastelands, which in a sense I guess we are.

I look to my left to the two children that walk past hitting each other as they go, huge grins like Doughnut's on their faces. Despite the fact that they look too thin, that their clothes are barely rags, that they probably haven't washed in months, if ever;

despite all that they're still smiling, still finding things to joke about.

Maybe that's what makes Our Leader so powerful. No matter how bad it gets in Sanctum, at least we're not out there having to face *them*.

"Whoa!" Doughnut's mouth is practically hanging open and I have to admit that mine is getting that way too. Doesn't matter how many times you enter the Square, it's always the same feeling; awe.

I guess it's like the centre of the city, at least the areas that we're allowed anywhere near. Doesn't matter how windy and stretched out the lanes become, you know that if you follow their contours for long enough then eventually you'll come out somewhere that leads here.

I can't help but crane my neck to get a good look at the columns as we pass underneath. They must stand about thirty feet high; eight of them in all angled like an arrowhead with a large stone slab on the top, forming a huge entrance that everyone has to pass through. Etched in foot high letters that seem to stand out for miles around is the word *SANCTUM* and underneath in slightly smaller letters is the phrase; PEOPLE'S COURT.

"Hey! Wouldn't it be great to climb those posts! We could jump our way round to the Court. Imagine that!"

Ellie frowns at the idea but I can see from Doughnut's eyes that he's already picturing us doing it, and as I do the same I realise that once up onto the first column it wouldn't actually be that difficult to do exactly that. The other columns that line the Square leading to the court, acting as a kind of huge fence are smaller than the ones we just passed through but they too have slabs on top of them. Perfect for climbing.

"Why's it called the Square?" Doughnut's voice intrudes into my thoughts and I look at him blankly. "Seriously!" He shrugs and looks about with those wide eyes of his, "Why? It's more circular than square, isn't it?"

"I hate to say it, but he's right you know!" I frown as Ellie joins in and then I start looking at the other columns, at the way they sweep round in a sort of semi-circle. Never even thought of it before and I shrug as much to say 'I don't know either'.

What I do know is that the entire place is an extremely effective way of Our Leader showing off his power. You can't help but be amazed by the size of the place, the sheer number of people.

And by the mass of red uniforms lining the sides.

Chapter 6

There are even more guards in here than there were on the way and we instinctively move closer together, worried that we'll get split up and lost in the crowd. Safety is most definitely in numbers. It's just another on the long list of reasons why I'm glad I have these two by my side.

"Whoa! How many people?" Doughnut's mouth is wide open again.

"All of them I think!"

There must be a thousand people here if not more and I can't help but think that this is all for something a little more than the usual pre-recorded slogans that we have to listen to. Something else is happening; I'm sure of it.

I look around as if I've been talking out loud anticipating the looming figure of a guard, stick raised above his head. I'm lucky that my dad raised me to trust my own instincts and not slavishly follow other people's ideas. He taught me that on the outside it is good to appear modest and respectful but the inside, well that's for us to do with as we please.

As if on queue the music starts up as it always does from the huge black boxes attached to the columns; softly at first, a few wind instruments fluttering about before the huge drums kick in. It sounds like it's coming at us from all angles and I'm amazed at the physical effect it has.

I can see it in the way both Ellie and Doughnut seem to stand that little bit straighter, that little bit more to attention than before. I know I do it as well, without even thinking, as if the music, the strings that are now stabbing away, the trumpets and God knows what else that are making every hair on the back of my neck stand up, as if it's all somehow more inside than out.

For me it has the same effect as the siren's do when the sun falls in the sky. It somehow changes behaviour as if the sound of the siren *is* a Wastelander chasing us back to wherever we lay our heads. As if this music *is* Our Leader commanding us to listen and obey.

I search my brain for what my dad used to call it. He had a saying for this kind of thing, when people use other methods to get you to do what they want.

Conditioning. That was it. He called it conditioning.

At the far end of the square in front of the building the huge screen, even from back where I stand, looms over everyone. I am always amazed at how they do it, how they manage to put it up and then take it down, something of that size without anyone knowing.

It's another example of Our Leader's power I guess, like the Guards, the Inner Sanctum, the sirens, the very walls that hold us all in place. We all belong to him in one way or another and it's very rare that anyone is allowed to forget that.

Whatever technology was left over after the Great Light, he controls. And don't we know it.

"How does all this happen?" The words come from my mouth before I have a chance to stop them and I look around sheepishly expecting Ellie or Doughnut to make fun but they're staring too as we are buffeted by the sea of people all around us.

"Are there more people here than usual?" Ellie's voice is quieter than usual and I nod agreement.

"I've got a weird feeling about this you know? Doesn't feel like the usual type of meeting!" I expect her to shoot me a glance like earlier or to tell me to be quiet and have some respect but she doesn't. Instead she glances at me from the corner of her eye and I see the same doubt reflected back at me.

The huge boxes momentarily crackle as the music builds like a storm about to break. There is an air of anticipation as more and more people file in, the Guards directing people to row upon row, although we all know what is expected of us, we've been lining up like this to hear Our Leader speak since the moment we could walk.

That's another thing about these events; you only have to step out into the street for a second to hear just how much noise is being made, a lot of it by children running around. Here though it's as if they instinctively know that they've got to be quiet, that it's no place for playing around.

I sometimes wonder if there's more to it than my dad's idea of conditioning. I sometimes wonder if we're born with this capacity for blind obedience, for conformity. If it's actually what we prefer. At least then we don't have to take responsibility for our choices.

The great screen flickers, horizontal lines running from top to bottom as Our Leader's face comes into view to great cheers. His hair is scraped up into the familiar dome on the top of his head and his orange robes spread out behind him practically filling the screen. It gives the impression that his face, with its pointed nose and square chin, is the centre of the sun.

Set against the back drop of the grey brown dust that clings to everything else in this place, it's like an explosion, a lightning strike in front of our very eyes.

As the screen widens so the yellow robes of the Senators that sit behind him add to the overwhelming spectacle, their faces a mixture of fear and entitlement. Dad used to say that at the beginning the Senators were created to represent the people in local matters, that they were actually approachable at the Peoples' Court House.

He used to act as if it was the most amazing thing in the world that you could actually make an appointment with them and air your grievances. The idea was that they would then seek an audience with Our Leader to try and resolve the issue.

Imagine that! As far as I'm concerned all they do is live within the inner Sanctum, sending the

Guards here and there to do their bidding. Ceremonial is what I've heard some people call them, used as another show of strength on the part of Our Leader. Leeches is how I'd describe them.

"CITIZENS OF SANCTUM!" As he begins to speak a great hush descends on the vast crowd and he pauses until there is absolute silence "It has been thirty years since we emerged from The Great Light!" He pauses dramatically for the number to sink into each and every one of us. "Thirty years since we stood back from the chasm of *annihilation* and *destruction* and, friends, we have achieved a *great* deal!"

Each word is deliberately emphasised for maximum impact bringing gasps and cries as sections of the crowd break out into a spontaneous cheer that sweeps everyone else along with it, even us. It's amazing how you can know that you're being manipulated but at the very same time be powerless to do anything about it.

"We have shown that *mankind* can come back from the brink, that *mankind* can rebuild from the ashes of ruin, that *mankind* can once again determine his own destiny!" The crowd roars again. The face on the screen, now seemingly brighter than ever looks around, scanning the whole Square from left to right. Cries rise up from the crowd.

"We love you!"

"God save Our Great Leader!"

The crowd settles again as Our Leader's words resume but this time they are softer, somehow more sorrowful and it's as if the whole crowd begins to lean forward, straining to hear what he has to say.

"But it has not been without hardship and it has not been without sacrifice. A great many of us have been touched by tragedy in one way or another as the Wastelanders have tightened their grip on the land beyond our wall. There are barely any amongst us who have not been tainted by their evil, been in fear from their devilry! We have all seen the notes left behind, pinned to the boards at the crossroads; faces of loved ones that have been stolen from us!"

The crowd is electrified and a lone voice somewhere to my left breaks the spell.

"Help us my Leader! Please help us against these DEVILS!"

A chant of "DEVILS" rises up and my whole body tenses, Doughnut and Ellie pressing against me from either side.

"More and more they attack our city, taking our loved ones and it is time we fought back! It is time we showed them that this is our land and *not theirs!*" I've never heard Our Leader speak like this, I don't think anyone has, and although another cheer goes up I can see people turning to one another, confusion in the air.

I look at Ellie and Doughnut but their eyes are fixed on the screen, jaw muscles tightened. The meetings are usually a time when we are told to keep working hard, to keep the dream of a new world alive.

We usually have to sit through a number of 'normal' citizens as they of how their lives had been terrible, how they had barely enough to eat. How, by some miracle that we're never actually told about, Our Leader came to their rescue and saved them from almost certain starvation and death. It is this same story that we are told over and over again until it doesn't really matter if you believe it or not, it just sort of becomes so familiar that you don't even question it.

But this, this talk of aggression. No one was ready for *this*.

No one knows what he will say next and as he resumes scanning the crowd there is a collective intake of breath as to what the next pronouncement will be.

"The time has come for us to fight back and fight back we will! We have come to a fork in the road my friends! We must *do* something!" The tension is unbearable as he takes a breath. "We," he tilts his head towards the Senator's sitting behind him, "have been considering the nature of our next move for a long time Citizens, a very long time. Agonizing over what to do."

"Tell us my leader! Please tell us!" A smile plays on his lips as he allows the crowd to cry out as one, to plead with him for an answer, for a solution. He raises a hand and the square falls silent.

"Each new full moon we will open our gates and release our worst prisoners, those amongst us who do not share our passion for this new society and they will be afforded the greatest gift of all, the chance of redemption, the chance to fight. There will surely be no longer a need for the Wastelanders to find ways around our Great Wall if we give them what they want; FOOD!"

Cheers ring out and the chant of "DEVILS!" is replaced by "FOOD!" rising to an almost ear splitting volume. I'm confused and I can tell the others are too. Music has begun playing again and people are openly weeping. It feels like something is being allowed out, some sort of emotion that had been locked up for too long. As I look around at peoples tear streaked faces and their wide eyes as they continue to stare at the screen I realise that for some of them it must be a feeling of hope.

For some of them.

But not for me.

As I look at Ellie and Doughnut, the feeling I have is different. I usually feel it when the sirens go off and my mind automatically fills with images of whatever is out *there* trying to get inside the Walls.

But for some reason I'm feeling it right now like a fist squeezing my stomach.

I'm feeling fear.

White hot fear.

Chapter 7

Our Leader's head moves slowly from left to right and for a split second it feels like he is looking directly at each and every one of us as if he's deciding if we should be among the first to go. And then he holds his hands up to silence the crowd and you can hear a pin drop.

"Of course we would not be the society we claim to be if we did not hold out an olive branch to those who have broken our rules." Voices sweep the crowd as people try to second guess what he is saying. "If anyone of our criminals fights for survival like a true citizen…" He sweeps his hand from left to right, "…like anyone of *YOU!* If anyone of our damned *KILLS WASTELANDERS AND LIVES…*" Our Leader knows his audience and pauses, leaving every single one of us hanging on his next few words, "…then that person would have paid their debt to us, and shall be pardoned, their expertise used to train others!"

The music grows louder, swelling to a fever pitch and I see people hugging each other and shouting out in joy. The feeling is infectious and even though I haven't really processed what's just happened, despite the lead weight that has settled in the pit of my stomach, I can't resist joining in.

For so many of us it's the magic of Our Leader in a nutshell. Just when you begin to doubt him, he comes up with something that helps renew your faith.

I grin at Doughnut, despite myself, who returns the smile but Ellie is just staring ahead as if she's trying to work out what's behind the words. I want to say something to her but it's too noisy, too much going on. It'll have to wait.

The crowd begins to hush and we turn back to the screen as people wait in anticipation of just what he will say next.

"Every full moon we will celebrate the defence of our city, of our lives. It will be every Citizens duty to bare witness to this glorious rebirth, to look from our walls to the wastelands beyond, to our criminals as they fight for their lives. I hereby declare this day to be a public holiday for one and all."

Cheers begin but are quickly hushed as people strain to hear his next few words. "A Festival, to celebrate the best of us. To celebrate the day when we, as a unified people fight back. A day when we can proudly celebrate the city of *SANCTUM!*"

The last word echoes throughout the Square and then suddenly a chant breaks out.

"SANCTUM! SANCTUM! SANCTUM!" For a single moment I hold my breath as if time itself has stopped, emotion surging through the crowd like electricity. It's like nothing I've ever heard before and for the first time since I can remember I finally give myself up to the moment.

"SANCTUM! SANCTUM."

As the huge screen fades to black I am left with the chanting ringing in my ears and the image of

Our Leader imprinted in my mind's eye, glowing like the sun. Slowly shaking my head clear I realise that the music has started up again, our cue to start leaving the Square; the urgency of the drums, the blasting of the trumpets keeping my heart beating fast, adrenalin still coursing through my veins.

The atmosphere is charged as we begin the slow process of filing out of the square. The sheer numbers that have been hemmed in make each of the six exits nothing more than bottle necks, but the volume of Guards on the perimeter, coupled with the excitement generated by Our Leader's message means that no one minds that the going is slow.

When I look at Ellie and Doughnut to discuss what on earth just happened, I can tell that they're still taking it all in as well. I can see from the faces all around, wide eyes and open mouths, that no one was expecting anything remotely like this. It's as if we've all been drugged somehow, lulled into another state of mind by his words.

Criminals facing the Wastelanders! A day's holiday for all.

It's a kind of public sacrifice in a way, and the more I think about it the more it seems like a stroke of genius; simplicity itself. But I need to frame Our leader's words in my mind because I don't want to have misunderstood anything. It's too important for that.

Problem: *The Wastelander's are mounting more and more attacks inside the Walled defences of Sanctum.*

Solution: Offer up our worst criminals, those that do not share in our dream for a better future. Get the fight back outside, give the Wastelanders a regular source of food so they don't need to find a way in.

Outcome:

- *Less criminals to look after*
- *Hopefully fewer Wastelanders to fear.*
- *Built in possibility of redemption and martyrdom.*

I want to talk to the others, check that I'm right but they're a few steps ahead and the noise from the crowd makes it impossible to be heard close up. Hustling to catch up I move beside them and get Ellie's attention.

"We need to talk about what just happened! Can you *believe* what he just said?"

Ellie nods but I can tell she's still trying to take everything in, like the rest of us so I back off a little, still buzzing. Then another thought enters my head, a darker one that acts like a cloud passing over the sun. Never trust anyone, not even Our Leader. That's what my dad used to say. But if there's another ulterior motive for all this then I'll be damned if I know what it is! I quieten the thought and keep my head down because until we can get somewhere where we can talk it pays to fade into the background.

The crowd has slowed down now we're nearing one of the exits, walking reduced to shuffling. I can see more and more red uniforms up ahead but they seem somehow bunched up, and then I feel the surge from the crowd, a bristle of anticipation and fear.

Suddenly people begin pushing back and I can hear some stifled screams as a couple of people are pushed to the floor. I manage to stay on my feet and grab Ellie towards me who does the same to Doughnut and we huddle together as the crowd surges and pushes us about. Then, for a split second, the sea of bodies in front of us parts and no more than thirty yards away I see a bundle of rags on the floor barely moving as the Guards repeatedly raise their batons and bring them down with force.

"They're going to kill him!"

"What did he do?"

The voices come from all around us but all I can focus on is the blood that is beginning to pool around the rags on the floor and for the briefest of moments I see a man's face, bloodied and bruised, and then it's gone, swallowed up by the crowd.

My heart's racing but I keep on moving, keeping Ellie between the two of us so she doesn't get caught up in any of this. Not that's it's anything we haven't seen before but it's like an instinct to protect her. We all know that the Guards have to keep order and Our Leader keeps telling us that without their protection we would be like 'sheep to the wolves'.

But despite all that, no one intervenes on the man's behalf.

No one ever does.

As we pass the Guards to our right the crowd gets moving again; people eager to get on with the days scavenging. Slowly the spell of the Square begins to lift as if the nearer we get to the Lanes, the nearer we get to a sense of normality; the whole day seeming more and more like a kind of dream, a figment of the imagination.

"Holy shit! Can you believe what just happened?" Doughnut's voice is high with excitement. "Do you think anyone will win their freedom? Can you just imagine how much will be bet on the biggest looking criminal out there?" Ellie spots Doughnut's eyes widening and immediately slaps him down.

"Now just you stop there!" She drags him to one side, out of the march of the others, towards a space in between the shacks. I follow grinning and shaking my head, but when I catch up with them I see real fear in her eyes. "This is real, do you understand? It isn't throwing dice against a wall for coins!"

"Alright, alright! Gees…" Doughnut backs off from her, his eyes narrowing, as he starts kicking the ground. Ellie means well but sometimes she overdoes it a little, especially with regards to Doughnut. She treats him like her little brother, I guess we both do, but the reality is that he survived long enough out here on his own. It's plain stupid to think that he can't look after himself.

"Forget about that," I smile at both of them. "a Public holiday! Have you ever heard of such a thing?"

Doughnut tries to lighten up a little, flicking that grin of his, "Every day's a holiday for us Jake!" But Ellie's face remains stern, as if there's something she can't quite reconcile in her own mind.

"How will they make everyone stop working and living? What are they going to do, drag us to the Wall or something? Force us to watch?" There's no real answer to that and I look at Doughnut who shrugs and looks at his feet. "I mean..." Ellie looks at both of us, her eyes ablaze, "What's to stop people from stealing when others are watching this, this fight or whatever it is? When Sanctum's empty I mean."

I meet Ellie's glare but don't answer because I can't.

"Won't the..." Doughnut's voice is quiet, as if he's not sure of how to say what's on his mind and he looks around to check who's near us. "Won't the Wastelander's be too strong for the criminals?" Doughnut quickly looks down at the floor again, as if he's said something he shouldn't have, but the silence that greets the question suggests that we've all thought the same thing at some point. "What if they don't want to fight?"

Ellie clears her throat. "I guess we've just got to trust in Our Leader! Things have gotten real bad and he's trying to answer our prayers, trying to give us a solution." But I can see in her eyes, for the first time that I can remember, that she doesn't entirely believe her own words.

I can see, for the first time, doubt.

Chapter 8

We walk on in silence into the Lanes, for us at least, where Sanctum really begins, each of us lost in our own thoughts. It's as if the buzz of the meeting has worn off leaving only a series of doubts and questions that we have no way of answering.

The strained silence is broken by Doughnut coughing and rubbing his stomach. "Tell you what." He looks back at us, his face cheerier this time, like the Doughnut we all know and love. "Doesn't matter what's going to happen at the next full moon 'cos I'm not going to be around to see it if I don't get some food inside me!"

I smile as he continues patting his stomach but he has a point and I look around at where we are, scouting for the opportunities in our midst. I spot a blanket on the floor with what looks like fruit on it, jealously guarded over by three burly looking men who growl even when people approach *with* the means to pay.

"Maybe I could…" The rest of the sentence disappears as Ellie strides past me with purpose towards the blanket. Doughnut makes to follow but I stretch out my hand and hold his arm. "Watch and learn!"

I walk out to about half way between the two of them in the middle of the lane, dodging all the people still filing out from the Square. On cue Ellie begins to limp as she reaches the blanket before falling into one of the men who goes to push her.

My heart skips as I think he's rumbled what's going on and is going to give her a hiding, but instead he catches her and as the others begin to crowd in, she manages to flick out with her heel at the nearest fruit sending it scuttling across the lane towards me.

Dodging between the crowd I scoop it up before anyone can spot what we've done, or worse, anyone can grab it before me, and I'm back next to Doughnut in time to see Ellie thanking the men profusely as she limps off on the other side.

"What a girl! Let's meet her up by the corner." Doughnut looks at me out of the corner of his eye, a big stupid grin beginning to form on his face.

"When you gonna tell her?"

I pretend I don't know what he means and keep on walking. "When you gonna tell her that you love her?" The word makes my cheeks burn bright red and for a moment I have no idea what to do or say next. Doughnut catches up with me and peers up into my face but I refuse to be goaded. "I might not be as clever as you are but don't you dare tell me I'm wrong on this one. I've seen you mooning after her with that soppy look on your face!"

"What soppy…" The rest of the sentence trails off to nothing as I realise he means the red cheeked one I'm currently wearing. "Anyway shut up now because she can almost hear you. And if you so much as breath a word!" He nods and backs off but inside I'm cursing because I haven't even admitted it to myself yet and here he is with something on me that he can use to tease whenever he likes.

Looking up as we reach Ellie I fix a smile to my face. "Well done you! A perfect score I think!" She grins as I hand them both a big lump of the fruit. Starving as we are it's just about the best damn thing we've ever eaten.

As we fill our stomachs I can't help thinking that we need to get our hands on some money and a proper meal, because even though we always manage to find *something* we could all do with some real meat, preferably hot, Ellie more so than the rest of us.

I noticed it when we had the bird to eat last night, how Ellie was coughing and then again this morning, that sort of low rumble deep down in her chest. I also couldn't help but notice, when she was curled up next to me, how thin and bony she was. Of all the things that can kill you out here, hunger and thirst are the things you've got to watch out for the most.

Doughnut looks up from the fruit he's busy devouring and winks at me before looking at Ellie and then smiling that stupid, smug grin of his. I look away, trying to the best of my ability to ignore him because I need to figure out how I'm going to bring up this plan of mine, a plan that I know Ellie will be dead against.

When you're fifteen in the Lanes you don't have much choice over what you can do. If you're lucky and you've got parents with a trade like baking or carpentry then you might be able to follow them into some kind of business, at the very least you'll have some kind of trade that you can use to get food and shelter.

If you're an orphan like us then you take your chances on the streets, scavenging what you can, maybe getting some work every now and again doing the stuff that no one else wants to do; like emptying the overflowing buckets of human waste that seem to be on every corner these days. There's supposed to be a team that does this but they're invariably late and one thing you don't want is a bucket of waste sitting in the hot sun too long; the flies, the maggots – the stench! I practically wretch just thinking about it because I've done it once or twice; emptied the buckets for a piece of bread, getting more of it on me than anywhere else.

There is, of course, another option, if you look old enough that is, and as I look up at the other two as they finish the last of our surprise meal I think I've hit on the angle I need.

"We need some money!" I look at Ellie who knows where I'm going with this because we've fought about it before. "I need to…"

"NO! Absolutely not! Doughnut, tell him!"

Ellie has her arms folded across her chest and her eyes turned away from me. I hate it when she gets like this but I can't think of any other way that we can get some money relatively quickly without endangering ourselves. "*Tell* him!"

Doughnut looks at his shoes because he doesn't like it when she's like this anymore than I do but as he raises his eyes I can see him slowly shaking his head.

"I'm sorry Ellie but I agree with Jake on this one."

"Doughnut!"

"Don't look at me like that – I'd do it if I looked old enough but Jake's the only one of us that actually does." He looks admiringly at the fuzz that's begun to appear under my nose and chin and high up on my cheeks. "Could pass for my dad he's so old!"

The joke makes me grin but Ellie's not having any of it and continues pouting into the distance. "I'll only take work that's no more than a walk away, that way if it's too much or anything happens I can run away and meet you guys." I look at Doughnut for help and then Ellie's voice intrudes surprising the both of us. I guess she's thinking about the cough, or more probably the fact that, on this occasion, I'm right.

"You'll meet us back at the hole, Jake." She turns and stares at me and I practically back off a step at the intensity of her piercing blue eyes as they bore a hole into my head. "You hear me! I mean it, Jake. You get back to the hole before curfew you hear, sooner if it gets out of hand!"

Doughnut grabs us both and we huddle in a tight circle, the boniness of Ellie's arms stiffening my resolve to earn some real money for a change.

"Jakey's gonna pretend to be a man at last. Who'd have though it!"

"Get back to the hole as soon as you can Jake. I'm not kidding!" And then Doughnut's mood changes as he realises that I'm going.

"I won't be any trouble! You'll barely know I'm there. Please let me go with you!" He knows the answer but I don't blame him for trying. I'd do exactly the same.

"I need you here." I look towards Ellie and then back at Doughnut and although he's kicking the dirt with his foot I know he understands perfectly well what I mean. I kneel down by his side as he deliberately looks down again at the ground because I don't want to leave under a cloud, not when I'll need my head clear for what I'm about to do. "You're the oldest male when I'm away. It's your responsibility to look after things while I'm gone."

I can tell I've chosen the right words because he's stopped kicking the ground and is now looking at me from the corner of his eyes. He's at that age I guess when he's stuck somewhere between a boy and a man. I guess we both are.

Standing up straight I see Ellie smiling at the two of us and I start to feel a little embarrassed, as if I've been way too soppy and the two of them are about to explode with laughter at me, but it's Doughnut who breaks the awkwardness as he looks up, eyes shining, and grabs Ellie by the arm.

"Come on then! We've got work to do before Jake gets back." And then before I know what I'm doing I turn and start off down the lanes, weaving in and out of people, because having made all this fuss I don't want to hang around and wait for my courage to dissolve.

The lanes twist and turn and I step carefully to avoid the remnants of rotting food and who knows what else that litters the way. The area I'm making for is a patch of open ground that acts as a meeting place, dumping ground and in the last few years one of the unofficial recruitment areas that have sprung up all over. If you're one of the lucky ones then you can earn some proper money; fixing the precious water pipes that still work, helping to build shelters, if not then you're more than likely to be left face down in a ditch somewhere.

Guards are supposed to be present to maintain control but are less visible than elsewhere and despite the risks of entering, it's actually one of the few places, other than the roof tops, that you get a feeling of freedom, however fleeting and illusory. It's like a no man's land where the rules are totally different to out here in the lanes and the Guard's prefer to keep their distance. In fact, there's pretty much only one rule I've ever heard of; no kids.

Apparently people still have some humanity.

I know Ellie hates it and Doughnut, for all his brave talk would rather cross the street than be anywhere near it, but I like it here. There's always something going on; people on the make, trading anything they can get their hands on, looking to buy, sell or steal.

It's as real as life gets here.

We call it *The Pit,* and I brace myself as I enter.

Chapter 9

Ellie won't go near it and I know that Doughnut never really wants to either, regardless of what he says but on occasion I've ventured to the rooftops that overlook *The Pit* despite the danger of being caught. I've sat there for hours watching the comings and goings, knowing that someday, more than likely, I'd have to take my chances down there just like everybody else.

The Pit itself is a large area of land that over time has been used for many things. I've heard stories that at first they wanted to build some sort of facility for the Guards but it was deemed to be too close to the Lanes. Our Leader has always wanted those that rule to be separate, hence the inner city beyond the Neutral Zone I guess.

From time to time, so the stories go, people have tried to live on it, building their shacks as best they can like the rest of us do from whatever materials they could lay their hands on. But the houses never stayed for long as if some unspoken rule had been violated, as if the land was somehow not for living on.

The rumour I heard that did the most to strike fear into me was that the land had been, in the time before the Great Light, a burial ground, some kind of cemetery, and those who were old enough to remember when it was hated the idea of anyone building on the graves of their loved ones.

Whatever the real reason over time the land became separated from the rest of the City, barricades slowly built up from sheet metal to old burnt out cars until it became a no go area, a sort of black market, different from the day to day street trading in the Lanes. If you want food and water, protection, whatever it is then you can find it here. But you've got to be willing to pay for it and mostly the price is not worth the hassle.

From time to time the Guards are sent in to clean the place up and they take down the barricades, open the land up for communal use, but it doesn't take long for people to creep back, for the place to grow again.

Head down and hands in pockets I aim slowly for the entrance up ahead. The gap I'm aiming for is in between two burnt out wrecks that have been turned onto their side, wood and metal forming the rest of the barricade, at least the part that I can see. Taking a deep breath I can see a group of men laughing and smoking and I suddenly feel like the youngest person here, as if any minute now someone's going to grab me and drag me off God knows where or some sort of alarm is going to sound alerting everyone to my presence.

From the roof I've seen countless numbers of people flow in and out of The Pit and although it's common knowledge that gangs control certain areas, no one person controls who gets to come in. I guess the theory is that anyone can enter. It's leaving that's the problem, at least with what you came with in any case.

As I near the group I can hear them talking about Our leader's words from earlier and with their attention on other things I look up a little from the ground, not much but enough to see them this close up; their tatty clothes, ripped and dirty like the rest of us. Faces smeared with dirt and dust.

"Why doesn't he send the damn Guards out there! Give 'em something to do other than bother us…"

"When they gonna come here? You know they're gonna start rounding up people sooner rather than later!"

"Only a few days until the next full moon!"

The last comment makes them look up and for a split second all of them are looking directly at me and I almost trip on my own feet with fright until I realise that they're looking beyond me to the Guards that are about fifty yards behind me, towards the Lanes.

I hold my breath as I slip by them, squeezing by the rusty car on the right until I'm a few yards away but the expected sense of relief doesn't come. How could it, considering where I am?

The rules here are pretty simple and straightforward; keep yourself to yourself and don't interfere in other people's business, especially if you're my age. Avoiding eye contact I push on through the people who are scattered about intent in their business but almost immediately out of the corner of my eye I see three men making a line for me; traders, scavengers and they're every bit as dangerous as they look.

I don't have anything of value on me but it won't stop them trying. They'll take the clothes off your back if you've nothing else to give.

I know.

I've seen them do it.

I smell them before they get to me, people getting out of their way as they push through. "Hey there kid, you're a long way from home aren't you?" The one in front, toothless save for a black stump at the front of his mouth is eyeing me up, looking for any tell tale bulges in my clothing that suggest I'm hiding something. Another one, smaller with a scarred face, steps to his left.

"Fresh water, boy? Best you'll find round here! Got anything to trade?" The third one steps to the back and I see that they've cut off not only me but a guy who entered The Pit just before I did. He looks nervous, as if he's hiding something and they start to jostle us both, spinning us around, trying to disorient us as people continue walking right by, minding their business, unwilling to get involved.

I've seen it from the rooftops countless times, hell I see it everywhere, everyday; people praying on the weak, nipping at them until they've got nothing left to give, and even then it doesn't stop them, doesn't make them give up. Out in the Lanes, on some rare occasion one of the old timer's will step in if things are getting out of control, as if they have a sudden memory of what it was like before the Great Light, where from what I've been told, people tried to look after each other rather than relying on the power of just one man.

In here? Forget it! It's everyone for themselves. Survival of the fittest.

The man to my left looks scared, unable keep the fear out of his eyes. "I…I don't want any trouble…please…" The scavengers laugh and mock his voice and then from nowhere they knock him to the ground and start to rummage through his pockets. The atmosphere had changed in an instant as all eyes turn towards our group. The one with the blackened tooth stops for a moment and turns to no one in particular.

"Disrespect me in my own house!" He catches my eye and begins to stand. "This is MY house! You hearing me boy? You're in MY piece of the city now!" He turns and drills his fist into the man's face, blood erupting from his lip and dripping onto the floor. He screams and covers his face as the others laugh and continue checking him for anything useful.

I choke back the fear and back away, slowly turning until I'm facing the area of The Pit that I need to be in. The hand that grabs my shoulder makes my heart practically jump from my chest.

"Where you going little fish?" I feel myself pulled back as hands enter my pockets and feel along my arms and legs for anything sown into the lining. I look at the bloodied figure on the floor and brace myself for a beating that doesn't come. The hands disappear and for a split second I stand there, in the middle of The Pit with my eyes shut scared of what I might see if I open them.

Slowly my right eyelid lifts up against my will and I catch sight of them running off into the crowd. I'm filled with relief as I see them hone in on more new people, desperate to get to them before anyone else does. For a split second I lie here on the ground, dazed, before my mind starts telling me what to do.

And then I'm off, darting between bodies until I reach the far corner, bursting through a line of people and slamming into a low wall, my right shoulder taking the impact. The pain shoots up and I half turn, half stumble, holding my hand up by way of an apology to those I've just knocked into, gasping for air and shaking like a leaf. I can see the man through the crowd, a small figure on the floor, others beginning to move in on the off chance something might be left for them.

Part of me feels guilty for not helping him but I know that there's nothing I could have done except get myself into even more trouble and that's simply not an option. Gasping for air, I look around, tensing in anticipation of more confrontation but despite the grumbling from some, their hollow eyes tell me that I'm not worth the trouble it would bring to start anything.

Looking down at the ground, my chest heaving with recent efforts I begin to smile but it's more like a grimace if truth be told because I picture Ellie with her arms crossed over her chest and that withering, sideways look. She'd kill me if she knew I'd already gotten myself into trouble.

Relaxing a little I slump against the wall and breath deeply and although I'm more than pleased to be out of harms way, the sheer number of people gathered in this corner deflates me a little. The area I'm in is at the corner of the waste ground and it's where, if you're lucky, those in need of cheap labour will come to choose the best of what's on offer; heavy lifting, clearing rubbish, digging what's left of the oil out of the ground.

It could be anything, or it could be nothing, but for a fifteen year old it's about as good as it gets.

General rules? The more people the less your chance of work. If you're lucky enough to be at the front then the following happens; you wait around and hope that a truck pulls up, or what passes for a truck in any case.

Despite dad telling me many times how, before the Light, the roads used to be full of cars of all different shapes and sizes I can't imagine it, certainly not when I see the thing that's belching out black smoke and looks like it's been made from just about anything that came to hand.

As it lurches and leans to one side I wonder just what the hell it's running on and how it's creating the foul black smoke that's beginning to cover those of us over here. As far as I'm aware, in these parts oil and gas are as rare as fresh drinking water, at least for us in any case.

From what I've seen from the rooftops, the next part of the process is when the Bossman looks at the gathering of people and calls out what work is available and how many bodies he needs for the day. Some days the trucks don't arrive at all and then people are simply left to their own devices – that's when most trouble happens, when the realisation hits that there's going to be no money that day. I've seen plenty of brawls breaking out precisely because the thought of another day without any money is just too much to take.

However, even if there's plenty of work and you're at the front of the queue, it's still no guarantee that you'll get anything. If you're face doesn't fit, if they're looking for a particular type of person, if they *know* you. There's a multitude of factors that go into getting on the trucks. That's why, as I look at the numbers in front of me, I don't rate my chances very highly at all.

I try pushing my way through but the way is firmly closed and with a few grunts and stares I'm pushed to the back again. I can hear the truck groan to a halt, sense the crowd beginning to move; people yelling and shoving trying to get seen and heard, faces yearning to be the ones picked.

Pushing again I near the front and think I've got a chance until the truck begins to pull away already full to the brim, at least four people hanging onto the sides. One of them slips and falls to the ground much to the amusement of everyone else and he howls at the sky before bowing his head and returning to the fold.

Now the group has thinned a little I figure that I've got a much better chance than before but the heat's getting really bad now and my throat is burning for some water, especially after the beating I very nearly took just to get here.

I try to put it out of my mind because I know full well that the chances of anyone actually taking pity on me and handing over a water canteen are about as remote as it's possible to get. In fact the chances of anyone having any water on them at all is pretty far-fetched.

As I stand there considering my options there's another surge and this time I'm the one being pushed from behind. The second truck, even more battered looking than the first, if such a thing were possible, chugs into view as if it's about to lay down and die, pulling up about ten yards from where we stand.

The man that gets out of the truck looks about as old as people get in Sanctum, and as fat, and by the way he's stretching his back and legs he doesn't look like he'll be doing too much today.

He clears his throat and spits a long stream into the dust. Looking up through squinty eyes he looks around, surveying what's on offer. "Who wants to work today?" Those remaining jostle again for attention. Shouts ring out;

"Pick me!"

"I do!"

"This way!"

"I need two people to work the water tunnels!" Immediately the clamour dies down as if everyone is suddenly hesitating and a cold sweat breaks out on my body because I'd rather shovel someone else's toilet than work down there. The tunnels are notorious for collapsing; their dangerous and claustrophobic and everyone knows of someone's relative or friend that's been trapped down there at one time or another.

And then there's the Wastelanders and the rumours that they've some how been using the very same tunnels to get inside the walls.

But Ellie needs to eat!

I picture her and how thin she's gotten and before my mind is allowed any more time to think my body has made the decision for me as my feet propel me away from the safety of the group and towards the Bossman.

Seeing me move forwards acts like a spur to the others and they begin to follow, fear of empty stomachs too much to bear but I've already been seen and I guess, being young, I'm more what he's after. He gives me the nod and I look around, momentarily uncertain as to who he means.

"You coming or what, son?" And then I run the last few yards to the truck and jump in before my place is taken.

Chapter 10

This is only my second time working for someone else. I don't really count when I picked up that bucket of waste because the stench was overpowering and I didn't even last long enough to get paid anything at all. The first *real* time was a short walk from the Pit clearing and burning rubbish. It was hard work but there were ten of us and the time seemed to fly by.

I didn't tell Ellie or Doughnut I was going to do it and the look on their face when I returned to our little hovel, a makeshift home of cardboard and branches, was priceless because I had made enough for a bottle of clean water and some bread. Doughnut didn't know which way to look and Ellie momentarily forgot she was supposed to tell me off as we all set about feasting.

As the truck pulls out along the north lane I smile as I picture the two of them and realise that I'm already missing them. It's like going into the unknown and although I'm nervous for sure, I'm also excited at what lies ahead. The truck's full to the brim like the other one and I'm squashed against a dirty window by three other people sharing two seats. The smell of stale sweat is almost overwhelming and no one's really speaking, I guess no one really wants to.

Every half mile or so the truck stops and various people get off and on, a real flow of labour being distributed around the Lanes. Everyone looks more or less the same; same gaunt expression, same tired eyes, same dirty patchwork clothing. They're all scavengers and when I look down at the holes in my clothes I half smile because they all look just like me; you forget I guess, when you spend your whole life in a small little area of Sanctum, you forget that there's more out there than your little, tiny corner of the world, even if it all looks exactly the same.

Two of the new ones start talking and I catch various snippets about Our Leader's speech and the plans for the criminals but I'm not really paying much attention, I'm too interested in what's going on beyond the window.

I'm used to flying over the roof tops with Ellie and Doughnut, I'm used to the cramped conditions of the lanes, or at least the parts that we stick to; I know them like the back of my hand, could make my way about with my eyes closed, no problems at all.

What I'm not used to is what I'm seeing now, the sheer *size* of it all, stretched out before me as the truck drives by row after row of half built shacks, of little kids playing in the dirt, of open sewers running by the sides of the tracks that weave in and out of the slums. They seem to go on forever, multiplying until I shut my eyes.

How can we all be living like this? Why hasn't more been done to improve things? I think back to the speech earlier, to Our Leader's words. Maybe this *fight back* or whatever he called it *is* the start of something? The start of a new era for Sanctum.

It's got to be.

The thought is cut short as the driver yells out *Tunnels* and my brain reminds me that this is my stop. I make my apologies as I squeeze past those that are left and I'm grateful to be off the truck and sucking in the relatively clean air.

As the truck drives off I see one other person, the one that was chosen alongside me in The Pit and we eye each other for a moment before nodding. Conversations are difficult. Why open up to someone you are unlikely to ever see again?

I look around and up ahead, through a line of shacks, I see the well that must service this particular area of the lanes, a ragged line of people waiting their turn. They're all the same, the wells; in the middle of a patch of wasteland so they can be clearly seen and guarded. In fact, mounted on blocks of concrete, I guess they're not really wells at all, more open pipes with a valve somewhere down below the ground.

A Guard stands there all day and is in charge of releasing the valve and allowing the water to flow through the pipe and out of the end, which has been beaten and bent until it can reach into the neck of most portable containers. You're not allowed much and the Guards are the ultimate deciders of who gets what at the end of the day.

Every now and again fights break out but for the most part people are just too damn hungry and tired to be bothered losing their place in the queue. Although there must be plenty of ways to get a little more, otherwise how would people be able to sell it at such extortionate prices?

"You what they sent me then?" The new Bossman appears from the bushes near the well as the sound of the truck disappears into the distance. He's been relieving himself as there are tell-tale splashes on his trousers and I try to stifle a smile as the two of us stand a little straighter and wait for instructions. I'm just hoping he doesn't send us both walking back.

It has been known if the decision is made that you're the wrong person for the job after all. Your main problem then of course is how you're going to get back home on foot. I watch him as he ambles over; he looks harmless enough, certainly older than I imagined with a balding head and a blue shirt that's stretching at the seams.

How do some people seem to remain so fat when most of us spend our time starving? But appearances can be deceiving and I don't know yet whether I'm going to like him or not, not that it really matters I suppose.

"Small enough I guess," He mutters looking us up and down, "although you're a little tall." He's looking directly at me and I start to get nervous, "It can be incredibly tight in places down there!" He pats his stomach and chuckles, "'Course I'm grown a little too large in the last few years, that's why we need some young fellas for this type of business!" I smile back and he doesn't seem to mind.

"I'm quick to learn sir and I'll work hard for you, I promise!" The words come out before I have time to stop them and for a moment I stand there with my heart in my throat. It's not the done thing to speak without being directly asked to by a Bossman and I have visions of the Guards coming over and dragging me off to 'teach me some manners'.

At first his face is stern as if he can't believe I've had the cheek to speak back to him but then slowly a grin spreads until I can see teeth at various angles poking through. Nodding he begins to walk away from us before stopping and half turning. "Well, what are you waiting for? Our Leader to choose you for the full moon fun and games?" He chuckles and heads off, shaking his head, "Seems to me he's got plenty to choose from already!"

As we walk past the well, faces from the raggedy queue of people look up, dark eyed and weary. They carry anything they can to hold the precious drops. The Guard next to the tap looks bored as he yawns, "Next!" and the people shuffle forward a few paces. No wonder people are so scared. They've barely got the energy to stand.

I'm full of mixed emotions as I know we need the money but at the same time I want to ask the Bossman questions about whether or not its true that the Wastelanders have been able to dig this far under the walls and whether they can simply come up from under the earth whenever they like. But then would they send us down there if there was a chance that those *things* were down there as well?

Surely protecting whatever water we do have is of paramount importance?

"You listening to me boy?"

My thoughts had gotten away from me and I snap to attention hoping I haven't ruined my chances. "I'm sorry sir." I hang my head and stare at my shoes.

"Look, we're all workers, right? Just trying to make an honest living! Don't worry about it." He pats his stomach and chuckles and I decide that I might get to like him after all.

He carries on walking and we dutifully follow. I throw a look at the other worker but he's staring ahead, really concentrating which is what I should be doing. I hear Ellie's voice in my head; *stop goofin' around*, and I stand that little bit straighter.

"Each well has a worker's hatch so that we can get down there and do any necessary repairs." We follow back to the bushes that he originally emerged from but this time from the other side and I see what he's talking about; a big concrete looking slab that must be a few metres wide, with a small wheel to the side of it. He kneels by the wheel and starts to lean into it, his face slowly turning purple with the effort as a smaller section of the slab slides open and I see the beginning of a set of steps descending down into the darkness below.

"The ladder goes down about forty yards until you reach the first level, that's where the equipment is stored for upkeep and maintenance, we'll stop there to get what we need. The pipes themselves are another fifty yards below that, relics of the past so to speak, before the Great Light when each home had its very own pipes for water."

The other worker smiles and I catch his eye. I know exactly what he's smiling at, the thought of piped water into every home, as much as you could ever want. It seems so, so far fetched. The Bossman wipes his face with his sleeve and looks back up at us both, brow furrowed.

"It can be dangerous down there and seeing as though we're looking for some damage that's occurred you need to be careful at all times!" The Bossman steps onto the top rung and begins to descend. "Don't worry about closing the lid, the Guards'll do that for us when we're down far enough."

I look back to the snake of people by the well waiting for their turn, for their meagre rations. What would happen if it completely dried up? Would there be chaos? Would there be riots? He stops and turns to face us, "But hey, where are my manners? Three men go down into the earth and none of them know each others names!" He shakes his head and tuts, "Won't do...won't do at all!"

For a moment we stand there in silence before I realise that he's waiting for one of us to go first. I look at the other worker and then clear my throat.

"Jake. My name's Jake." I half smile and look at both of them.

"Angus." The other worker looks back at me shyly from under his hair and I look at him properly for the first time, he's not that much older than I am; same thin face, same rags. The uniform of poverty.

Then the Bossman holds his hand out for us to shake and I find myself strangely touched by the gesture. Angus is the first to take up the offer like he does it all the time and steps forward, and then it's my turn and I get nervous again trying to remember what I've been told about first impressions, about not gripping too weakly, about not having a sweaty hand.

I'm suddenly convinced that my hands dripping and that he's going to think I've no strength in me. And then it's done and we're all standing there again as if we're just three regular guys that do this all the time.

"Glad to be working with you boys, glad to be working with you." And then the top of his bald head disappears into the gloom and we're left standing there on our own looking at each other until we hear him calling out from below.

"The name's Jeremiah by the way. Now get your asses down here!"

Chapter 11

Adrenalin starts to surge as I begin to descend the steps. It really feels like going into the unknown, like travelling back into Sanctum's past. There's no kid in the city that hasn't gone hunting for access below ground but it's difficult to find and the Guards are always there to stop you.

I've also heard stories that there may even be great lakes under the ground as if when we were fighting, when we scorched the earth, the water retreated below like us humans tried to.

Can't imagine it myself, that much water being underground. I can't picture what it would look like. I just run my tongue over my dry, cracked lips and hope before the day's out that I get to drink some.

"Fifteen metres to go, lads!" Jeremiah's voice echoes all around and I try to stay calm as the gloom gets darker still. I look up to see Angus a few feet away from me, his face ghost like as a light from below flickers casting great long shadows that seem to have a life of their own.

As I near the last rung of the ladder my foot begins to explore the air, groping for a firm platform and I step off and to the side to allow Angus to get by.

We're in a relatively small room that I take to be the equipment room Jeremiah spoke of earlier given that there are all sorts of things hanging on the walls. The lamp opposite is still flickering, still sucking in air and spewing out shards of light but it's the object in the middle of the ceiling that's caught all our attention. As Jeremiah flicks a button on the wall so it too begins to blink life into itself before the whole room is bathed in light and he is able to turn the lamp down until it sparks and then dies.

Although there are plenty of places where light bulbs are to be found in the lanes, most of them either don't work or are only used for very special occasions for it costs a lot to light them. You really need your own generator but they run on fuel and fuel is as rare as water here; it's why we're all currently staring at the light bulb.

In its simplest form it represents the power and technology Our Leader has, like at the Square earlier, the big screen that shows his face, the music blaring out of the speakers, even the siren itself. He's been the one able to harness what was left after the Great Light, and with it he has the ultimate power I guess because he chooses who gets to use it.

"I know, I know! We all live up there where times are hard and getting harder, where we barely have enough to eat and if we have a fresh candle then we've done well indeed!"

Jeremiah spreads his arms wide, his voice taking on the tone of the preachers that you can see on almost every street corner, raising their arms and their voices to the sky, "Yet down here, under the ground, we have the latest in technology for your viewing pleasures!"

I want to question him about the light, about what it's doing down here and why it's not readily available above ground but he spins a wheel on the door opposite and the sound drowns out my chance.

"One more level to go lads! Angus, grab the gloves and the rope. It's all we'll need for the time being."

I'm more secure with my footing this time and our descent is further helped by bulbs at intervals that link the light to form an almost continuous glow. I think back to the occasional bulbs and the torches and lamps that I'm used to. How they light only a certain area around them, plunging everything beyond into an even richer darkness.

Do others know about this?

I feel like I'm being shown secrets that not many people know and it's making me uneasy.

When we touch ground we're in a smaller room than the one above but it still has the same door with a wheel that Jeremiah begins to turn. We hear the same click as before but instead of opening it he hesitates and turns to us. "This is the door boys, to another world! You need to keep to the left and watch your footing, the damage should be around fifty meters or so up ahead if I've done my sums right. Ready?"

I don't know what to think really. I can't imagine what's beyond the door. More tunnel is my only guess. What did Jeremiah say earlier? Something about using the remnants of what was left behind after the Great Light?

As the door opens my eyes widen and for a few seconds I'm unable to move. The door leads us into a long tunnel, about the height and width of at least three men, a thin walkway suspended outwards from the rock the only thing between us and the water that's running down from the gloom on the right and passing into the darkness on the left.

Running water.

The lights that shine at intervals on the walkway don't do much else in this huge cavern than point the way we need to go. "Told you it'd be a surprise!" I can barely hear Jeremiah above the noise of the thoughts in my head and speed up so I can hear what he's saying. It's about the water that's retreated down here, how Our Leader has been trying to harness its power for years.

I begin to wonder if the reason above the ground is so poor is due to the amount it must cost to keep something like this going. I look back and catch Angus who smiles weakly at me and then shrugs and looks around. He is having as much difficulty with all this as I am and this knowledge helps calm me down a little.

"Settler's moved into these tunnels all those years ago to get away from the danger above ground. Found out about the water and started to divert it up there."

Jeremiah points to the ceiling of the tunnel with his hand and I barely know what to do with myself; continue listening to his stories or dive right in and drink until my stomach bursts. "'Course, over the years, as the sun's beat down on us the water's gone even deeper down as if it knows we need it now more than ever and it's decided to play some sort of cruel trick on us!"

He half turns and grins as we follow, hanging on every word. "There's lakes beneath us boys, down there in the dark. Just need to find a way to harness them!"

"How many of these, these tunnels are there?" Angus has caught up with me on the walkway. He's asked the very question I was beginning to form in my mind.

"Ever seen a beehive?" Jeremiah yells over his shoulder.

I haven't personally. Don't think anyone has for a very long time but I vaguely remember dad telling us one of his stories about the old times about what he termed 'wildlife'. I recall being pretty sceptical about some of the stuff he was trying to convince us of like, I've forgotten it's name but it had wings but couldn't fly – I mean why in God's name would nature create something like that?

But I remember him being most passionate about something he would always call the cycle of life and how certain little creatures had an enormous impact on the world around them, far more influence than their size would perhaps suggest they would. I think it was his way of trying to tell me to look after everyone no matter how weak they were;

You never know when they might turn out to be important to you!

I remember dad talking about bees one evening, about how they used to fly around and move seeds from one plant to another and I would sit on his knees so I could look at what he was drawing with an old crumbly charcoal stick. I can see his face lighting up with a smile as he would draw box after box on their edges all interlinked. Cells he called them and he said they contained something sweet called honey that you could eat.

I imagine the tunnels that Jeremiah speaks of to be similar to those drawings and I half wonder how the ground has not caved in beneath our feet.

Jeremiah stops abruptly on the walkway and I almost bump into Angus. "Should be near enough there by now!" He scratches the top of his head and takes a piece of paper from his top pocket, unfolding what turns out to be quite a large map with dozens of scribbles and pictures that I reckon he's added to over time, no doubt to try and keep up with the pace of development.

He continues muttering to himself but both Angus and I are looking at the water beneath our feet and for a moment, when our eyes meet, we grin as if part of some secret society that only the three of us are members of. Don't care if Jeremiah says it's a trickle because it's more water than I've ever seen in my life.

To me it could be an ocean for all I know and it flashes up again and again in my mind the only real question worth asking. If there's all this water down here, why on earth is there so little up there? And what would people do, *really do*, if they knew the truth?

After a few minutes of thought Jeremiah turns to us, folding the map and placing it back in his pocket. "Should be up ahead a little way, look for disturbances in the water flow."

Instinctively we all look down but I half hear Jeremiah mutter something else, something like, "Bastards get everywhere." and I know exactly what he's talking about. It's the subject none of us have wanted to raise.

"Sir. Sir!"

He calls back over his shoulder, "Jeremiah's my name son."

"I'm sorry, Jeremiah, what do you think caused the early settler's to try and go underground?" I know the answer. Hell, everybody knows the answer but I'm hoping it will cause him to talk a little more. Most old folk I've come across can't resist an invitation to talk about how it used to be and I don't know if I'm ever going to get this opportunity again.

Turning slightly he eyes me as if weighing up how much to say and then turns back around. I've missed my chance and I begin to kick myself about it.

"Wastelanders, son. Wastelanders." Then he's off and I walk as close as possible in an attempt to hear every word. "We're not the only ones as made use of the old settler tunnels. Time was the original town was to be further along the valley floor," He points to the left with his hand, "but the rocks harder that way, tunnels were abandoned in the end, everything ended up being shifted to softer ground."

I take in everything he's saying, trying to picture it in my head. "So these tunnels, like sort of beehives, stretch beyond the city walls?"

"Sure do, son. Sure do."

I try to concentrate but all I can picture is the rest of us standing by the well waiting for our meagre rations, oblivious to the world beneath her feet.

"The Wastelander's have been using them, haven't they?" Angus' question breaks the spell as Jeremiah points to the wall up ahead. It has a large hole in it, enough to fit two or three men through and the water is gushing all around it, frothing and spilling out of this tunnel and going who knows where. "They've been using them to get in, that's why Our Leader wants to fight them out in the open to stop them getting in under our feet!"

It's more of a question than a statement but it makes perfect sense down here.

"That's about the size of it, son. That's about the size of it."

Chapter 12

Jeremiah looks out over the walkway and rubs the side of his face with a large, fleshy palm. I know what he's thinking; how on earth are we going to get to that damn hole? And when I look towards Angus I can tell he's thinking exactly the same thing.

"Didn't think this one through really lads!" He leans over and draws in a deep breath, "We're supposed to get down there and measure the thing, see what we need to fix it." The rest is lost as he continues to rub his face in puzzled thought.

Jeremiah looks back the way we came as if minded to return to ground level and contemplate another course of action. My heart pounds as I step forward, raising my voice so it can be heard above the water.

"If we work together," I look towards Angus who is still peering over the side looking at where we've got to go. "then it shouldn't be too difficult to get down there." Jeremiah doesn't say anything, he just continues to rub his face, his eyes darting from the walkway back to the hole.

I want to say to him that no one would care if he returned to the outside alone, that we're as expendable as any other work material, but as he turns to face us both I can see from the look in his eye that he's thought of this already.

We end up swinging from the edge of the walkway, lowering ourselves until we're holding on with our fingers and then gaining momentum with each swing until letting go and landing on a ledge on the tunnel wall. Angus only really needs to swing once to reach the ledge but I can see he's nervous and as he lands on the wall his leg slips and dangles in the water for a moment.

"Gees it's cold!"

"You boys be careful! I should never have agreed to this." I can hear the concern in his voice.

"We made it, don't worry!" But I am, about Angus and how we're going to get him back onto the walkway. There's about a five foot gap between the top of the hole and the ceiling of the tunnel and I spot some good hand holds and start to make my way across.

"Be careful Jake!" I acknowledge the sentiment but I need to concentrate because the wall's slippy and I don't fancy taking a plunge. The fall itself would be no problem as the water looks to be knee deep at best. You can see from the waterline that it should be at least two feet higher. I can't help but wondering where all the water has gone? Surely it can't just disappear back into the rock?

My eyes are drawn back to the hole, to the darkness beyond and the noise that I've never heard before. It sounds like a low, deep rumbling and I try to imagine what I've been told about there being lakes underground but I just can't picture it.

Shaking my head clear I trace a route with my eyes, happy where the next hand hold is and stretch to reach one with the fingertips of my right hand. I'm at full stretch but with my left knee bent in I get a strong foot hold which enables me to use my fingers as a pivot point and I stretch over with my left hand for the more secure hold.

I think of the fun Ellie and Doughnut would have down here, climbing and running about but I push the thought away; I can't get distracted, not now, not down here!

I noticed earlier, when peering over the side of the walkway to get a better look, that there were some deep indentations on the tunnel wall and I was right because as I figure out my next move I can see that a few cross steps and I'll be able to secure myself against the face of the wall. It's a little tricky with the water all around but I put my left leg around the back of my right until it feels secure and then slip the right one through, my arms following lightly across a couple of easy holds until I'm securely in.

"Way to go Jake!" Angus grins and waves from the other side and I sheepishly put my hand up in a sort of half shrug, half apology. Ellie and Doughnut would laugh their heads off if they knew that I was taking praise for such an easy climb. Wiping the sweat from my forehead I untie the rope from my waist and pull it as tight as possible.

"Can you read the knots?" I know Jeremiah is shouting but I can barely hear him, the noise coming from the dark hole is getting louder and louder and in the time it's taken me to climb across I'm sure the water has crept up the side of the wall a little further. Angus leans out some more and I pull the rope because it's gone slack.

"Pull it a little tighter, Angus, otherwise the reading won't be accurate."

Another thought pushes its way into my mind; why are we trying so hard? Why are we putting ourselves in danger? I have no answer apart from that I guess it's nice to feel a part of something, a team effort. Or maybe it's just that concentrating so hard on what we're doing is taking my mind of all the other crap we usually have to deal with? And then there's the money of course.

Looking over I see Angus nod acknowledgment and try to push himself back up straight but his hand slips on the greasy surface of the wall missing the open crack that would have easily helped him up. I see it almost before it happens; he tries to catch the hold again but slips further and with a sharp yell lands awkwardly on the lip of the hole.

For a split second all I can see are the whites of his eyes as he teeters on the edge of the darkness, his right hand scrabbling for the wall, fingers slipping over the smooth surface.

"Angus, hold on!"

And then he's gone. The darkness enveloping him.

"ANGUS!"

I can hear him coughing as his right hand reaches up out of the gloom and as I squint into the darkness, my eyes beginning to adjust to the lack of light, I begin to make out that he's holding on with his other hand to an outcrop just beneath the hole.

"Hold onto him Jake! Hold on to him!" I crouch as low as I can, my left arm at full stretch and we manage to catch hold of each other's hands. The roaring is louder now that I'm half through the hole. God knows how much water is down there.

"Don't let go! Don't let go!" I look around and see another good hold near the water level and try to lift him so he can get a better grip but he's too heavy. "There's a hold to the right of your shoulder, grab it!" But the water's making everything too wet and his hand begins to slip from my grasp. My shoulder is screaming with the weight and I try desperately to hold on but I can't.

I see his face for the last time. He's trying to say something.

And then he's gone.

I know Jeremiah's calling out but all I can hear is Angus as he shouts for help. But even that doesn't last for long because as the darkness engulfs him there's one last scream.

And then nothing.

"We'll follow the map and find him where the water stops!" Jeremiah is pleading with me but all I can think about is his hand slipping through mine. And the screaming.

Ellie's face fills my mind because I know what she would expect me to do, "*You've got to help him Jake! You've got to!*" and my body makes the decision before my brain has time to think of a reason not to.

Gripping the hold with my right hand I take one last look up towards Jeremiah on the walkway and then push my legs out and swing through the hole. Momentum takes over and I hold on for as long as I can before my hand lets go. The fall must only take a few seconds but it seems like a lifetime as I hang, suspended in the gloom, not knowing what awaits me below.

The cold is the first thing I notice as I hit, but I fight against the urge to thrash around, instead letting the water take me where it will. My head breaks the surface and I take a lungful of air before I'm turned again and my shoulder crashes against the side of the tunnel. The water's speeding up, I'm sure of it, which means it must be going downhill.

I imagine that Angus is holding onto a protruding rock and that the water will start to slow down but as I surface again I make out a bend up ahead and what little light there is left from the hole above shows me that if anything the tunnel is getting narrower. As I fight to keep my head above water I start to cough, inhaling more than I should.

The roar of the water is getting louder.

And then I'm free falling.

The ground opens up beneath me as my legs and arms windmill, propelling me forward. I can't be in the air for more than three or four seconds at most but it feels like forever.

Hitting the water forces what little air is left out of my lungs and I fight the urge to inhale again, my legs kicking for what I hope is the surface. Breaking through I gasp and brace myself for a fresh onslaught but nothing happens and as I roll over it's all I can do not to sink to the bottom.

"Quite a ride isn't it?"

The voice makes me jump and I cough more water up as I lose my stroke and briefly slip under again. "Straighten your legs, you should be able to touch the bottom with your toes." I do as I'm told managing to use the last of my energy to get close enough to the side to haul myself out before the rest of the water drags me further towards the darkness and roaring beyond.

I'm so exhausted I don't even acknowledge the fact that Angus is still alive. Instead I just lie there, my chest heaving up and down and my mind racing to unscramble itself.

When the roaring in my head subsides I turn onto my side and try to get my bearings. I can make out Angus across the water about thirty yards away and I raise my hand wearily and then let it flop back down across my chest. He smiles.

"Thought I was a gonner when I went over that little waterfall, thought I was just gonna keep on falling!" For a moment I wonder whether he's hit his head on something before looking back at where I've just come from to see the white froth churning away. It's not really a waterfall at all more like a water slide but it's still enough to take my breath away for a second time.

"We're in some kind of underground lake or river system like Jeremiah was talking about is the best I can figure!" There's something else behind his voice, something other than fatigue and when I manage to prop myself up on my elbows I can see Angus properly for the first time.

"You alright?" He's on a ledge opposite, the lake or whatever it is drifting off into the darkness. The sound of more churning water far off in the distance.

"It's my leg." He leans forward a little and then sits back sharply trying to suppress a cry, "I think it's broken! I slammed into the rocks pretty hard." He stops for a second and I worry that he's passing out and then he speaks again but this time is far softer than before and I can barely hear him above the noise of the water. "I can see some bone sticking out."

My strength is beginning to return and I start to think of what to do. If Angus has broken his leg than he needs help and fast. The only light we have is the faint glow from the other tunnel and that's only enough to see outlines at best. If he can't move then it's up to me to go for help but as I look into the darkness that's seems to be closing in on all sides I shiver and wrap my arms around my legs and face reality.

I don't have the first clue how to get out.

Chapter 13

Slipping into the water takes my breath away and I grit my teeth against the cold. When I reach Angus and pull myself up I only need to look at his leg for a second to realise that it's bad. I had been thinking about helping him back up the side of the waterfall, trying to make our way back to Jeremiah, but there's no way he's moving.

Looking again I can see dark water around his leg as if blood has been pooling, the bone a clear centimetre out from the shin, the skin all around torn and ragged. He's grinning but I can see that he's very pale and his teeth are beginning to chatter. None of which is a good sign.

"We need to get you out of the water otherwise you're going to get colder and colder." I'm talking to myself more than anything and I begin to look at the ledge above which mean he needs to be moved about half a foot. Lying in a slight hollow as he is means he'll never be out of the water; I'm no doctor but it seems the most sensible thing to do.

"Let's do it then shall we!" Taking a deep breath and bending his arms behind him he's able to shuffle a little until his back is touching the ledge.

"If you can get your hands up then I can lift your legs." I don't say that I think it's going to involve more pain than he's ever experienced before but I don't think I really need to. He's already grimacing from shuffling backwards.

"I like the confidence, Jake, I really do!" Raising his left leg at the knee I slip an arm quickly under, the same thing at the top of his thigh. He tries to lift the injured leg but cries out in pain and frustration.

"Dammit!" He chokes the rest of the sentence off and tries again. Yelling out again he looks at me and I see panic in his eyes. "I can't move the bloody thing. I can't do it!"

My dad once pulled a splinter from my finger by pretending there was a spider crawling on my shoulder. By the time I worked out there was no spider the splinter was out and the tears had stopped. Before I've time to think any more I'm looking over Angus' shoulder in mock horror as if something is creeping up behind us. I open my mouth as if to scream.

"What? What is it?" He half turns and as he looks back I take my chance and lift him up onto the higher ledge. The movement in his leg causes him to scream out louder than before and I can feel warm blood oozing out over my fingers. But his arms automatically help lever his body up until he collapses on the upper ledge, my arms still under his legs.

As I slide my hands out from under him he's no longer screaming, instead all I can hear is a whimpering sound as he lays his head back against the rock. But he's out of the cold water and that's what matters.

For now.

Suddenly a thought hits me from nowhere, like a hunting arrow; *they* can smell blood from miles away, at least that what we're always told. My skin tightens as a shudder rips through my body.

Craning my head I look back at where we came from forcing the fear back down. The water's still tumbling over and although steep I see that there is a potentially climbable area to the right. I follow the contours of the rock and although it feels like it's getting darker I think I can see some undulations that might make good holds, maybe a crack running to the top that I could manoeuvre myself against.

Fear crowds my mind but I push it back and turn to Angus.

"How you holding up?" The answer's obvious but it's all I can think to say. He looks up at me and grins through the pain.

"Beats working I guess!" We both laugh and it feels good to fill the gloom with something other than screaming.

"I'm going for help." I look back at the waterfall, "If I can climb up then maybe I can make it part way back to Jeremiah. I'm sure by now he's got help, some ropes maybe…" My voice trails off because I don't want to end up making promises I might not be able to keep.

"Try not to be too long!" I smile and slip back into the water pushing off with my feet. As I near the waterfall I see an obvious flaw in my plan that I should have thought of earlier. The spray from the waterfall has made everything damp and when I swim to the side of the white froth, to where I thought I might be able to climb, it's glistening with water.

Taking a deep breath I reach up and my fingers find a possible hold but as soon as I put any weight onto it I slip back into the water. I try again but this time I use my left leg against the rock to propel me up; for a moment I'm almost completely out until my right foot slips sending me flying back into the water again.

"Damn it!"

I float for a while on my back. I think Angus is saying something but the water in my ears obscures the words and for a moment I submerge and let the current take me away from the wall, trying to clear my head, trying to think, until I feel the water begin to churn me about. I kick for the surface and emerge directly under the waterfall, the force of the water trying to push me back under. Blinking rapidly as the water spits out at me I feel disoriented.

Again I think I hear Angus shout something but I can't make out what he's saying and I start to worry about his leg and whether the pain has increased.

Taking a breath I dive under the water and kick until I think I'm clear of the waterfall before emerging and shaking the water from my eyes. When I blink them open, for a moment I have no idea where I am, the way is dark and narrow and I don't recognise it at all. The roaring seems to be behind me and as I turn I realise that the disorientation I felt under the water was for real as

I've gone through the screen of water to the other side.

I need to get back to Angus and check that he's okay, try and find another route out, but as I bob up and down my mind nags at me as if it's trying to tell me something and I rotate in the water straining to listen. Blinking rapidly I look into the darkness of the passageway that lies beyond the waterfall, wiping my face of water droplets, a nagging thought trying to make itself known.

And then the thought propels itself to the front of my mind.

Air.

I can feel a breeze on my face, it's faint but it's there making my skin feel cold and tight. If there's a breeze then there must be a way out.

The thought sends a surge of energy through my body and I turn back to the screen of water. I know it could be a trick. There are probably enough tunnels to create their own wind. It could be a false alarm, it could be anything, but it's a glimmer of hope and that's all I need.

Taking a few deep breaths I dive below the surface and under the churning water from the fall until I surface a few metres away. My mind is already made up. I'm going to tell Angus and then see where the breeze takes me – what have I got to lose?

I surface and begin to swim over to the ledge when I see Angus' arm pointing up in the air. I follow the direction until I see a small opening high on the right hand side of the cavern, a tiny orange glow coming from deep within.

"HELP! HELP US PLEASE! WE'RE DOWN HERE!" His voice is so loud it scares me. We've been speaking so quietly that as the words echo around the chamber I begin to feel uneasy. Who is it? What if we get in trouble for being down here? Where the hell are we anyway?

I try to quieten my mind as Angus yells again. "MY LEG'S BROKEN. PLEASE COME QUICK!" I look back at the tunnel. The glow has stopped as if whoever is there is trying to decide what to do.

And then I hear it.

Faint at first but then louder and louder until the whole chamber seems filled with a gnashing sound, as if some sort of animal has found its way down here as well. Confusion fills my head and I look back at Angus but this time he's not looking at the hole with hope as he was before. This time his face is contorted, his eyes as wide as they can go, and I see his mouth open and then close as if even the very words he wants to speak refuse to come out.

The gnashing, gnarling sound is closer now and I feel my body lock as if refusing to turn around; refusing to face what I know is up there waiting for us.

Slowly my head swivels until I see a deformed silhouette cast on the opposite wall of the chamber by whatever is causing the glow.

Wastelanders.

It's true. They *have* got under the Wall!

I'm a least twenty meters from Angus when it jumps and I catch it out of the corner of my eye as it clings to the rock. It moves its head from left to right, clawing at the wall until it stops and then all I can hear is it taking great snorts of air as if trying to sniff out its prey.

The rattling as it inhales sounds as if something's broken inside but it's soon drowned out by the scream to my left.

I turn to where Angus is lying and for a split second I don't know what I'm looking at. It's as if he's somehow grown larger, grown more arms until something detaches from his leg.

The grinding of teeth on bone fills the cavern as Angus screams again. I see a second beast, it's deformed head shaking from side to side.

Ripping.

Tearing.

I can't move. I'm frozen to the spot as I hear the other one scraping its claws across the wall. Panic grips. And then I see Angus' face, blood streaked in the gloom as he turns in my direction, his mouth opening and closing.

I want to move nearer. I want to fight them off but I don't know what to do. He's trying to tell me something as the Wastelander pulls something from his lower leg and crunches.

"RUUUUN!"

Chapter 14

Fear roots me to the spot and my head starts to pound. The scream echoes round the cavern but I still hear the splash to my right as the water erupts in a shower of spray. The second Wastelander has dropped from the side of the wall.

I'm its prey.

This time I move.

Diving under I swim as hard as I can for the waterfall. The splash was to my right but far enough away that I have a slight head start. I need to make it count. Angus' scream is still in my ears as I strain every sinew in my body to get ahead, forcing away the thoughts that threaten to overwhelm.

Feeling the push of the surf I redouble my efforts. Every second that goes by I expect teeth to clamp around my ankle, claws to rake the side of my body.

Water pressure starts pushing me down which tells me I'm under the waterfall. My lungs are bursting at the seams but I daren't surface yet, my body pushing me further, hoping that the breeze wasn't a figment of my imagination.

As I get further away from the pull the gap narrows until my arms begin to scrape the sides. My lungs are burning and it's only a matter of time before I breathe in as a matter of instinct. Claustrophobia adds to the panic and I begin to thrash around.

Breaking the surface my lungs scream as I inhale deeply. Glancing behind I see the water rippling and bunching up a few metres behind me and redouble my efforts. The passageway narrows until my head's almost scraping the ceiling and I start to feel the pull of the water as it drags me nearer the darkness beyond.

I can't get my thoughts into any coherent order, my mind filling with Angus' face as he screams at me, the splash of water to my left.

Where has the damn thing come from? What is it doing here?

And then I'm tumbling.

The passageway turns to the left as the water begins to roll me about and I bounce off the wall wincing at the pain that shoots from my shoulder. But if I'm having trouble then so too is the Wastelander. I try to keep my head above water as I race along. If I can somehow find a place to stop, somehow let the thing fly past then it'll buy me some time. Allow me to regroup.

The thought gives me hope but I can barely see anything in the gloom and the pace of the water has picked up considerably.

For a second I expect to smell the fetid air of the Wastelander's breath on the back of my neck as it bears down on me and I thrash my arms about me as if I can somehow hold back the water, stop myself from being pulled even further in. It can't be happening! It can't be!

I can't allow myself to think about it. I've got to focus on what's going on right now.

As my arms fly up in the air I tumble again and my hand scrapes along the ceiling of the tunnel or whatever it is. It's only for a moment before I'm rotated under again but it's enough for me to feel the bumps and ridges of potential handholds.

The idea makes me thrash around even more trying to right myself but the action only seems to make me slip and slide further. All the while a noise that's been intruding in the back of my mind forces its way to the front as I sense something else up ahead in the gloom. A sound. A booming sound.

More water?

But this time the sound is far deeper, more menacing as if it's coming from way down deep within the earth itself. I throw my arms at the wall, try to slow myself down but there's nothing to grab hold off. *It* could be right behind me for all I know but the noise up ahead is getting louder, like a roaring, gurgling sound that I've never heard before. If I go over a bigger fall then I'll be lucky if it's only my leg that gets broken but I can't let even this happen.

If I do I'm dead.

I try to steady myself in the water as best I can and shoot my left arm out towards the ceiling, my fingers scraping along the grooves and bumps, but I'm going too fast to get any purchase on a hold.

I try again, lunging out of the water but again my grip is too wet and my fingers slide over the rock as I plunge back beneath the water. As my head bobs up I can hear the noise getting louder and louder.

It's now or never.

Tensing my body for one last lunge before I'm swallowed up I launch myself as far up as I can go. My left hand slides along the ceiling as the water pushes me to the left turning me over as my hand closes around a small lump of rock on the wall of the tunnel.

My body jolts to the side and I'm half out of the water but I know that I'm not going to be able to hold on. My hand is already slipping and the current's too strong. Throwing my left leg out ahead my foot slides across the wall and hits against a ledge just as my hand slips off the hold. For a split second I'm pinned against the wall as the force of the water locks my foot in place.

I push my back against the wall pressing my hands down hard and inch myself out of the water until only my right shoulder is submerged and looking up, manage to jam my left hand into a crack above my head. Taking the pressure on my arm I shift my foot until I've got both on the ledge.

Three points of contact. At last I'm able to catch my breath and I heave my chest up and down as I cough the last of the water up from my lungs.

And then I see it, in the gloom.

The Wastelander.

Tumbling in the water, half screaming, half choking, its arms outstretched as its talons scrape along the wall. I hold firm as the stench of rotten flesh fills my nostrils, pressing myself further against the wall as if the rock will somehow absorb me. It slips beneath the churning water and for a moment I can't see it, can't even smell it.

Then the surface breaks and a claw extends from the water. I look down and I can see that it hasn't got any purchase, hasn't found any hand holds as its shadow slides past me near enough to touch and I resist the urge to kick out, to help it on its way.

But I can do nothing as the claw reaches out from the water, as the Wastelander makes one last lunge, scraping its talons down the side of my body.

I feel my skin opening up and I shout in pain. And then it slips back under the water and is gone into the darkness, its screams fading as it plunges over the edge.

Trying to ignore the searing pain along my side I stretch up along the wall with my left hand for a better grip, all the while images of more claws breaking the surface cloud my mind.

I try to concentrate because if I slip I'm gone, just like the Wastelander. My fingers quickly locate another grip and I start to straighten up, keeping my feet firmly held against the rock but straightening my torso until I'm almost vertical, crouching on the small outcrop of stone inches above the water line.

My body aches with pain but it's not as bad as it looks. There are three lines from my underarm to my waist and they curve around to the point where the creature was sucked under for the last time. I shiver against the cold and stare at the wounds, it's gloomy in here but I can tell that they're not as deep as I first feared.

Closing my eyes I try to block out the images that float around because the longer I stay perched on this tiny bit of rock, the worse my situation gets. Shivering, I try not to think of Angus but the effort only forces his image to the front of my mind; his head turning towards me, the creature feasting on his leg.

RUUUUUN!

The image drives me on and I turn my face to the side to try and get an idea of what I'm faced with. The waterfall is only twenty yards away at most and it looks like there's enough jagged outcrops to make getting there relatively easy compared with what's gone on before but what do I do when I get there? Where do I go?

I can't answer the question in my current position so I pivot my left leg across my body and onto a firm hold that turns me face down on the rock and then begin to inch my way towards the mouth of the falls. My foot slips into the water but the other holds are good and I'm able to carry on until the narrow tunnel widens.

The roar is incredible and as I hang off the rock I try to extend myself as far as possible, to get a look at what's above me but it's so wet that I have to change holds every few seconds or my fingers will slip.

Straining every sinew in my body I stretch back until I can see out of the tunnel and up into the darkness of the chamber above. I can see chinks of light breaking through high above, they're only vague little dots but they're there all right; could be something or nothing. Could be exhaustion playing tricks on me but I'm not about to start climbing down that's for sure!

My legs are still inside the tunnel on the side of the wall but with my head and neck out in the chamber I need to extend an arm above me so that I can pivot my legs out. It's the most dangerous move of all because for the briefest of moments I'll only have one point of contact with the wall, my left hand which is grasping onto a hold on the ceiling of the tunnel.

Seeing the other hold I need in the chamber about a foot from my head I move back in slightly and take turns holding on with only one hand, letting the other drop down so I can shake blood into it and try to get rid of the fatigue that is threatening to drop me over the edge.

I picture Ellie and Doughnut high above me, talking me through it, telling me where the holds are, Doughnut looking down on me with that goofy, lopsided grin of his.

"Come on slowcoach! Give me some kind of competition at least!"

It helps and with a deep breath I begin to climb.

Extending my head and shoulders as far as they will go into the chamber, I ignore the froth that is spitting up at me and I let go. The weight of both legs dropping from their holds pivots me on my right hand and my head shoots up towards the side of the chamber. With my left hand high above me I slam onto the rock face and for a split second I think I've missed my chance.

My right wrist is still taking my weight but now instead of being vertical, I'm horizontal and all my weight is pressing down. I scramble with my left hand until I find something else, it's not the original hold but it will do and I raise my left knee until I have three points of contact and I'm out of the tunnel.

I daren't look over my shoulder in the direction of the booming sound beneath me and I start to move as quickly as possible. The rock is drier the further I go and in terms of climbing it's relatively easy with various holds and cracks to use but my adrenalin has left me and I find even raising my arm above waste height an almost impossible task.

With fatigue comes pain and I start to feel every knock I've taken but the one that's concerning me is the pain in my side from the creature claws. I try my best to ignore it as I inch up the rock towards the shafts of light that cross each other above me but I can't help my mind from pouring over everything else; Our Leader's speech, the full moon festival or whatever they're going to call it, Angus and the other Wastelander.

Do they know about the creatures, about the extent of these tunnels and caves? Do they know they have gotten this far into Sanctum?

The enormity of each thought threatens to drag me from the rock face and I shake my head clear in an attempt to redouble my efforts.

As I reach the first beam I can feel the warmth of the sun on me as I pass through it and I have to grip the rock to prevent my body from relaxing too much. Fatigue is beginning to take hold and I know that I'm in the most danger now that I'm almost out. If I lose concentration for a moment I fall.

And if I fall I die.

I bring my hand down hard on my side and the pain from the wounds wakes all my senses, momentarily shaking off the drowsiness. I can still hear the roar of the water but it's getting further away and as I near one of the beams of light I stretch my hand towards it and the tiny pin prick of warmth feels like heaven.

The rock is thinner up here, more layered and as I move nearer the beam I stretch my hand out again and start feeling around the damp rock until my fingers strike a patch of something far moister and soft.

Soil!

The thought is almost too much to bear and I try to wriggle my fingers between the rock, bits of earth falling on my face. The hole I make isn't big enough for my hand let alone the rest of me but the beam of light is much larger now and I begin to feel a breeze on my skin.

"You've almost made it, Jake! Keep going. Keep going."

Ellie and Doughnut's voices sing out to me in my mind and I frantically look around for the other beams, scrambling across to check the rock, to see if the gap is bigger. Once or twice my hands slip and despite the length of the fall it's all I can do to keep myself attached to the holds, a mixture of excitement and fatigue threatening to plunge me back down into the gloom.

It takes an age for me to find a sizeable gap, but when I do, my fingers break through the soil and I manage to position my legs so I can pull my torso through as well. The sun threatens to blind me as my face instinctively turns towards the warmth and I start to spit out the soil that's fallen into my mouth. I feel a rush of emotion more intense than I've ever felt before.

It takes an age for my weary limbs to drag the rest of my body out until I'm lying on my back, my chest heaving up and down as my lungs greedily gulp in the clean air. At first I think it's a big ball of laughter that's begun to build up inside, as if all the tension needs a release, but then I realise it's not laughter at all, and as I blink into the sun, the tears start to fall.

I have no energy to stop them.

Chapter 15

As my eyelids flutter open and I try to push myself up on my elbows I'm at a loss to explain where I am or what has happened. It's as if I've just been picked up and thrown here, like some kind of pebble or rock.

Shielding my face with a hand I wince as the pain in my shoulder stabs away. Moving's even worse as I feel my side screams at me to remain absolutely still. Looking down I see scratches and cuts all over my hands and arms. My shirt is in shreds and I have three gouges that seem to run from under my arm to the top of my hip. What the hell happened?

And then the images flood my mind; the Wastelander hunched over Angus, the tearing and chewing. I shut my eyes, hands over my ears, but I can't stop the noise and I stand unsteadily on my feet ignoring the pain.

The image changes and I picture the Wastelander scaling the side of the cavern, sniffing the air, following my scent, its clawed hand breaking through the soil, reaching for me, grabbing at my legs.

My legs propel me forward and I half run, half stumble down the hill. The movement is opening up the cuts, especially on my side but I don't care because I've no idea how long I've been out for, for all I know they could be all over the place.

They could be looking at me right now.

The thought fills me with fear and my head whips round half expecting to be greeted by dozens of slathering creatures bearing down on me. I need to find help, I need to tell someone what's going on.

They're here!

They're under the ground!

I look up to get my bearings but I don't recognise where I am, there are no shacks, no roads, no people, just clumps of dying trees and bushes, gnarled and skinny, parched by the never ending sun. I try to picture where we first went underground, try to think how far we walked along the passageways but it's all too scrambled, it's all…

I'm outside the Wall!

The thought terrifies me and I stumble forward through a clump of bushes. They tear at my clothes and skin but I ignore the pain and run until I'm limping along, my side twisted as I hold my hand to the claw marks on my body. The water must have swept me further than I thought. Who knows where the tunnels lead to?

I break through the bushes and find myself in another stretch of open ground but there's something up ahead and although my eyes are still a little blurry I keep going, my legs pumping as hard as they can before I fall on my knees, chest heaving, fingers resting on the fence in front of me. Relief floods through my body.

I'm in the Neutral Zone.

Leaning my back against the fence I slump forward but the euphoria is short lived because the position of the sun in the sky tells me that it's somewhere between four and five in the afternoon. I must have passed out for longer than I thought because the Siren will be sounding soon.

And then another thought hits me as the words of Our Leader fill my head.

"Criminals! Our Damned will face the Wastelanders!"

Criminals.

What if I get in trouble for even being on this side of the fence? What if no one believes what I've got to say?

The thought ties my stomach in knots and I wish Ellie was here because she'd know where to find a way through. She always knows about this kind of thing. My heart swells and I choke back the tears.

Wincing at the pain I start lurching towards the fence line. Emerging from the trees, I see people far in the distance, a line of shacks beyond them. The Lanes. I start yelling at the top of my voice but my throat is scratchy and dry and nothing really comes out.

I start to wave and bang on the fence, trying to make as much noise as possible. I can see people beginning to look over.

"HELP ME, PLEASE HELP ME!"

My legs begin to wobble as I slump to the ground grimacing at the searing pain that explodes from my side. I can see people pointing towards me and surge of hope runs through my body but then I see one woman, she's come a little closer, maybe thirty yards or more away.

It's the expression on her face that concerns me. She's keeps turning and shouting something over her shoulder and I can see a blur of people running to her side. I can't hear her properly, maybe it's too much water in my ear so I can't really make out what she's saying but her lips keep forming the same word over and over again as she moves back away, fear in her eyes.

Wastelander.

That's what she's repeating and I whip my head round expecting the worst but nothing's there. Confusion clouds my mind and I turn back. The crowd that's gathered has separated and a blur of red speeds towards me, batons raised. Again I turn my head and again, nothing. So why are they…and then my mind makes the connections.

I look down at myself, at my torn, filthy clothes and my ripped and bloody skin smeared with dirt that has now dried. I try to yell and hold my hands up but it's too late. The Guards have reached the fence and I can feel the baton blows as they rain down.

They think *I'm* a Wastelander!

It's the last thought I have before everything goes blank.

Hours blend into one another as day becomes night. I'm vaguely aware of the beating stopping as the Guards look down at me, confusion etched on their faces. Of being picked up and thrown in the back of a Guard truck but it's like my mind is dislocated from everything around me, like it's all muffled and I'm not really there at all.

Everything's a whirl of images; the fence, the baton, Angus screaming and then nothing as if the trauma's been too great and my body needs to shut down and regroup.

I have no idea how long I'm out for but when I do manage to open my eyes or lift my head, pain pours in from every angle and I have no choice but to retreat back into the darkness.

I'm being taken somewhere, that much I do know, as the rolling of the truck lulls me into a kind of half sleep. I dream of faces leering at me, of hands carrying me God knows where, until the roll of the truck is replaced with something else, something bumpier.

And then I'm gone. Falling into a black hole and all I can hear is screaming.

When I come to again I sense lights and faces and people talking at me, but none of it fully wakes me, none of it brings me back. All I know is I'm cold and far from home. And scared.

"Hey it's okay, it's okay! Shhhh!"

"Get him some water!"

"Someone wake him up for God's sake!"

I feel water on my face and start to cough. Arms help me to sit up and I slowly open my eyes but all I can see are dim shapes that refuse to take form. Closing them again I'm shuffled back until I can lean against a cold hard wall.

"Watch he doesn't lash out, we don't know who he is or what he's been through."

"I think it's pretty bloody obvious what he's been through, don't you?"

I don't recognise the voices and as I open my eyes again I can see people in front of me. I instinctively pull my knees up towards my chest, the Wastelander's image still fresh in my mind.

"Hey, it's okay, you're safe."

"That's a joke!"

"Hey! Shut up! Can't you see he's struggling, poor thing doesn't even know where he is!"

As my vision begins to clear and my eyes focus my body reminds me of its various injuries and I hold my hand against my side but there's something new, a sharp pain on the side of my face. It hurts to the touch, as if my face is swollen.

"Let's leave him be for now, not like he's gonna go anywhere is it!"

Where am I?

I think back and remember the fence, remember calling out and then the red blurs running towards me. What was I doing? And then images intrude again as I try to stand.

Blood. Bone. Teeth

I slip back down the wall but immediately try again because I need to tell someone what I've seen.

Because I need to get home. I need to get back to Ellie and Doughnut.

"I…I've seen them! They're under the ground." I hold my hand out and use the wall to guide me. Maybe I'm in some kind of hospital or something? I push the thought aside because I've got to get out. I've got to tell Ellie and Doughnut. I've got to warn them.

I see faces in the gloom looking out at me. No one is saying anything but they look at me with sad eyes. Now the panic starts to return and I fumble for a door, any door but there doesn't seem to be one. In fact it doesn't look like any room I've seen before.

"C…can someone show me the door? I…I need to get home." I drunkenly spin around but no one helps and then a deep voice comes from the shadows.

"Door's over here boy." I follow the voice and see a large metal door at the far end of the room. "But it won't do you no good." I don't understand what he's saying I just concentrate on crossing the floor without collapsing, each step shooting pain from every inch of me, until I reach out for the door and push.

Nothing happens. The door won't budge. I try again, jarring my shoulder as anger takes over.

The deep voice sounds again. "You could do that all day, won't make any difference, I've tried! It's a prison door, son." I frown and try to say something but the words won't come.

"Designed to keep you in, not let you out!"

Chapter 16

Prison.

"But I've gotta get out! I've gotta warn people!" I turn to the direction of the voice, try to ignore what he's just said and concentrate on wiping my face of tears as best I can. The area I'm in seems to be underground, full of columns that have been crudely dug, alcoves that I'm beginning to realise are where the faces keep appearing from. The gloom is casting huge shadows, the only light coming from a small window high up on the wall by the door.

"You need to preserve your energy. You've been in the wars by the looks of things!" The voice comes from the gloom to my right and as I squint to get a better look as a body emerges; torn, filthy clothes, matted hair. I take a step back and then remember the vision I had; the faces staring at me open mouthed, horror stricken through the Neutral Zone fence, fingers pointing...

Wastelander! Wastelander!

I look down at my own torn and ragged clothes as images from the water tunnels fill my mind.

"I...I saw them...under the ground! Angus was..." I slide down the wall and come to rest heavily on the floor.

"You've been saying the same thing since you were brought here!" The figure moves over to where I am, kneeling by my side. "But you need to rest up some more." The face looks down at my side. "You've go some nasty wounds! Got yourself in some real trouble didn't you!"

I follow the gaze and see cloth has been wound round my torso from the hip to the shoulder. Blood has stained some of it and my hand instinctively rises to my head, gently feeling over the lumps and cuts that crisscross my brow. My mind is struggling to work things out but I'm losing whatever energy I had fast. I can't remember the last time I ate or drank something.

"How long have I been here?" I look up at the face besides me and for the first time I notice warmth and sympathy.

"Three days." Sadness fills the eyes, "You've been here three days."

"Lucky you're alive boy! If it wasn't for the girl here you'd have been a victim of those injuries I dare say."

I look up and see a large man emerging from the gloom, followed by several others as if they were waiting for the right moment to reveal themselves, and then I look back to the figure beside me. The dirt on the face all but obscures her features but now I'm looking properly I can see green eyes and a red flush under all the filth. They all look the same; tattered, torn, bruised.

I look back at the girl. "Where the hell am I?" and she grins and then stands up spreading her arms and slowly rotating.

"Why, your host is Our Glorious Leader! He's looking after you now! He's looking after all of us, for the next few days at least!" The others grin and I can't help but join in. "The Guards bought you in. Pretty beaten up you were too."

"We thought you were dead, what with all them cuts and bruises!" The voice belongs to an older women over to my left and she nods, grinning at me toothlessly.

"The Guards have brought us all to this place, wherever the hell that is! They've been moving people for days now." The girl is speaking from the shadows and then she darts across the floor and falls to my side. I notice her piercing green eyes. "You a *criminal* boy?" She spits the word out like it's acid in her mouth. "You a criminal like the rest of us?"

She slides back across the floor, eyeing me up and down before turning to the others, "Although I'm having a hard time seeing how!" She laughs and some of the others join in when the old woman raises a hand and a hush descends.

"Quit teasing him girl! Can't you see poor pup's confused." The old woman turns to the others and they eye the floor, "Just like all of us when we first arrived." Then she fixes me with a stare. He eyes are watery but vivid and speak of a lifetime's experience. "You're here for the Festival, like we all are in one way or another! Full moons in three days boy, three days and then we'll all get to show them what we're made of!"

Three days! Is it that soon? Are we that close?

And then she tells me. About how the Guards have been taking more and more people, not just from the prisons but from the streets and the poor houses too. About how they've been funnelling them to places like this all over Sanctum, long before Our Leader made his first speech, what seems now to be a life time ago.

"You don't think this grand idea of his, this festival came to him in one big moment of inspiration! He's been planning this, this *clear out* for months I'll bet! He wants rid of us. He wants less mouths to feed! He's planning something that he's yet to reveal to us, you'll see! There's more to this than he wants us to know!"

I sense some unease as others start to mutter and mumble under their breath. The old woman looks around, her cheeks flushing red.

"I don't care what he says and I don't care what you all think, it's nothing to do with killing Wastelanders and everything to do with killing Citizens!"

The room falls silent again as people retreat to their alcoves, the old woman's words ringing in their ears. Everyone except the girl who is sitting a few feet away with her knees up by her chest, rocking gently.

"She's right." She stares ahead at the floor, her green eyes moistening. "It's happening everywhere, we're not the only ones, thousands of us being led to slaughter and HE has the front to say that we can be martyrs, that we can be heroes."

"Wastelanders will tear us apart soon as look at us!" The voice comes from the shadows, murmured agreement ringing out around the room.

I shake my head, refusing to believe what I'm hearing, refusing to believe I'll never see the Lanes again, that I'll never see Ellie or Doughnut. The old woman begins to stand and the girl immediately springs into action, holding her elbow, guiding her arm as she rises unsteadily.

"We're all to blame! We've let him do this to us!" Silence descends as she looks around the room. "Who amongst us turned a blind eye to the beatings for the sake of a cup full of water?" She waits for a challenge but none comes. "Who amongst us stood up to the red uniforms? Said, you DO NOT have my permission. We have NOT given our consent!"

Silence.

"None of us!" Her voice falls to a whisper. "None of us. We were grateful for the protection. We rejoiced at the sight of the uniforms as they kept the wretched at bay. We praised to the heavens when he dug those wells, when he gave us pits to get our work from, when the wall went up to protect us from *them.*"

She raises a hand and holds on tight to the girl as if her energy is leaving her. "We raised him up to be our God and now he is displeased with what he sees. Our punishment? To be fed to the lions. It's not his fault at all – it's ours."

The old woman slumps forward and the girl leads her gently to the wall by the side of the door, to a bundle of rags on the cold, hard floor. The room is silent as if there's nothing more to say and I am left alone in this cold corner with nothing but my thoughts, and the old woman's words whizzing around my head at a hundred miles an hour.

"It must be some kind of mistake, I'm not a criminal! I've done nothing wrong!" My mind ticks over, fractured images from the past few days crashing in on themselves, and then the words tumble from my mouth before I have a chance to stop them.

"But I've seen them! They're under the ground already!" Every face turns towards me as my words pierce the silence. I'm as astonished as everyone else that I've spoken out and before I can stop myself more pours forth, as if desperate to jump from my mouth; about Angus, about the tunnels and the creatures coming from nowhere.

About everything.

"You've been dreaming boy is all! You've had a hell of a beating by the looks of things. Got your brain all messed up." I panic as the faces begin to turn away like I'm telling a bed time story, as if I'm to be pitied but not taken seriously. As if I don't matter to them. And then my hands start to fumble at the rags on my body, at the bandages stretched over my side. Indignation rising up within me, making my face burn red.

"Then who did this?" I claw at the bandages until the whole of my side is exposed and I can see from their eyes, from the way some of them begin to recoil back into the shadows that they weren't prepared for this.

A silence descends as if no one wants to talk about it and I begin to slump against the wall, my body weak, my mind aching.

Suddenly there is a low whistle and a stained blanket is thrown across the floor. I know it's from her and I whisper a thank you but there's no reply.

It barely covers my body but I'm grateful for the little warmth it provides and as soon as I lay my head on my knees I can feel tiredness engulf every sinew of my body.

My dreams are full of horrors that plague me like so many shadows creeping along the floor and try as I do to stop thinking of dad, waiting for me at home, it's impossible. I see him sitting at the table, or standing at the door wandering where I've gone. And then the picture changes and I see Ellie and Doughnut, worry etched on their faces.

It's this strength of love that will keep me going and as I call out to them in my dreams I hope that somehow they can hear me.

Chapter 17

I don't even notice the door is opening until it hits the stone wall and echoes around the room. The sleep has done me good because my eyes are immediately open and I feel more alert than I have in a while.

The Guards file into the room and quickly set about ripping blankets off bodies and pushing people towards the door. I can hear raised voices and screaming from far off in another part of the building. Something big is happening.

"Hey! Get your hands off me!" The big guy I saw briefly yesterday emerges from the shadows and I notice that the guards don't bother touching him, not like the rest of us that they are manhandling roughly.

"What do you want with us?"

"What have we done? You said you'd send criminals out there! You said you'd send criminals!"

The questions ring out and for a moment the atmosphere changes as hands twitch above batons and voice rise to a fever pitch and then the Guards begin to part as another one enters the room. From the way they behave I take him to be some kind officer or something as the other Guards step into line.

"Our Leader requests your company out in the yard." He looks around taking his time before turning back to his men, "Anyone resists they get carried out!" The smiles that break out make us compliant and I wonder if maybe the old woman was right, that maybe somehow it *is* all our fault.

The Guards run us out into a large courtyard and I have to shield my eyes from the bright sunshine that pours down onto us. I look around trying to take in as much information as possible, the sleep I had last night, the dream of dad, of Ellie and Doughnut. I know they're waiting for me and I know what they would want me to do; they would want me to watch and wait, wait for an opening that will eventually come.

As I look at some of the others around me now that I can see them properly I am struck by how many look defeated already and I make a silent promise to myself.

Whatever happens I will not give up. I will not give in.

I see the familiar line of red uniforms hemming us in and a raised platform at the far end of the court. But I've never seen this kind of building before, the columns of stone that lie everywhere, the statues, the sense of grandeur, of wealth.

As I continue to take everything in my eyes are drawn to the baskets of flowers that hang from the columns, the vivid explosion of greens and reds against the backdrop of stone. It looks like a miniature version of the Peoples' Court.

"What the hell do they want with us now?" The question comes from my left and as I go to answer my words are drowned out by the ripple of noise that goes up as a group of guards sweep in from behind the columns to the left and up towards the podium.

Just before the steps they part and a figure draped in bright yellow robes continues on unaided.

The colour represents the Senators who speak for Our Leader in local matters and an air of anticipation settles over everyone as he turns to face us holding both hands in the air. I've only ever seen them on the big screen at The Square. I can barely believe that one's standing in front of me right now.

"CITIZENS!" His voice booms out around the courtyard, "You are here because you have transgressed, in different ways and for different reasons, the laws of Sanctum, laws that Our Leader has created for us in order that we may live in peace and harmony."

He pauses and this time, unlike in the town square earlier in the week, there are no cheers or booing, instead there is an almost deafening silence. "But I am not here to punish you, as is my right and duty! I am here to help extend to each and everyone of you the second chance that has been given you, a second chance to renew your faith and service to the ideals of Sanctum."

"I've done nothing wrong!" The voice comes from within the crowd, the courage of anonymity, as murmurings sweep around.

"Do you trade in The Pit? Do you harbour thoughts of stealing what you can't afford?"

Despite all that I have experienced in the past few days I find it almost impossible not to be swept up in his words, in the power of his voice. Maybe it's being in a crowd, standing amongst a number of people but I felt it in the Square as well, a sense of no longer being an individual but somehow being linked to a group, a kind of collective mind.

Suddenly I'm alive to the cleverness of it all, the red uniforms that represent danger but also a sense of security. The bright yellow robes of the speaker and how they reflect the sunlight bathing him in an almost religious aura. We stand here rapt in the sights and sounds that have been cleverly chosen to represent different things, to send different images to our brain. To trick us. The words of the old woman echo in my mind.

"We raise him up to be our God! It's not his fault – it's ours!"

"You should feel pride that you are here! You are amongst the chosen who are to fight for the honour and safety of Sanctum and its citizens."

"To be sacrifices you mean!"

I brace myself for the onslaught of Guards into the crowd to seek out the lone voice, to demonstrate the power of the Leader. Surely he can't tolerate these interruptions? A collective breath is taken.

But nothing happens.

The Senator casts a glance around the crowd as if to challenge anyone else to shout something but nothing is forthcoming.

"You all heard Our Leader's words! Do you doubt them? Do you doubt HIM?" This time there is no comment from the crowd. The power of words cast their peculiar spell. "You will be given food and shelter, things many of you have not had for a long time. You will be trained to fight, given as good a chance as is possible, a chance that many of you do not deserve."

He pauses again and looks around the courtyard, lowering his voice until it is barely above a whisper. "It is of paramount importance that you take hold of it with both hands, for many of us have been affected by this plague that lies outside our walls. They are multiplying at a dangerous rate and they want what we have; our food, our water, our children!" I can hear wailing from some of the older women in the crowd.

"Please help our children! Please help our little ones!"

When he speaks again it is in a softer tone and I have to strain to hear every word.

"It is Our Leader who is calling on *you* for help. He calls on each and everyone of you to make amends for past deeds, to seek forgiveness for wrong doing – if necessary to give your life in the defence of Sanctum. And those of you that pass this test, those amongst you that survive out there will be granted your freedom because you will have faced the very demons of hell…and survived."

There are tears in peoples eyes, heads nodding in agreement. What do they have to lose when life is so cheap, when for them each day offers little food and warmth?

With his words ringing around our heads, the Senator sweeps from the podium, his yellow robes quickly swallowed by the red of his bodyguards as they stride from the square and disappear beyond the stone columns.

For a split second it's like we've been forgotten about and then the guards descend with their batons held high. However this time, instead of chasing us back to where we came from we're separated into groups, in some cases literally dragged to different areas of the large courtyard.

I'm pushed towards a group at the back and frantically look around for anyone I recognise but everything is happening so fast; the intensity of the Senator's words now lost amidst the screaming and yelling that has erupted.

I've got to dig in. I've got to survive.

I find myself in a smaller group, maybe twenty strong and the first thing I notice is that we are all young; some look aged by their lifestyle, by the lifestyle that is forced upon them but no one seems over the age of eighteen. Maybe they're grouping us, but why?

Voices start whispering; questions in search of answers. A girl to my right is crying.

"What do they want now? What are they doing with everyone else?" And then the crowds begin to part as even the guards who are down on our level stop and turn to see what else is happening.

At first no one appears, heads beginning to turn away and then a figure emerges at least a foot taller than anyone else in the yard, his bare chest revealing equal parts muscles and scars. Turning his thick neck I am close enough to catch sight of an angry welt where his left eye should, behind him other monsters emerging, one for each group.

Was this the plan all along? To herd us together, to kill us all where we stand?

I see the guards that are still lining the courtyard begin to move revealing half a dozen gaps all around and then, out of the corner of my eye I see something drop from the giant's hands, something that unfurls and hits the floor with a light *thud*, disturbing the dust.

Whips.

Chapter 18

As soon as the thought settles I hear the *swish* as the whip whizzes through the air extending until all but horizontal before snapping back with a sharp crack. And then all hell breaks loose as the giants wade into their respective groups, the sounds of the whips competing with the sound or screaming, people covering their faces, herded towards the gaps that have opened up in the guards.

"MOVE!"

Blind panic forces obedience as I try to stay towards the middle of my group to avoid the whips as we stumble up the steps and past the columns. I can see people falling over in the rush, the giants bent over them, whips raised and then the courtyard disappears from view as we're run along the line of stone pillars. The noise is disorienting as it bounces off the stone walls but we keep our heads down as the sound of the whips drives us on.

Soon we're out in the sunshine again but I've lost my bearings. It's like this whole place is some kind of puzzle box with hidden compartments and secret alcoves, and as we enter what appears to be a smaller courtyard, those in front seem to slow down, as the giant with the scarred face walks past us, the muscles on his arms the thickness of my entire body. He's about twenty yards away from us when he turns and stands there, slowly rolling up each whip in turn until they sit in the palm of his hand.

"He's going to kill us!"

"Shut up! They would have done that ages ago if they wanted to."

"It's some kind of test."

I look around and realise we've been backed up against a large stone wall as a boy to my left is pulled roughly from the line by a Guard and pushed towards the giant before crumpling to the ground.

"Hey! What are you doing?" The voice comes from the middle of the line as the boy snivels where he sits, dust clinging to his torn clothes.

"FIGHT OR DIE!"

The words explode from the giant's mouth as he nods to one of the Guards who steps forward and throws a baton down on the ground a yard or so from the boy. He looks around pleadingly as if one of us is going to step up and help him out but the line doesn't move and he eventually turns back towards the giant.

"Pick it up! Use it on him!" I turn with surprise to a hard looking face a few people down from me. He has nearly as many scars as the giant and I remind myself that many of the people I am here with are real criminals and a lot of them have had to handle themselves in all kinds of situations from a young age. "Pick it up and use it Godammit!"

The giant steps forward, crouching slightly at the knees as if ready to spring. The whips unfurl from the hands and I instinctively press my back against the wall almost willing it to swallow me up. The boy curls in on himself as the guard smiles down upon him from his great height and then the familiar sound, the crack of the whip in the air above the boy's head.

"PICK IT UP!" Our voices are almost as one as we will the boy to do something, anything to prolong the inevitable. The whips are sent flying again but this time, from the angle of the wrist it is clear that they are meant to hurt when suddenly the boy explodes into life, leaping to his right using his hand as a pivot on which to rotate his body until he lands three feet away, knees bent, eyes fixed dead ahead.

He was faking it all along; the tears, the begging, he was faking it to buy time, to suss out his options. Clever.

The whip ends join together in the exact space his head had occupied moments earlier and the cracking sound draws gasps from the line mixed in with the cheers that rise up for the boy's audacity. I can see him eyeing the baton on the floor which now lies between them both as the guard growls and begins to roll in the whips, all the while moving slowly to his left hand side. The boy does the same, still crouching low, mimicking his movement until the two of them are circling one another.

The line has gone quiet as the reality of what's happening sinks in. By now it's obvious that we've all got to face this rite of passage, this ritual or whatever the hell it is. But none of us can second guess how far it's meant to go.

What happens if you stumble? What happens if it's clear you're not up to the mark? Are they going to kill us one by one until they've got what they need?

The whip sounds again and the boy spins to his left this time, the ground exploding into a shower of dust, but this time the giant follows up quickly with two enormous strides and with right fist clenched bends in at the waste and pivots, swinging down in a wide arc.

The blow catches the boy on the shoulder and sends him sliding across the ground and the line lets out a groan as if we've been hit as well. It's clear he's shaken and in pain and the voices start up again urging him to his feet as the giant steps forward once again.

"Move kid! Get the baton!" I'm surprised by the urgency in my voice but he represents us all out there. There's also the plain fact that the longer he lasts the more tired the giant becomes and the more hope for the rest of us further down the line. A pang of guilt tries to rise up but I squash it back down. Weak emotions have no place here. They never have.

The boy delays until the huge figure is nearly upon him before rolling quickly away to his right. He's gambling on speed versus strength, a gamble I guess we're all going to have to make, and it appears to pay off as the giant is slow to react and he is able to skip around the back. From nowhere the whip darts out again from behind the gnarled wrist catching the boy somewhere on his calf.

The cry is loud and sharp as he rolls onto his shoulder but the move has worked because the baton is now within arm's reach. Diving for the baton the boy grabs it with his left hand before throwing it with all his might at the turning figure of the giant. The baton spirals through the air and catches him just above his kidney causing him to grunt loudly, grimacing with pain.

I hold my breath as the boy lands with a thud on the ground and rolls onto his back, his chest heaving up and down. The giant regroups and pulls himself up to his full height casting a shadow that all but engulfs the figure now lying at his feet. None of us can tear our eyes away from what is about to happen.

The giant stops and nods to one of the guards lining the side of the courtyard.

"Mark him!"

The Guard scuttles forward carrying a bucket and before anyone's had time to work out what's happening he pulls out a brush and wipes it across the boys chest leaving a bright smear of red for all to see. Two other Guards drag him to his feet and march him out of sight and I'm left staring at the space he occupied.

It's a test of bravery. I was right. They *are* grouping us!

"NEXT!"

As the boy second from my left is pulled out of the line and shoved into the dirt my mind starts pouring over the last few days, knitting ideas together, discarding things that no longer seem to fit. The Wastelanders are a problem, that much was clear even before I encountered them in the chambers beneath the earth.

The problem is we don't know what numbers they have, we can only figure the worst; that they're out there, lurking underground or in the mist, waiting for the sun to fall in the sky. Waiting to feed.

Facing them out in the open, outside the walls would be much better than underground in all those tunnels and caverns, that's for sure. Wasn't Jeremiah getting us to repair tunnels that had been damaged? If they were damaged by the Wastelanders then maybe the plan has been to chase them back out, get them out in the open again where we stand the best chance.

Maybe they're like dogs, always going back to where they think the food is? Get them above ground fighting, send in the weakest of us first to lull them, to give them fresh meat and then…maybe that's what's happening? We're being sized up and then divided; the weakest ones of us to lure *them* in, the strongest ones to fight!

My train of thought is interrupted as I see the boy being dragged off by the Guards, blood staining the ground. I notice that there's no marking on his chest.

And then I feel myself grabbed and pulled out of the line, but I'm not prepared, I'm not ready for this and my heart beats against my rib cage until it's all I can hear.

"W…wait, please!" I look at the blood trail and then back at the line but whatever collective energy there was has gone. Maybe they've figured out things like I have. Maybe their just scared for their lives, but I can see it in their faces, smeared with dirt and tears. I can see fear.

I look up at the giant, wincing in anticipation of the now familiar whip crack but all I can see is his huge frame as it bears down on me, two batons swinging in either hand. I look for the whips but they've been discarded to his right.

They're changing things up so we don't second guess them.

A loud, deep voice emerges from the scarred face, but it's not just to me, he means it to be heard by everybody.

"WHAT ARE YOU GOING TO DO WHEN THEY'RE COMING AT YOU FROM ALL SIDES?" All the while he's twirling the batons and slowly circling me as I crouch in the dirt watching him like a hawk.

"ARE YOU GOING TO OUTRUN THEM WHEN YOUR THROAT IS DRY AND YOUR BODY TIRED?" He steps forward causing me to scrabble backwards. "WHAT ABOUT WHEN YOU'RE INJURED?" The baton flies through the air catching me high up on my right shoulder. The pain is sharp and intense but I know it could have been worse.

He's toying with me like the others but I'm not going to scream. I'm not going to cry. Instead I hold his gaze and place a hand protectively over my shoulder. He wants to break me down, show the others how easy it is. I eye the baton on the ground but my legs refuse to move towards it.

"WHEN THEY'RE BEARING DOWN ON YOU, THE SMELL OF YOUR BLOOD IN THE AIR." He lunges again and I'm a fraction too slow too escape his fist arching its way through the air. It catches me on my ribs as I try to roll out of the way and I land with a grunt in the dust. Before I have a chance to regroup he's pulling me up by my clothes, bunched in his huge fist, until I'm inches away from his face and can smell the putrid breath.

"WHAT ARE YOU GOING TO DO WHEN YOU'RE ALIVE AS THEY STRIP THE SKIN FROM YOUR BONES?" Raising his right hand he means to break my skull, I can see it in his eyes and I move quickly. I hold the baton I took from the floor high in front of me and it meets his fist, shattering into pieces, shards of wood missing my face by the slimmest of margins.

For an instant I see rage in his eyes before I sense his fist relax and he throws me back to the ground, his voice calmer than before.

"You adapt. You buy yourself a precious few seconds because that's all you've got!"

My heart's in my mouth because I haven't been at my best and I'm waiting for what he's going to do. For a split second nothing happens, no one moves, and then the giant slowly turns his head and nods. I'm quickly dragged to my feet before receiving the splash of paint across my chest. The mark that I hope will give me access to those few seconds he's been speaking of.

I'm pushed in the direction of the others, towards the columns and just before I disappear I glance back towards the line and catch the briefest glimpse of the next person in line and then I'm gone, my feet trailing behind me as the stone pillars pass me by.

I don't recognise the face but I recognise the emotion it's showing.

It's fear, and it's all around us.

Chapter 19

Gaining my feet I'm marched down the avenue of columns. Any fight left in me has evaporated and it's all I can do to keep one foot in front of another. My shoulder and ribs are beginning to sing out but that's nothing compared to the rumbling coming from my stomach. No wonder I'm so exhausted. I haven't eaten for what feels like days.

As we near the end of the avenue I see a large wooden doorway up ahead, at least twenty foot high, with two Guards standing in front, dwarfed by its size. I'm handed over as the one on the left strains against the large door, pushing until it gives in and begins to open. I feel a hand on my back as I'm pushed forward and glancing back I see the other Guards retreating down the avenue. For a moment I'm alone with two of them. What if…

"Not worth it boy. There's nowhere to run to." I catch sight of a mischievous look in the Guard's eye. "Another brave warrior! You wouldn't want to run away now, not when Our Leader invites you to get your strength back!"

Confusion clouds my mind as I'm pushed through the doorway and then it hits me; the smell of meat, warm, salty meat. My mouth instantly fills with saliva and I swallow hard before looking back at the Guard hovering by the door. He stops at the threshold like he's remembered some long given command before nodding towards the long wooden table. "Join the other one then! Eat your fill! You *deserve* it."

The word is practically spat out but it doesn't register as I stand there, in the doorway, looking at the kid at the far end crouched over a bowl. He was the first of us to face the giant and he looks to be as hungry as I am. He looks up at me and then back down at the bowl, his arm protecting it like it's all he's got in the world.

"It's good. Get yourself some, never know when they'll take it from us!"

Even before he finishes talking I'm already striding over to the pot at the far end of the table. I can see the Guard still hovering by the door but all I care about is the food and I pick a bowl from the table and ladle in the thick stew until it spills over the sides and onto the floor. I don't question it, even though instinct tells me I should.

We must look quite a sight; the two of us, sitting there crouched over our bowls wolfing the food down. I begin to cough as the stew collects at the back of my throat and I can hear Ellie telling me to slow down but I carry on, swallowing hard to get the food down. It feels like it's dropping in from a great height but when it finally hits my stomach there's more growling and grumbling than earlier.

I should know better than this. I've seen enough people make themselves ill from eating too much too quickly, especially when their body is not used to it but it tastes so good! The gravy is thick and the meat melts as soon as it touches the tongue.

Movement by the door attracts my attention and I look up briefly as voices are raised, another person appearing at the head of the table like I did; bloody, bruised and confused, before he too joins in the feast.

When my stomach feels it can't take anymore I breath deeply stretching my back as straight as it will go and then force down two more large spoonfuls before pushing the bowl away and slouching in my chair.

There are now four of us at the table but there's at least room for another ten and as I look at each one, their heads bowed as if in solemn prayer, I see quite clearly the thing that links us all; the bright slash of paint across our torsos. I look down at my own markings and then back up, catching the glance of the face opposite me.

"What do you think's happening to the others?" His voice is low, no more than a whisper. I shrug and sit uncomfortably back in the seat, my stomach deciding whether it needs to create room for itself or not.

"Dunno – I've given up trying to figure everything out." I look up at the Guard who's still standing by the doorway waiting for others to arrive. "Just trying to keep my head down and get out, get back to…"

My voice trails off as I picture Ellie and Doughnut all alone, waiting for me to return. I try to push away the feelings of guilt, the thought that if only I'd stayed away from the Pit, if only I hadn't taken that stupid job in the water tunnels.

"Name's River by the way!" I look up, lost in my own thoughts. The boy opposite is smiling apologetically. "My parents named me and my sister after things from the old days." His smile broadens, "She's called Rainbow – guess I was the lucky one!"

He looks to his left at the person sitting next to him, for a moment the figure looks up and then back down to the bowl of food. I hadn't even realised she was a girl. We all look so alike.

I smile back as the thoughts from earlier begin to fade, the feeling of guilt receding into the background. "Jake. Good to meet you!"

"Do you reckon they've got more tests for us? I mean," River looks around at the others, "why would they feed us if they weren't planning something else? And that giant Guard! I thought I was a gonner, I thought he was going to crush my head in one of his big fat hands!"

He opens and closes his hand as if squeezing hard and I can't help but giggle at the sight. The others look up before going back to their bowls, they haven't eaten their fill yet, they've still got room for more.

"It's our best chance, you know." He must have seen me gazing at the doorway before, imagining running through it, leaping across the roof tops, making a bid for escape. "Out there in the Wasteland."

The word makes me cringe inside and I sense that the whole table is listening in. "What do you mean?"

"You ever know of anyone taken by the Guards being returned?" River shakes his head, "If we don't keep on proving ourselves then we'll either be dead in here or dead out there! At least out there we'll have a chance."

"What! With hundreds of those...*things* running at us? Are you mad?" Rainbow doesn't even look up from her bowl, instead she stares straight ahead, straggles of lank, greasy hair acting as a barrier between her and the outside world.

Both River and I fall silent as I hear the Guard talking to another figure and then pushing him through the door and towards the table. "It's all a load of bull anyway, all of it!" She pushes the bowl out of the way and flicks the hair away from her face. She's younger than I thought. No more than thirteen at a guess. "You heard Our Leader and that fat idiot Senator! We're all expendable! This food, this, this place. It's all a con. It's all a damn trick!"

I wasn't expecting such ferocity, none of us were and I think River recognises this because he's grinning as if he's seen all this before. Shrugging he looks around the table.

"Sorry about this. She gets cranky when she's angry!" But it's obvious she wants to be heard as if the food has given her an extra charge, an extra jolt of electricity.

"I'm telling you – the whole thing stinks to high heaven!" Getting into her stride she sits forward in her chair looking around the table.

"Here we go!" River rolls his eyes.

"Why don't they send out those damn Guards if the Wastelander's are that much of a problem? Have you ever thought about that?"

A figure for the far end of the table speaks up. "Our Leader said he wants to use the criminals to do it, that way it doesn't matter how many people die, as long as a few of *them* are taken as well."

"Exactly my point!"

I'm confused and I can see that others are confused too. "I don't see what you mean." I look at the Guard who's still by the door and I suddenly get a flush of nerves, as if any moment now we're going to be set upon like we're talking treason or something.

"She's saying that there's something else going on. Something we don't know about yet." The voice comes from the last person to come through the door. River nods agreement.

"What did you all do to be here?" The question brings an immediate hush to the table as the figure approaches looking at each of us in turn. "Did you murder someone? Have you been plotting against the leader?"

The silence continues, fear suddenly holding people's tongues, until a small voice sounds from somewhere to my left.

"I stole some water? I saw it near the well." The face looks at us, tears welling up, "I didn't mean to! There was such a queue and we hadn't had any for days." The voice tails off into a series of low sobs and for a moment I want to be anywhere but here.

"My mum couldn't afford to look after me. I was sent to a workhouse. They came in the middle of the night and loaded us into trucks and brought us here!" Another sad face. Another look of defiance.

The next voice is River's. "Us too. We're orphans." He looks at Rainbow and smiles. "They rounded us up a few days ago and I've got to tell you – the food here's much better!" His big smile breaks the tension that's been building.

And then it's my turn.

"I still don't really know why I'm here? I mean, I guess it's because I was caught in the Neutral Zone." Eyes widen at the mention of the words, " Maybe it's because I saw one of *them*!"

And then I tell them my story.

It pours out as if it's been bursting to be heard. I tell them about getting work, about going down into the tunnels and I can see their eyes widen as they try and picture Angus being washed away. I tell them about the waterfall, about the Wastelanders and how they attacked us and about how I managed to escape.

"Jesus, Jake! How the hell are you still alive?"

I look up at River and shrug. "I have absolutely no idea but after reaching the fence and waving at the people up ahead I don't really remember much else until waking up here." I realise I haven't talked like this for a while, not since I was last with Ellie and Doughnut and it feels good, it feels like a relief.

"Point is do we look or sound like a bunch of hardened criminals that deserve to face the Wastelanders?" Rainbow looks around the table but no one needs to answer. "There's something else going on, that's all I'm saying!"

The clanging sound shakes us out of our discussion as the door strikes the back wall and reverberates around the hall. The two Guards file in and stride towards the table and I think to myself that it's all over, that they've heard us talking and have decided to end it right here and now.

"What's going on?" Rainbow's voice is loud and firm and for a moment I expect the worst as the Guard nearest the table seems to hover over his baton as if deciding how far to take things.

"Time for more training!" The Guard grins revealing a crooked row of yellow teeth. "Can't have you disappointing the crowd now can we?"

Chapter 20

The giant from earlier is waiting for us at the end of the stone pillars and I sense all of us instinctively recoil when we see him. From the original group there's now only twelve of us left but with food in my belly I feel a lot more prepared for whatever is in store.

We reach the top of the stairs that lead down into the courtyard before the Guard to my right calls the others to halt. I've always wondered what makes the Guards tick, where they come from, how they got to be Guards but before I consider it any further the giant speaks to us.

"You have proven yourselves to be resourceful and brave and Our Leader has no wish to see you all killed within the first few minutes of fighting. He has even provided you with warm food to build your strength."

His voice is still commanding but there's a difference somehow, an intelligence that wasn't there this morning. "If you are to truly have a chance of making Sanctum and its Citizens proud…if you are truly to win your freedom then, thanks to Our Leader's ongoing generosity, he has seen fit to furnish you with weapons that will increase your capacity to kill, for make NO

MISTAKE, that is the reason you are here; TO KILL WASTELANDERS!"

The words are almost hypnotic and I feel my adrenalin levels increase despite not knowing what's coming next. I look at the others and I sense the same confusion as we begin to descend the steps.

The giant was blocking our view but as he steps aside and the Guards escort us down the whole courtyard comes into view, alive with small groups of people already fighting and it acts as a reminder that we are not the only ones here, that similar 'trainings' could be taking place all over Sanctum. Like an army being readied.

As we move down the stone steps I try to take in as much as possible; to my right in the far corner I see someone with a net practising throwing it over a pile of large rocks. Near them is another group who are throwing knives at various targets, beyond them a line of four who seem to be hitting poles that are sticking out of the ground, except the poles seem to have other things coming out of them at various intervals.

At first it seems like mayhem, there must be at least fifty people, probably more, all divided into small groups of no more than three. I catch Rainbow's eye and she shakes her head in disbelief I can tell what she's thinking because it's the same thing I am.

Why not turn the weapons on the Guards themselves?

But as soon as I think the words my own brain starts to doubt them. Am I here because I'm supposed to have done something wrong, or am I here because Sanctum needs my help to defeat the threat of the Wastelanders, a threat that I have seen close up?

I guess this is exactly what Our Leader thrives on; hesitation caused by fear, doubt and the ever present threat that allows him to dominate everyone's lives.

As soon as we reach the bottom of the stairs the Guards separate us into pairs and push us in different directions. I'm with River as he anxiously looks over his shoulder trying to see where Rainbow is.

"YOU!" The voice takes me by surprise and I turn to see a hard stare coming back at me and the blur of something whizzing by my face. "Ever used a net before? Those freaks out there are quick but if you knock 'em off balance then it kind of scrambles their brains a bit, gives you time to then step in for the kill!"

I must be looking at him with fear in my eyes because I can see his face soften a little as he eyes the big Guard passing by and waits until he's out of earshot. "We here to train you kid, not punish you." He nods to the Guards with the whips, the ones we fought against earlier. "That's their job. I'm here to try and give you a fighting chance."

Another Guard comes into view and he immediately straightens up. "You've got to hold the net by its edge but it's no good having the rest of it hanging by your knees, too much drag and the damn thing won't go anywhere." He demonstrates by holding another net by his fingertips, the material flat against his legs and then throws it towards River who raises his arms and ducks out of the way. The net falls about a foot from the trainer and he points to it as River uncoils his arms and I try my best not to smirk at him. "Too much air resistance, plus I was standing straight on so I had no real momentum in the throw.

He steps forward, gathering the net up from the floor and rolling it until it's a thick rope in his hands. Next thing he does is to stand side on before beckoning to River. "Run!"

For a second River frowns and stays exactly where he is.

"RUN!"

Then he's off heading back for the stairs careful to dodge out of the way of the various other weapon stations.

I hold my breath thinking that one of the Guards is going to whip him to the ground. I want to shout after him, to tell him to stop but I daren't and when he whizzes past one of the giants, there's no reaction and then he's by the steps and I'm willing River to continue.

Whoosh.

The sound is close by my head as the trainer pivots his hip and then throws his arms forward and as the net leaves his hands it looks nothing more than a wavy rope that has no chance of reaching

River, not now that he's almost twenty yards ahead and about to leap the steps two at a time.

But as my head turns to follow the rope it starts to unravel, the down force pushing it even quicker through the air, the flick of his wrist sending it spinning through the air until it seems to float above River's head before dropping like a stone, tangling him up until he lands in the dust with a *thump*.

"Whoa! How did you do that?" I look back at the trainer as he smiles to himself.

"Practice makes perfect." before setting off to release River from the net. We take it in turns throwing the net as the other tries to make it to the steps. As time goes by I notice three things; that I'll never get the hang of throwing the damn thing, not if I practiced for a lifetime, as I seem capable only of throwing it either over myself or about a yard in front of me.

Secondly, that River has taken to it like he was born for it or something, needing only to watch the trainer a few times before flicking his wrists like a pro and sending it sailing out above my head time after time.

But the last thing I notice is how much focus everyone is giving this task. As I snatch glances around the courtyard it doesn't matter whether I recognise the person or not, everyone has a look of concentration on their faces that I've rarely seen on so many people before – certainly not all at the same time like this.

As I wind the net in for another attempt an ear piercing whistle sounds out around the courtyard and I hold my free hand up to my ear. "MOVE ROUND. NEXT WEAPON!" The order is barked by one of the giants with the whips and River looks at me before following the trainers pointed arm to the next station. As I walk past him he steps forward, speaking low, almost whispering.

"Remember to try everything, you never know when a weapon might be needed, even one you think you can't use." I nod thanks but I'm a little puzzled as to what he means. River stops my train of thought progressing any further by shouting out.

"Jake!" He's grinning for ear to ear in front of a large table that stands near a wooden pole with a board on it. "Knives!"

As I reach the table I see more knives than I thought possible; long handles, jagged edges, thin like a point, all of them glinting in the bright sunlight. The new trainer also grins as we stand there staring.

"Your dad's never take you out hunting?" We look at each other and then turn back to him, our voices in unison.

"Hunting what?" And then he smiles almost apologetically.

"Guess I'm an old man." He sighs and stares off into the distance. "Remember when these lands were full of things to hunt; rabbits, birds."

I remember dad telling us similar stories, drawing us pictures of weird animals with long ears. The way he tells it you only had to step out of your door and you'd trip over the damn things. Seems to me you didn't need to be skilled back then; just having your eyes open would be enough.

"Well," The trainer fiddles with his belt, pulling it up over his ample stomach. "shall we!"

Chapter 21

The next trainer takes one of the knives from the table and makes like he's weighing it in his hand. "These are great for close up work." He holds it up to the sky and the blade glints in the light. "Go through skin and flesh like it's paper!"

He then looks at both of us as if remembering something from long ago. "Of course, you don't want to see *them* up close and personal if you can help it, much better if you can hit them from a distance."

In the blink of an eye his hand flashes out and there's a thud as the knife hits a board that's at least thirty feet away. "Slow them up, then you can do what you want to them!"

I look at River who is staring, jaw open and then back at the table. I'm determined to master this weapon. No way he's getting the better of me again.

"Start with this type." The trainer hands me a small knife, handle first and I take it, surprised at how light it is. Turning around I see the board in front and try and block out all the noise and activity that's going on in my peripheral vision. "Trick is to empty your mind of everything else that's going on around you." he snorts, "Easier said than done mind, when your heart's in your mouth and sweat's pouring in your eyes. Plus these *things* can jump and swerve as good as any of us, guess they've learnt over time or something."

I want to ask him more, I want to ask him how he knows so much about them, but it's not the time or place for a casual chat and as if I need reminding I catch sight of one of the giants cracking the air with his whips, letting us know that they're still there.

"Visualise the target, imagine the knife slicing the air and hitting it bang between the eyes!" I try to do just that, try to focus on the board in front but it looks a long way away and I can feel my palm getting sweaty, the knife ready to slip. "Most important of all is to take a deep breath and hold it in before you throw. It'll help you concentrate and steady your heart."

I do as he says. I try to block everything out and as I wipe my greasy palm on my clothes I take a deep breath and hold it. As I look at the board it's as if holding my breath has somehow sharpened my senses and I reckon I can see it a little clearer than I could before.

"Now pinch the end of the handle and hold it backwards so the blade almost touches your wrist. That's it! And when you feel ready, let her go."

I begin to exhale slowly and suddenly my arm flings forward sending the knife hurtling through the air. I wince as I imagine it missing by a mile or embedding in the ground metres from my feet like the net, but instead I hear a thud and when I look up I see the knife in the board. It's nowhere near the middle like the trainer's throw, in fact, a centimetre further to the left and it would have ended up missing completely. But it didn't, it hit the board and I feel an immense sense of achievement.

"That's it son, well done!"

"That was awesome, Jake!" I grin and take a step to my left leaving to floor to River who turns and takes the knife from the trainer's hand.

"Same thing, sonny. Focus, breath deeply and let it fly." River takes a few deep breaths as he tries to steady his nerves, looking at the floor, trying to block everything out and then he draws his head up and I see a look of concentration on his face that tells me he means business.

Thwump

His knife lands in between mine and the trainer's and he looks back at me as if to say 'how the hell did that happen?'

We spend the next few minutes trying out various different knives and it becomes quickly apparent that the smaller, lighter knives are the best for throwing, the heavier ones are harder to control in the air, starting out straight but soon veering off until they land in the ground meters before the board.

"What about if you're throwing from your side, if say you have to jump out of the way of something or you need to move to the side to get a better angle?"

"Excellent question my young friend, and the principle remains the same, you just have to maintain your focus and adjust to whatever angle you're aiming from." He takes up a knife and then holds it as if his arm is pinned to his side, moving his forearm and pivoting his hip.

He then raises his arm until it's almost straight above his head before leaning his shoulder into the movement. "The angle of the throw dictates which muscle group you need to use the most."

As we're busy staring back at the table fantasising about flying through the air, the trainer walks around the side until he's standing next to us, hands by his sides, knives in each. He takes a single breath and then explodes into action; tucking his chin towards his chest he rolls forward over his right shoulder, flicks his wrist out and then repeats the process on the left side until he's standing back next to us, barely out of breath.

I look at River and then towards the board and see two new knives each side of the original one he threw. "How the hell did you do that?" River's eyes are wide open and a grin is breaking out on both our faces.

The whistle sounds again cutting through the air and we reluctantly move towards the next station, not before he gives us a last piece of advice. "Remember to get your breathing right." I look over my shoulder but there's already two others at the table and I turn back to River, his face reddening like he's ready to explode.

"How are we supposed to master any of these skills if they only give us a few minutes on each one? And how do we know they're even going to give us these weapons when we're out *there*?" River looks over and I can sense the frustration but don't know what I can really say to help. He looks around at the activity going on in each corner of the courtyard. "Seems to me they're in a hurry to introduce us to everything!"

He's still talking but I've stopped listening. In fact I've stopped walking and he practically bumps into me. "Hey Jake, what…" And then he stops as well and looks in the same direction as I am, at the man with the beaming grin who is rubbing his hands together. In front of us a body is being dragged away by two Guards, a thin trail of red blood staining the brown dust.

"Welcome to *The Gauntlet*, boys! Let's see how *you* both do!"

Chapter 22

"It's a test of balance and nerve and it demands your respect!"

The trainer looks us up and down as if weighing up our prospects but his face gives nothing away. The nets and knives have awoken a competitive spirit in both me and River and the more time I spend with him the more I like him.

I think Ellie and Doughnut would too but as I give him a sideways glance I detect for the first time something other than confidence exuding from him. It's not exactly fear, more concern as to what he's about to do.

"Have you ever seen anything like this?" I shake my head.

"No I haven't. You?"

"God no! Would have run a mile in the opposite direction if I had!"

So far the stations have mostly been tables with weapons on them or mats that people are throwing themselves about on. Each one far enough apart to enable us to move freely without getting in the way of anyone else; Guards moving between everything with their whips never too far away.

There's no need for crowd control because everyone understands that their soon going to be fighting for their lives. Better to save your energy for out there.

But what's in front of us is completely different. It looks like a series of wooden beams suspended about three feet off the ground crisscrossing at various intervals and at various heights. Each looks to be no more than a few inches wide so balancing is going to be difficult to say the least. It looks like some kind of demented climbing frame, but it's what's hanging all around that's really got my attention.

The first beam looks solid enough and I know that I could jump it no problem, I've been doing this kind of thing with Ellie and Doughnut all my life. I run my eyes along the beam and see that it has a pivot in the middle which means that it's most likely weight sensitive. Positioning is going to be all important because as soon as you make it to the middle it's going to tip down forcing you to speed up or get off.

"If we fall in *that* we're not getting up again in a hurry!" River reads my mind and I can see him looking at the same thing that I now am; broken glass placed directly under the structure, as if any further incentive is needed to keep your focus.

I can't really make out the rest of the 'Gauntlet' or whatever the trainer called it because it stretches off into the distance and I'm at the wrong angle but I'm nervous. This isn't just throwing nets and knives.

"I see you like my little design?" The trainer is grinning from ear to ear looking over the beams with a fondness I normally associate with a father for his children. "You've got to be fearless when you face them, your body's got to know what to do instinctively, before your brain has time to slow everything down, to think each move through. Think too much and your dead; don't think at all and you're not much better off!"

I look at River; words at this point are useless.

"Well, who's up next?" He looks in the direction the Guards dragged the body just as we were arriving. "Let's see if you can do any better than the last one!"

I sense the giant Guard nearby ready to pounce if he detects weakness or hesitation and surprise myself when my legs move me to the first beam. I can hear River behind me, whispering, "Are you sure? They can't make us do this?" but I know he doesn't really believe that. After all I've experienced in the last few days the only thing that's got me through it is a refusal to back down, a refusal to be broken by what they throw at us.

And I'm not about to begin now.

"Remember, it's a test of mind and body." I acknowledge the trainer's words with a nod and back up about fifteen feet from the first beam. I need good speed to make the initial jump onto it but not too much that I stumble forward and lose my balance. I glance at the glass on the floor and then back at the beam, swallowing hard, trying to calm my heart beat like the previous trainer showed us; long deep breaths – in through the nose, out through the mouth.

Walking backwards I've taken thirteen steps but I know that my stride will be longer when I start running so I calculate that eight steps will see me to the best place to jump from. I'm right footed so I need to take off exactly on the eighth stride if I'm to make it.

My legs start twitching, telling me that they want to move, that I've got to stop thinking about it. What did the trainer say?

A test of mind and body.

Leaning back on my heels to get as much spring as I can I push off, blocking out the noise from all around me, counting each step in my head.

1...2...3

I've got to jump on the eighth. If I get it wrong I'm in the glass.

4...5...6

My body tenses as it readies itself for the next phase; the transition from running to jumping.

7...8

My right foot and ankle take the weight of my entire body as I hit the ground hard and push myself up. My left leg spirals round as if there's another step about a foot in the air and for a split second I think I've gone on the wrong one, there's no way I've given myself enough room or speed to make it up to the beam!

I start to wobble in the air rotating my arms to keep me upright. The beam is fast approaching and as my left leg moves back up I'm convinced my shin is going to crash into it and send me flying.

But it doesn't. It clears the edge by a matter of millimetres before landing with a thump. My brain reminds me of the pivot in the middle and as my right foot makes contact as well I try to push my weight down so I don't run on too far and upset the balance. I take two small steps and then throw my arms straight out at my sides, wobbling slightly as the beam threatens to tip on the pivot before balancing out.

I hear River call out something from below but I don't acknowledge. I can't afford any distractions. Leaning forward I inch along the beam until it starts to pivot.

When I think I've made it more or less to the middle I lower my centre of gravity and inch forward some more hoping that the friction between the wood and the warn soles of my shoes will prevent me sliding forward any quicker.

The next beam up ahead is another foot or so higher and leads slightly to the left, the one beyond that is lower and angles to the right. Before I reach the end of this one I take two longer strides and just about make it onto the next beam, again using my arms as counter weights, crouching low like before.

The next two are easier than the first; they're just a case of remembering your footing and not being put off by the height because I'm now about eight feet in the air and although it's not much it's more than enough to break bones. It's like I'm climbing on something Doughnut put together, but when I look ahead at the next section the thought vanishes.

The beam itself is not a problem. It's long and straight and by far the easiest of the lot; it's what's dangling above it that's got my heart hammering against my ribs!

Spaced out at intervals, suspended from a parallel beam at least three feet above me, are what look like long metal poles, some with spikes on, some that looked wrapped with a kind of wire. I guess if I walk slowly enough I could somehow manoeuvre them out of the way, maybe if I sit down and inch myself along I might be able to…

The thought is halted as the wood begins to rotate. I look down below to see a Guard winding a handle and then my eyes go back to the beam.

I see now how the poles are at different lengths, the rocking motion making them swing at different times; it's not only a test of balance, it's a test of fear or more realistically, my ability to control it.

The noise from the others in the courtyard intrudes and I try to block it out. I've got to concentrate because the body that was being dragged away as we approached this station looked in bad shape and I don't want the same thing happening to me!

I take a deep breath and step out onto the next beam. The pole above me is grinding and clicking as it rotates, swinging the objects I have to navigate. As I inch towards the first pole I can see the nails spread out across its surface more clearly now, some of them coloured a rusty red, some of them with rags of cloth still stuck to them.

The movement of my head as I turn my neck in time with the pole begins to make me dizzy and for a moment I look up to the sky in an attempt to clear my mind.

When I'm ready to look again I begin to count in time with the swing.

One Mississippi.

Two Mississippi.

Three Mississippi.

It takes the pole five seconds to complete one swing from left to right, ten to make it back to where it started. That means I've only got a couple of seconds to move by it.

I look beyond to see another pole past this one glistening in the sunshine. It looks more like a sword but the problem I'm going to face is that somehow it's swinging the opposite way, so that when one is swinging to the left the other is swinging to the right and if my eyes don't deceive me, there are at least four more poles after that one.

Stop stalling!

Inching my right shoe forward I begin to feel the breeze stirred up by the pole as it swings past my face.

I follow the pole of nails until it's on the highest point of its journey to my right and then step forward. My body aches with tension and I move my other leg as quickly as possible as it swings closer behind me than I thought it would.

I wince as I imagine the nails catching me on my side or digging into my back and look back at the rags of cloth that flutter as it passes by again trying not to imagine how they got there.

The breath that escapes my lungs is ragged and I wipe sweat from my forehead as I look ahead to the next one. My initial thought was right; it is some kind of sword and it seems to be swinging at a slightly faster rate than the previous pole. It's only fractional but as I count again, it's more like eight seconds and I'm already inching forward as close as I can get because there's even less margin of error than before.

MOVE!

I take three quick steps in succession and feel the blade rustle the hair on the back of my head as it swings down. My hand instinctively reaches up and around and then I look at my palm, fearing that it will be full of clumps of hair and blood, but there's nothing, except sweat and dirt.

Flexing my hands I try to focus as exhaustion threatens to topple me off the beam.

It's like my body's had enough.

We've been kept on the edge for what seems like days, but why now? Why do I have to feel like this now, up here where I can least afford to?

I picture the blood soaked floor below, the body being dragged away as we approached. Is that what's going to happen to me?

Am I going to die up here?

Chapter 23

My mind is still fuzzy when the next obstacle clips my shoulder blade as I skip along the pole, spinning me to my left. I instinctively lower my body and hold onto the beam with both hands until the initial surprise fades, grimacing at the sharp pain that shoots down my arm. There are no nails or shards of glass sticking out of this one and a quick check reveals no blood but I hold on as tight as I can as my body sways from side to side.

I can make out River below and imagine him to be memorising all my moves for when he has to navigate the beams. I think he's trying to say something to me but I can't hear him. All my energy is focused on my next move.

Standing up I see three more swinging obstacles and take my chance. Skipping past the first one, keeping count in my head, I near the second one; this one definitely does have shards of something glinting in the sun and as I follow its pendulum motion I can't help the dizziness that begins to spread throughout my body.

I need to focus. I'm almost at the end and as I count off, *3..2..1*, my left foot slips off the beam and I land on my chest knocking the wind out of me.

My face is turned to the left and I can see the pole swinging back down towards me. If I inch forward the hunching of my shoulders will provide too much of an area to hit, if I don't move at all…

There's no more time for thinking as the pole swings down and a piece of glass misses my cheek by a matter of inches. And then I'm off, scuttling across the pole on my hands and knees before falling flat on my stomach as the last pole makes its way towards me.

As I twist my head to take a look I realise that it is longer than the previous one and although I can't see any nails on it, it doesn't really matter because if it hits me I'm flying off this pole and God knows what happens then.

I instinctively roll to my left side as the pole bares down and before I know what's happening I slip of the beam entirely, only my hands are still holding on and they threaten to drop me as they take the full weight of my body.

Dangling beneath the beam I begin to inch my way forward towards the end; if I fall I end up like the body that we saw dragged away so my only hope is to make it to the end and hope that they take into account the fact that I completed the challenge.

Ahead of me I see a series of beams like the beginning, each crossing the other at different heights until the last one is no more than a foot or so off the ground. I pass hand over hand until I've almost reached the end and then begin to swing my body back and forth. If I can get enough momentum then I should be able to swing towards the lower one and grab on tight. That's the theory anyway.

Shifting my legs I begin to rock back and forward. It's something I've done a million times with Ellie and Doughnut as we run along the rooftops of Sanctum. But never with this pressure.

I wait until I think I've got enough momentum, but my fingers won't unlock themselves and I swing back, my arms burning with the strain.

I try again but this time I can feel my fingers beginning to lose their grip on the beam so I let go before I'm fully stretched. I've got to show them I can adapt, that I'm worthy and although there's no way I can now get both hands to the next beam, if I can grab hold with one and then turn my body using the momentum I've already got, I should be able to land on the one below and then drop to the ground.

Shooting my left hand out and up it hits the beam and I grab on for only a second but it's enough to change my direction and with all my strength I reach for the next one but I'm too far away. My body begins to tuck itself in as if it's already taken this into account and I turn in the air and brace myself for the impact.

Hit and roll! Hit and roll!

The ground rushes up and as I slam into it I push with my feet and spring forward, rolling over my shoulder until I come skidding to a halt in a cloud of dust.

"That was AMAZING!" River is the first by my side grinning like an idiot, "I thought you were a gonner when you slipped from that beam but the way you swung through the air!" He begins to mimic my movements, flapping his arms like a bird, and for a moment I think the two of us forget where we are and what we're trying to do as I sit there in the dust and begin to giggle.

The mood is abruptly darkened as the shadow of the big Guard looms into view, and from the look on River's face he's suddenly remembered the bleeding body being dragged from the same place earlier. I see the whip fall from his hand but I'm so shattered as the adrenalin leaves my body that it's all I can do to raise a hand weakly in his direction, wincing as I anticipate the pain that's about to be unleashed.

"He finished the challenge!" The voice comes from my left and as I open my eyes and look up I see the trainer who had been turning the wheel stepping beside me. River joins too and the three of us look up at the huge guard, a look of puzzlement passing across his scarred face. "I don't mean to, I mean – I'm sorry to speak in this way," The trainer fiddles with the ends of his shirt; he looks pale and scared his greying hair loose around his shoulders. "but we're supposed to train these boys and this one showed he has the ability to think on his feet, to adapt."

The Guard tenses his upper arm and for the first time I see beyond him to the other training stations in the courtyard. They're all looking this way as if we've challenged authority, as if we're defying Our Leader. Even the Guard begins to look around as if not quite sure what to do.

I'm still in the dirt, one hand on the ground but inside I'm struggling to keep fear at bay and then a loud whistle, not unlike the siren call back in Sanctum sounds and the courtyard erupts into life again as we're pushed and pulled back towards the columns.

I turn to say thanks to the trainer but he too has been swept up in the mass of bodies and as I get hustled towards the middle I can still feel people's eyes on me, as if there's unfinished business between me and the Guard and their eager to see it completed.

I lose track of how long we're kept out there being pushed from station to station, forced to try whatever weapon is in front of us until the whistle blows and we have to switch again. But I do know, as we're led back to the cells in the gloom of dusk, that we're all exhausted, the long faces and the lack of talking tells me all I need to know about how we all feel.

I'm so tired I barely register the new faces amongst the group, the fact that we all seem to have the same slash of paint across our chests.

Once inside the cold, dark cell people quickly retreat to the shadows trying to find whatever rest they can as we make our way to the far wall beneath the small barred window, River the first to slump down onto the floor, his head resting on his arms. I don't really want to disturb him because he needs his rest, we all do, but I can't stop my brain from ticking over.

If I'm right with my dates then the day after tomorrow will be the full moon. In *two* days we will be facing whatever lies beyond the Wall. Even thinking about it makes my skin want to shrink from my bones and I look over to River to see if he's still awake but I can tell from the way his breathing has become slower and deeper that he's managed to fall asleep.

Two days.

It doesn't seem possible and as I think back to the knives, the nets, the other things we've been made to do today I come up against the same thought as before. We don't have enough time to really master any of these skills. So if the idea is that we're able to put on some sort of great show for everyone then I just can't see it happening!

But then maybe that's not what it's really about and as I stretch out on the floor, my hands behind my head, a word begins to form in my mind, a word that I haven't thought about since the meeting in the Square.

Conditioning.

It's what dad used to say was the real point of the stupid meetings in the first place and as I think back to the quiet that had descended towards the end of the day. As I picture the resignation on people's faces, I start to wonder if the training is more about keeping us focused, getting us in the mood for fighting.

To *condition* us to accept our fate.

Closing my eyes I desperately want sleep to come and wash over my aching body, to stop my mind from pouring over the last few days but already know that that's not going to happen any time soon.

Squirming around on the floor trying to find a position of comfort, I can't help but still feel we're not being told the whole truth. That there's more to all this than meets the eye, and as my eyelids become heavy I try to picture Ellie and Doughnut lying in the cave, a small fire smouldering next to them and for what feels like the first time in an age, a smile begins to form at the corners of my mouth.

Chapter 24

I don't know how much sleep I've had, but I do know that it's nowhere near enough. As we're pushed from the cells along the corridors it begins to feel like I haven't had any at all. I don't know if it's all the training yesterday or the fact that we're expected to curl up on cold hard floors all night, but my body aches like I've already faced the Wastelanders.

The light is harsh as we emerge coughing and wincing into the morning air but what's most noticeable is the quiet that's descended over everyone. The other day when we first arrived there was a lot more shouting, a lot more defiance, but as I look around at people's faces, the overwhelming feeling is one of resignation.

The Guards herd us back into the Courtyard, the Senator already standing on his podium, but this time I don't hear any whip cracks. They're no longer necessary.

We've all become so compliant.

"Those of you still with us have already proven yourselves to be worthy of Our Leader's great generosity!"

The Senator's words ring out and I can't help but wonder how many times *he's* had to fight for his life, or for the food that he so obviously enjoys.

"And I have GREAT news directly from Our Leader!" He spreads his arms in a gesture of welcome, palms up to the sky, "The day of reckoning is almost upon us! When you redeem yourselves for the crimes you have committed. The day when you stand out there, outside the Great Walls of our city and say to the Wastelanders, NO! YOU WILL NOT PASS!"

His words are powerful and I feel the hairs on the back of my neck rise up as if he's somehow bypassing my sense of reason, the part of me that feels a burning sense of injustice that I'm here at all, the part of me that wants to see Ellie and Doughnut again.

"As we speak the Citizens of Sanctum are readying the way for your arrival, preparing the roads for your progression from this place, vying for the best vantage point along the wall to witness this great festival first hand. But there is no time to waste, for sources tell us *they* are gathering on the horizon, waiting for the mist to descend, waiting to feed." He drops his arms and sweeps his head slowly from left to right.

"Tomorrow." The word rings out around the courtyard, "Tomorrow the whole city will be waiting for your arrival, willing *you* to be the one who defends their homes and by doing so win your freedom!" The Senator turns to the Guard next to him and nods and you can hear a pin drop as we all take in the reality of what we're being told.

It's happening. It's really happening!

The Guards begin to slowly descend from the steps towards us and I feel the crowd as one begin to shrink back.

"But for now allow the Guards to show you something that may just help to save your life. I think you'll find it rather interesting!" He sweeps from the platform as the Guards begin to separate us back into our smaller groups and I notice how, this time, there's no need for whips and screams. This time we pretty much group ourselves and I can't help but wonder at how quickly we have become so docile, so compliant, so weak.

As we are marched from the courtyard along the same stone pillars as before the stench is almost unbearable and I can't help but tense because something is nagging away at the back of my mind. I look around and see River and Rainbow. In fact I recognise most of the people from the big room and the food that now seems so long ago. Others may have perished in the 'training' but it seems that we have managed to survive this far.

My adrenalin levels are still high from the beams and I flex my shoulder that still aches from the hit it took.

"Thought you were a gonner!" River keeps his voice low and looks at me with a side on glance and the hint of a smile.

"I was just showing you how to do it, that's all!" I return the smile but it's half-hearted because I'm still playing the Senator's words over in my mind.

"Great   Festival…procession…lining   the streets."

I don't think any of us has got the faintest idea of what's going to happen, but *tomorrow*! I don't know why but I thought we were to have longer to prepare for things. I guess in the back of my mind I was hoping that someone would find me, that somehow Ellie and Doughnut would…

"Jake are you okay?" It's Rainbow, she's moved next to me in the line and I instinctively look towards the Guards, to see if they are looking this way. "Can you believe we're going to be facing them *tomorrow*!" I can see fear in her eyes, we've all got that, but there's also something else, something nearer excitement that's making her eyes shine a brilliant green.

"I know, I can't really…" My words falter as I wonder why I'm feeling so uneasy next to her and then it hits me; it's the same feeling I have when I stand next to Ellie and before I know it I've got her image in my mind's eye, tapping her feet with her arms folded as if she's mad as hell, and I suddenly feel my cheeks burning hotter and hotter and imagine Doughnut to be somewhere nearby ready to grin and point at me.

Looking back I see Rainbow staring straight ahead. As the Guards lead us beyond the stone pillars onto a patch of stony ground I'm still aware of the thought that's been nagging away at the back of my mind, and then it begins to dawn on me…it's the smell! It's the same smell that flooded the caverns moments before I saw what was crouching over Angus. I can see people putting their hands to their face, some retching and spitting onto the floor.

It's the Wastelanders.

"I don't believe it!" The words escape my mouth and I see heads turn as we follow towards a crumbling wall that stands about head height. The Guards have stopped and the large one with the scar turns to face us, a smile playing on the parts of his lips that he can still move.

A murmur breaks out amongst us. "They've got one of them. They've got one of them beyond that wall!"

"What do you mean *them?*" Rainbow is the first to ask the question but my mind is replaying the events in the underground tunnels and I can barely hear her or anyone else, as the Guard with the scar begins to speak.

"It's tied up securely so none of you are in any danger! Our Leader has decreed that those fighting outside of the wall tomorrow should be able to study the enemy up close." He nods his great scarred head towards the end of the wall, inviting us to take a look and for a split second no one moves a muscle, as if the horror of what awaits is too much for everyone.

But I've seen them already. I've fought them and survived, barely, and something in me, some force moves my feet and before I know what I'm doing I'm walking towards the Guard and then past him to the horror that awaits.

There are two crumbling walls running parallel to one another about ten feet apart and as I look around, trying to stop my heart from leaping out of my ribcage, I'm confused. I assumed that it would be there, waiting to pounce but all I see are the scattered remnants of animals that have been fed to it; strips of rotting meat and shards of bone covering most of the dusty ground under my feet.

Sensing movement behind me I register the gasps of some of the others as I imagine the Guards have pushed them to follow but I'm now concentrating on what's up ahead.

At the far end of the two low walls, about twenty feet away, some sort of canopy has been erected, a few wooden poles staked into the ground with some dirty sheets stretched across, I guess it makes sense because we're all told from the moment we're born that they don't like the sun. It's why they wait for the mist to descend before mounting any attacks.

My vision is obscured by the strips of material that are hanging down at the edges, as if it's tried to tear down the canopy and has only succeeded in shredding parts of it. Why would it try to do such a thing if the sun is dangerous to it?

The Guard moves past me and pulls on a chain that is looped through various rings attached to the wall and we all take a step backwards as a yelp sounds from within the darkness of the shelter.

"They cannot function properly in sunlight, their eyes and skin are deformed and unable to accept the sun's rays." As if to demonstrate the yelping continues as the Guard gives one final pull on the chains and a form emerges from the canopy, hunched over and screaming into the light. The

Guard has one foot on the wall for balance as we stand there watching the creature twist and writhe until its claws are shielding as much of it from the sun as possible.

The stuff of a million nightmares yelping and scrabbling in the dirt.

"Oh my God!"

"What the hell is it?"

And then another Guard pulls on more chains and the creature's arms are forced away from its face and down behind its back.

"It has NO mercy for you. It has NO sympathy." As the creature screams and spits, pulling at the chains that bind it we all get a clear view of its face; of the skin that is stretched so tight it shows the movement of every muscle, of the teeth that protrude from the mouth as if trying to escape.

But that's not what I'm looking at, I'm looking at the eyes.

"The radiation from the Great Light warped and deformed any who could not get out of its way, any who could not find shelter below the ground. But the will to survive is strong, the need to feed, to breed is as necessary for them as it is for us. They survived on the contaminated bodies of the dead."

He gives a nod to the other Guard who pulls the chain again, but this time it brings only one arm forward and the Wastelander flexes its claw in rage like a puppet on a string. "They have several distinct advantages; namely teeth and claws." The chain remains tight and the claws flex and open and we see clearly what he means.

Protruding from each finger is a three inch talon, curved at its tip.

No one really needs to be told what it is capable of achieving. All the while the jaws are clamping away like an animal trap, snapping down with a force I have already seen and for a moment my head is filled with the sound of chewing and tearing.

I see in my mind's eye one of them on top of Angus waving its head from side to side, ravenous and unyielding, as the Guard's voice continues. "They can also run fast, faster than we can."

"They can also swim."

The words leave my mouth before I have time to swallow them back down and I look around as all eyes are momentarily on me. A fresh scream from the Wastelander breaks the spell as the Guard on the left falls away from the wall clutching his hands as the chain rips through them.

Freeing one hand it then begins to pull on the other chain and although the larger Guard doesn't seem to be unduly worried, we all take a step back to the safety of the walls edge as two more Guards pass by and throw rotten meat from a bucket behind it into the shelter.

The Wastelander scrabbles at the ground, trying to get back to the safety of the sheets, the smell of flesh in its nostrils but the Guard doesn't let it go until the air is filled with the chilling sound of gnashing teeth and the shrill cry that comes from deep within its deformed chest.

And then the chain is let go and the creature scuttles back into the shadows until all we can hear is the sound of ripping and tearing as it hungrily devours the meat.

"But how can *we* kill *that*?" The voice comes from somewhere behind me and I hear a murmur of agreement ripple around as if it's the thought that's been on everyone's mind but that no one has wanted to voice. "If we come face to face with one of these *things* have we really got a chance?"

For a moment the Guards look at each other as if they don't quite know what to do or say and then slowly they pull on the chains and we hear the creature scrabbling and snapping its jaw as it's forced from the torn and broken shelter, back out into the sunlight. As it's pulled nearer I can't help but take a step back because I can see the flesh of its food still in its teeth, blood dripping onto the floor.

"It will kill you all without hesitation or mercy!" And as I look at its head, whipping from side to side, straining against the chains despair begins to take hold, despair that I was ever stupid enough to think that we had anything resembling the slimmest of chances out there against them.

The second Guard pulls a small knife from a leather sheath hanging from his belt and in one swift move takes a large step forward and I hold my breath as the knife arches in the air, blade glinting in the sun, in front of the Wastelander's face. The rest of the movement is obscured by the Guard's body and then he steps back and for a brief moment, nothing happens.

After a few seconds I begin to see blood. It starts as a thin line high up on the creature's face and then begins to spill down the cheek as a flap of skin peels away revealing the sinew and tendon beneath.

And then the Wastelander screams.

The pitch is like nothing I've ever heard before as it brings its claws up to its face shuffling backwards against the tension of the metal chains.

"If it bleeds it can be killed!"

The questions come thick and fast; "How are we supposed to get that close without chains? Are we given knives before we get out there? Where will the weapons be?"

But all I can do is look at the faces around me and then back at the Wastelander as it shrieks and moans, blood pooling around its feet, because as the others are taking some kind of comfort from this demonstration, I'm looking at its eyes, and all I can see is fear and confusion.

"They were like us once!" And for a split second I feel something that I never thought I would, not for these creatures in any case.

I feel compassion.

Chapter 25

The room is as gloomy and dark as it was the night before and we try our best to curl up and pretend that we're tired but the reality is that I don't think any of us will ever be able to sleep again. We were fed again earlier, just like the day before; Guards at the entrance to the hall, as we grabbed at the bowls and spooned the stew into our mouths.

How quickly we've become used to this way of life. How quickly it becomes almost *normal*.

Smiling, I remember River telling as we ate how I was dangling by my fingertips from the beam and then how I spun out and down onto the floor. The way he told it I did a few extra somersaults as well for good measure. Rainbow also told how she had learnt to fight with a sword and her trainer had shown her that it isn't necessarily how strong you are that wins a fight but how quick and agile.

Then she was up rolling her wooden spoon around, rotating her wrists and then bringing it down in a forward slashing movement. The laughter still echoes in my ears, but it didn't do what we all wanted it to do; it didn't stop us from thinking about tomorrow. And it didn't stop us thinking about what we saw this afternoon, the creature that stood no more than ten feet away.

Something's eating away at me as I lie here on the cold hard floor, like a word on the tip of my tongue or a thought that refuses to fully form and I fight the urge to shout out and disturb the silence.

I try to picture what tomorrow will be like; what the roads will look like with people lining the way. How will we be greeted? As criminals walking to our impending doom, or as the great hope for the city of Sanctum?

"Our only hope is to stick together." My voice is flat and it cuts through the quiet like a knife. I hadn't meant to speak out loud. I hadn't meant to disturb everyone and I look to the door, sure that the Guards are going to burst in at any moment, sure they can hear every word we utter. That they know everything we're thinking.

I hear murmurings from the gloom as if people aren't too happy that I've disturbed whatever peace they've been able to find for themselves on *this* night of all nights.

"He's right." I sense River turning towards me in the darkness and I blink until my eyes can see just about make out his face, but there's no smile on his lips, just the cold hard look of someone who's lived by their wits and knows that time is running out on them. "We've got to start thinking about what's up ahead."

"You think Our Leader is really going to give people their freedom if they survive?" The voice is almost a whisper and comes from a freckle faced kid who looks barely old enough to work let alone to be in here with the rest of us and then the realisation strikes; I don't really know any of these people. I don't even know all of their names.

How can I trust them when we're facing the Wastelanders? If we are to fight in a group, if my life depends on some of these people then how can I not know who they are?

"Whether it's true or not, it doesn't stop the fact that we'll be out *there* tomorrow facing *them*." I sense everyone flinch as they think back to what was behind the wall earlier on; the deformed face, the teeth that clamped open and shut like a metal trap.

The eyes.

"Damn right he will!" Rainbow's voice is strong and I am momentarily ashamed of bringing the mood down. "He's told the whole of Sanctum what the rules are! No way he'll go back on that! The people wouldn't stand for it!" Her voice rises on the last few words as if it's more of a question than a statement, and the silence that descends is even louder than before as we wait to see if the Guards have heard us.

"Hey, you know what?" I'm whispering as loudly as I dare because I'm the one who brought the subject up, who broke the silence in the room, and I feel like it's my job to try and raise the mood a little, if I can.

Sitting up I shuffle into the patch of moonlight on the floor and look around at the dim figures huddled together for warmth. "I can't believe my manners, I can't believe *our* manners! There are people in here I don't even know – can you believe that! Off on a great adventure tomorrow and I haven't even got the manners to find out everyone's name!"

I can tell from the flashes of teeth that people are smiling and I see a few beginning to shuffle towards me. "Tell you what! I'm going to begin; I'm Jake and as you've already been told." I shoot a glare at River who pretends to cover his face, "I'm pretty good at dangling by my fingertips, in fact I love running and jumping over things! I'll climb anything you care to put in my way. I take it as a personal challenge!"

Rainbow is the next as she moves alongside me in the patch of light and I swear I see a softness in her face I haven't seen before, a softness that makes my cheeks burn hotter than the sun.

"I'm Rainbow and you all know what I can do!" She swings an imaginary sword again, like the spoon earlier and a few chuckles begin to squeeze through peoples fingers as they try desperately to be quiet.

River's next and there's a good feeling in the room, the gloom momentarily lifting as we try to forget what's waiting for us.

"I'm River and I guess I've discovered that I can throw knives pretty well." He launches an imaginary blade and the faces in the gloom turn to follow its trajectory as if it's really flying through the air.

The freckle faced kid is up next and although he seems a little brighter than before, his face still betrays a sense of despair behind the eyes. "Name's Dodge." He shrugs and grins, "Least that's what my friends call me! Pretty good at hiding, seeing as though I'm so small. If I don't want to be found, I won't."

Another young kid shuffles into view, his hair thick around his shoulders and I can't help but think about the sense of having children this young in this place.

"Name's Samson...umm, guess I'm a quick runner, I mean no one's been able to catch me yet!" Faces smile and I'm struck by how quickly people's guards are coming down, like everyone is desperate to communicate something, anything about themselves. To feel for even the briefest moment, normal.

As we sit there in a makeshift circle in the dark, whispering our names, trying to find the words to describe who we are, I can't help but feel a little glad that I've met these people. I don't really know what the feeling is because my stomach's still knotted and when I think back to the Wastelander we saw earlier on I want to scream at the top of my lungs and beat my fists against the door. But there's something about sharing the experience, something about being here with others that stops the despair from becoming too overwhelming.

Shuffling back a little as the others continue to introduce themselves I realise that no one has refused to, that everyone has joined in and then I feel the warmth of Rainbow's body as she moves alongside me. "We'll be alright won't we Jake? Out there I mean?" For a moment I have no idea what to say and then the words slip from my mouth before I have time to consider them.

"Of course we'll be okay! Look around, as long as we're fighting for each other then we've got a chance, we've got a real chance!" I can see a smile break out on her face as she curls up beside me but my face refuses to follow suit because deep down I guess I don't really believe what I've just said.

Deep down I'm finding it hard to see any hope at all.

"Are we really in the Inner Sanctum?" The voice is a whisper and it comes from my left. I look down and see a pair of young eyes looking up at me. It's the kid who introduced himself as Dodge and as I begin to nod he tentatively moves nearer to Rainbow, as if prepared to be pushed away.

"Come and get some warmth!" Rainbow opens her arms and he sits there for a moment, his eyes narrowing before slowly moving against her leg, like an animal worried it will be scolded.

I look up and see the other kid, Samson I think he said he was, lying against River's legs and as our eyes meet River shrugs and smiles and for the first time in an age I feel like I do when I'm with Ellie and Doughnut.

Maybe it's the fear we're all being put through, the fact that this is like nothing any of us have ever experienced before, but its like bonds of friendship grow stronger in adversity or something.

It's like I'm beginning to feel protective towards them.

Chapter 26

I'm woken by the door clanging against the wall and before I can gather my thoughts, before I can even really check to see how the others are, Guards rush in and begin pulling and pushing people out into the corridor. I manage to grab Rainbow by the arm and pull her close because I don't want us separated, not today, and I see that River is doing the same for Samson and Dodge.

My senses are alert as we're jostled together but I can feel Rainbow straining to see the others. "It's okay! Keep by me. We'll be alright!"

"I can't see them! I can't see River and the others!" Panic grips Rainbow's throat as we stumble out onto the steps that lead out into the now familiar courtyard.

I turn and catch a glimpse of Dodge through the bodies and try to call out but the wind is forced out of me as someone is pushed into my back and I stumble onto my knee.

"YOU! GET UP!"

The Guard strides towards me, his whip unfurling to the floor and I hear others scream as flashes of red appear from behind the pillars, pushing and funnelling people towards the courtyard.

"Keep your eyes on me! Keep looking!" Rainbow nods although we're now separated by people as they rush forward and I manage to keep myself upright, showing the palms of my hands to the Guard. "I'm okay, Sir! I'm okay!"

"Keep moving! KEEP MOVING!" I nod and continue forward past the pillars until I reach the top of the steps that lead down to the previous days training area.

For a moment I don't recognise the place, there must be hundreds of people half running, half falling into different lines. It feels like the Guards have been told to tolerate no dissent because I can see people being hit for stepping out of line, whips cracking above our heads.

It feels like the first day we arrived.

Another push from behind sends me scuttling down the stairs and I duck just in time as another whip sounds inches from my ear. I try to look around for the others but it's all too frantic and when I reach the bottom of the stairs we're all forced into different lines, the Guards patrolling up and down as people cry out all around to newly made friends.

Looking up towards the end of the lines there must be at least ten tables set up, each under a canopy to protect the Guard from the sun's rays, each piled high with different coloured cloth.

"What do they want with us now?" I look down at the watery eyes that look at me searching for some comfort. I don't recognise the face but I recognise the fear.

"Maybe they're giving us uniforms?" I shuffle forward as the Guard walks past, my head moving all around searching for the others. "Wouldn't want to blend in out there, would you?" I want to smile, to try and relieve the tension but the best I can manage is a grimace as we're shoved forward again finally in earshot of the Guard behind the table.

"Take these and put them on! Can't have you going to the Peoples' Court looking like that now, can we!"

The Peoples' Court; The Square where we first heard from Our Leader about his plans. Is that where we're going? Is that where it all begins?

I'm still about ten people away from the table but I can see that beyond the canopies people are stripping out of their rags and putting on the clothes, simple woollen trousers and shirts, each a different colour.

Turning my head as I move closer to the table I catch a glimpse of Rainbow about twenty people behind in the line next to me. She doesn't see me but it doesn't matter because at least I know she's all right and I have to have faith in River looking after the other two. If I'm going to get through this then I guess I'm probably going to have to put my faith in a lot of things I wouldn't normally.

"YOU!" The voice jolts me from my thoughts and I turn to realise that I'm now at the head of the line. "Step forward and receive your gift." Looking to my left I see a Guard grinning as he watches the people undressing behind the canopies and I want to grab his baton and show him what it's like to be on the other side for a change.

Swallowing the anger I take a step and hold out my hands as I've seen the others do and then the Guard drops the itchy woollen clothes into them and pushes me by the side of the table.

"Wait. Please!" The words spring from my mouth and I half turn because we're being forced to change where the Senator has spoken to us the last few days. "W…where's the Senator? Does he not want to see us getting ready?" The Guard turns from the next person in the line and stares at me before his pale, spotty face breaks out into a grin.

"Plenty of time for that boy! Now MOVE!"

Stumbling forward I try to find space but we're all so tightly packed in that it's almost impossible. All I can hear are people sobbing and crying out the names of people they know, some half dressed in their new clothes, some naked. All with a look of fear.

And then I see them through the jumble of bodies; River, Samson and Dodge, struggling with their clothes, huddled close together and as I look down at mine I realise that they're the same colour, that they're green.

"Hey! River!" I push through the people in front of me until I see Dodge turn around, the smile on his face helping me regain some composure because if I can't be strong for myself then I've got to for him, for the others.

"Jake! Can you believe what they're making us do now?" He's grinning but I can tell that he's scared. We all are.

"Where's Rainbow?" I look behind me and then back at River who is struggling to put the woollen top on.

"She was in the line next to me." I turn around again and think I catch a glimpse of her by the tables. "Do you think she'll get the same uniform?"

"What the hell are these anyway? They itch all over!" Samson wriggles his finger inside the collar of the shirt and I see what he means when I put the trousers on. The material is coarse and rough on the skin. I can't imagine having to wear this stuff for long, but then I guess they're not really meant to last. Not where we're going.

I can tell River's not listening because he's still looking over my shoulder and then his whole face brightens.

"Rainbow! Rainbow! Over here!" I finish putting the rest of the clothes on and turn as she pushes her way towards us, the relief almost too much when I see that she's got green clothes in her hands too.

"We look like a bunch of damn trees in this stuff! Is this so we can be more easily seen out *there*?" But before any of us can reply the Guards begin to crack their whips, urging us to keep moving. Rainbow struggles with her new clothes as we stand in front of her to stop any prying eyes and then we're being funnelled again.

River takes the lead, holding his arms out in front to keep people from pushing into him. Voices sound all around. Rumours people have picked up along the way.

"…trucks are waiting for us…"

"…Wastelanders have already gotten in…"

"…gonna make us walk to the Wall…"

But I try and block them out because I need to focus on getting us all through whatever this is and if I let my mind wander too far then I'm afraid I won't be able to get it back.

We move along the edge of the courtyard and then up the wide stairs opposite and for the first time I get a look at the sprawling nature of the buildings we've been held in. It's like nothing I've ever seen before but the crowd is kept moving and my view disappears behind more stone columns.

I don't recognise where we're going, it doesn't look like any of the training areas of the first few days and then I begin to hear commotion up ahead as the path we're on begins to descend a little.

"What is it? What can you see?" Samson is trying to jump up and down because he's so much shorter than everyone else and I stretch onto my tiptoes before nearly falling into the person in front, and then the word gets passed along the crowd from the front about what they can see.

Trucks.

Dozens of them.

Chapter 27

By the time we reach the end of the descent even Samson can see the tops of the trucks that seem to extend on forever. When we see that they're filling up with people dressed in the same colour clothing, I feel a little weight lifting from my shoulders, as if for the time being I'm happy in the knowledge that we're not going to be separated.

The scene is mesmerizing; wriggling lines of blue, red and yellow all piling into the trucks. As I look at River and Rainbow I see weariness in their faces and imagine that I look much the same, in fact it feels like, after the shock of what's just happened that everyone's fallen a little flat as people allow themselves to be pushed onto the trucks with barely a murmur.

The journey to the Peoples' Court is in complete silence; the sheer number of trucks transporting everyone disappearing in one long snaking line almost to the horizon. I try to calculate numbers in my head. If this is going on all over Sanctum, if similar numbers of trucks are appearing from other places, snaking along roads like this one, then that means that we'll number in at least the hundreds, if not thousands.

Does that mean that there are that many Wastelanders? Does it mean that we're expected to die in great numbers?

I shut my eyes tight and try to chase away the images but it's no good and all I can see is the creature behind the wall, its bloodshot eyes, its teeth bared and snapping.

The truck rocks from side to side as it negotiates the rough terrain and I sit up, images still playing in my brain. I see River and Rainbow up ahead about four seats in front but I daren't say anything to them; there are almost as many Guards in the truck as there are us and the atmosphere is more like it was on the first day at the prison; tense and frightening.

Every now and again I see other people's faces, people that I haven't seen before, people that must have been in another part of the compound and I can tell straight off that they're going to struggle, that they're not going to last long. I don't know what it is; maybe it's their eyes, or the way their head hangs low, almost to their chest, but it's there all right, an air of doom, as if it's all a foregone conclusion.

As if they've already given up.

The truck rocks to the left on the uneven road and I shift in the small seat my mind turning back to the events of the morning; the tables piled high with clothing. It was like a production line; one table for shoes, one for trousers and one for tops and as the Guards filed us along the shouting and crying seemed to get worse and worse.

I can still hear the screams as people were forced into trucks, separated from friendships they made, maybe even people they knew from before and it try to shake my head clear. The woollen top proves a distraction as I pull at the material imagining my neck to be all different shades of angry red by now, trying hard not to scratch because I know that if I do, then I won't be able to stop. For some reason my mind conjures up the Senator's words of earlier.

"You are fighting firstly for the honour and safety of Sanctum and every citizen within its walls, and secondly for your own salvation. As such our Leader has been gracious enough to provide you with new clothing, clothing that better represents our city. Put this clothing on, wear the colours of your Leader and your old persona is gone, replaced by the new you, the better you, the you that is prepared to fight to the death for the greater good!"

I can't help but smile, but it's not born of joy more an acknowledgement of a simple truth. As we stood there in the cold morning air, stripping to our bare skin and putting on these new clothes, I couldn't help but look around, look at the colours as people slid into their costumes slowly and reluctantly; bright yellows, reds and greens.

We stood out like sore thumbs, as if they want us to be seen. We still do as we rock along the uneven road in these trucks, but it's not because we're representing anyone, it's not because *he's* being generous. It's because it makes us easier to see against the vast brown of the Wasteland. Easier to see when *they* bare down on us.

I wish I could speak to River or Rainbow but every time any of us so much as moves, the Guards snap round, and in any case, I don't think they would turn even if I did call out to them as they're probably as lost in their own thoughts as I am.

No one slept a wink last night as we all gave vent to the rumours we'd heard and the darkest thoughts in our heads about what lies ahead. Part of me still can't believe we've actually been beyond the Neutral Zone. The Inner Sanctum! Who'd have thought I'd ever get to see it?

My guess is that they're going to make us walk the rest of the way, it's about a mile or so to The Wall but try as I might I just can't picture the streets lined with people. I know it's stupid, I've been to the main square, seen the sheer numbers of people that have to file in and out. Maybe my brains refusing to go there! Maybe it knows that if I think about it all too much, I'm going to freeze or freak out, or something worse.

I stare back out of the window and try and calm my head down. The compound, or wherever we've been held these past few days has long since disappeared from view, the road stretching out before us as desolate and bumpy as the Lanes.

But that's where the similarity ends.

Where we live nothing really grows from the ground, unless it's dry and spindly and covered in brown dust. But here, as I look out of the window, lining the road are bushes and trees that I've rarely seen before, if ever. They're green and vibrant. They look somehow *fresh* and for a moment I try to picture what the Lanes would look like covered in the same vegetation, but I can't because it seems so improbable, so unlikely.

The truck passes by another gap in the trees revealing a winding path lined with more flowers leading up to another huge house. It disappears before I've got time to really take a look, but I saw it alright, just like the place we've come from.

A house fit for a Senator.

I feel anger rise up as I think of the fat, stupid Senator who spoke to us the other day, his robes stretched tight over his enormous stomach.

They don't have to scratch a living in the brown dust of the Lanes.

They don't have to fight for their lives.

And then I think back to the houses I've seen, the flowers, the green trees. Water.

They must have more water to use in the Inner Sanctum, otherwise how could everything look so healthy? We've always been told that the Senators must live apart from the rest of us, that the Inner Sanctum was necessary for them to have time and space, away from the crowded Lanes, to keep Sanctum safe. We are taught to have as much pride in them as we do Our Leader.

But now I've seen something of how they live. I've seen what they have and I don't feel pride.

I don't feel understanding.

I just feel hatred.

As the Peoples' Court looms into view from the truck window a thought that has been niggling away at me moves to the front of my mind. We must have been on these trucks for an hour, maybe two, who really knows, and in that time I haven't seen a single person staring back at us from the road. Nobody.

"Where are all the people?" My voice reverberates around the truck and for a moment I wish I could put the words back in my mouth as the Guards turn in my direction and I tense against the inevitable onslaught. Everyone has turned to me as if mad that I've broken the silence, as if the truck was going to forget that the Court is its destination and just keep on driving. I catch River's eye and he nods agreement.

"Why is nobody out there?" I can feel a murmur, a pulse from everyone as they begin to look properly, instead of remaining lost inside their own fear and then eyes turn back to me, wide and fretful as the back of the Court house looms up before us.

The big Guard at the front of the truck, the one who is handy with the whips begins to crane his thick, muscular neck round and I see the other Guards take their cue from him because as his face turns into view I see the raw scar on the side of his face move as he begins to chuckle. It's a low growling noise as if it's coming from somewhere deep inside, almost as if his body is trying hard to remember just what it sounds like.

Some of the other Guards look at each other and then start to smile as well until the whole truck is full of throaty laughter as if some long forgotten joke has just been remembered. What's crazier is that I can't help but be born aloft by this sudden outpouring of emotion and I find my mouth beginning to twitch as if it wants to join in.

And then the laughter stops.

The big Guard holds up a huge paw and it signals the end of the burst of emotion. He turns to face me still smiling but this time there's malevolence behind the upturned corners of his mouth and it makes my stomach knot itself even more than before.

"They're all waiting up ahead." He chuckles again but doesn't break eye contact and I shrink back into the seat under the heat of his gaze. "They're all waiting for you!"

Chapter 28

"MOVE!" The booming voice of the large Guard pushes me on as we file out of the trucks and into the large Square in front of the Peoples' Court. How different it all seems from the other day at the meeting when I stood here with Ellie and Doughnut, as the Guards resume their familiar ritual of yelling and cracking whips above our heads to herd us into groups.

I look around to check that everyone is close by, the bright coloured clothing we all wear lending the whole scene a touch of the absurd, as if we're a bunch of kids having fun.

"We look like a military force or something!" River whispers to my right and I don't turn to acknowledge him for fear of the Guard's seeing us but he's absolutely right and as I look to my left and right I count at least ten separate groups of people, all forming into squares of different colours, all kept subdued by the Guards. "They're going to walk us like this to the Wall. Show the Citizens who we are, get them all hyped up for the main event!"

I take a quick look at Samson and Dodge, both staring ahead, eyes wide open. I know they're scared. We all are. But there's something other than fear in their eyes and as I look closer, it's almost like I can sense excitement as well.

Pieces of the previous night's conversation in the gloom of the cell play in my head; about the orphanage, about the treatment they had received at the hands of so called carers and my surprise begins to fade. They've got the chance they wanted, the chance to do something, to actually have their own fate entirely in their hands for however short a period of time.

"WALK FORWARD!" The instruction is hardly necessary but the same words echo around the yard as each lead Guard shouts the same phrase and I feel the power of so many people taking the same step. I guess there's no longer anytime to think, there's no longer any hope of rescue or a change of heart from Our Leader.

Heart.

The word makes me grimace. He has no heart. If he did he would have stuck to his original message and sent only the worst kind of prisoners into the Wasteland and not emptied the orphanages and gathered up the homeless.

The sound of shuffling feet fills the air, followed by the ubiquitous crack of the whip, as if anyone has forgotten the threat that hangs over our heads. As we step out of the grounds of the Courthouse, each group following the other I turn to get a look at what is behind me.

Our group is the third from the front and as I turn I see the other blocks of colour snaking off into the distance, all trudging together as we make our way towards the huge stone pillars at the entrance to the Square. I can only imagine what it's going to be like for the Citizens that I guess are gathered up ahead somewhere waiting for our arrival.

The road we are taking is the main artery road that leads, eventually, to the Wall, and I can't help but think of what would happen if I tried to slip away? Would they catch me? Would they even know? As we push on our steps become more regular, a drum beat that settles us down.

The monotony of the sound steadies my mind and I begin to wonder how long the Guards would last if *they* were separated and on their own? Only so long as their batons and whips would keep the hungry and the sun crazed at bay. These kids that walk by my side have grown up in the shadows; they know every inch of the place, all the grime, all the filth, all the secret avenues and little short cuts.

A cry rises up from somewhere behind and I feel Samson and Dodge press against my side. It's quickly and brutally suppressed by the crack of the Guard's whip but it's got everybody's attention and as I look up ahead I can see why.

A huge banner has half fallen from its original placing which I imagine was high up strung across the sorry looking trees that stand, bedraggled and crest fallen in haphazard intervals at the side of the main road. The binding on the upper right hand side has come loose, probably in the wind, and has fallen, folding in on itself, obscuring some of the lettering but as we march past I sense everyone's head turn to look at the large, black letters.

WILDERNESS FESTIVAL

There's something else after the main heading but I can't quite make it out, something about the moon, but I can read what is written underneath in slightly smaller letters and I can fully understand the underlying message.

Participate in the Festival

Cheer them on

Try to pick who will survive and win their FREEDOM!

"Wow!" Dodge's voice is full of amazement. "They must have been preparing for a while. Have you ever seen anything like this?"

I want to answer but I can't. All I can do is picture people watching us, looking at us, weighing up our strength, our usefulness with a weapon, betting money and whatever else they have on who they think will win. But it goes further than that.

Anyone who has lived for any length of time in Sanctum knows that life is cheap and excitement is hard to come by; those same people betting on who will live will be the same people betting on who will die.

I look up to the sky, the blue an unbroken stretch from one side to the other and try not to think but it's too much, the unfairness of it all, the lack of choice we've all had in this.

My footsteps begin to falter and River grabs my elbow.

"Hey Jake! You okay?" I can hear his words but I'm unable to reply as the images in my mind continue to overwhelm me. I guess I've kept them back for so long, tried to be strong, tried to stay focused but the injustice of my being here, the thought of Ellie and Doughnut lining the street waiting to catch a glimpse of me or worse, watching as I step out into the Wasteland to face those *things*.

Stumbling a little River and Rainbow are quick to gather me up, supporting me under my arms as Samson and Dodge look up scared and confused.

"Hey!" A voice from behind whispers in a dark tone, "Keep him steady for God's sake or we're all done for!"

Samson turns round and glares at where the voice came from. "Keep talking and it won't just be the Wastelanders you'll need to fear!"

The voice goes quiet but it's right, I need to get a grip of myself, I can't lose it now, not if I want to see them all again. I look at Dodge who is staring up at me, his large green eyes willing me back from the brink. I can't let him down, I can't let any of them down.

My throat's dry as I speak. "I'm okay." I shrug my shoulders and River and Rainbow let go of me as I sway for a moment, waiting for the images to pass, for the thoughts to disappear. I can see a Guard looking over at the noise and I stand up straight, the cloud beginning to pass, and wink at Samson and Dodge. "I'm just so eager to fight. Nearly overcame me!"

"You'll get your wish soon, Jake!"

I grin but the words that come out sound hollow at best. "Can't wait. Just let me at them!"

Chapter 29

We've been marching for what seems like an age now and I can see a few people beginning to struggle with the heat and the lack of water. A woman to my left begins to teeter before falling onto the person in front and then to the floor, face down in the dirt.

We all turn to see if she's okay but almost as soon as her face hits the dirt the Guards are in amongst us screaming at us to continue marching, the air full of whip cracks and shouts from a few brave souls who I guess no longer think they've got anything to lose. Within a second the poor woman's body is dragged off and disappears as if nothing ever happened.

"I need water!" Dodge's voice is weak and scratchy and although he's only voicing what everyone else is thinking I wish he hadn't because now it's all I can think about. I can see heads beginning to drop as energy levels flag all around and part of me wants to yell at the Guards, to demand water.

After all, what the hell is the point of having us fight the Wastelanders near death from starvation and thirst? What sort of show would that be? Why feed us the other day if they're going to let us die of thirst anyway?

"I could do with a nice cold swim right now!" River shivers his shoulders together as if he's just jumped into a freezing lake or something and my initial response is to grab him by the ears because it's like torture to think about such things but then I hear Samson giggle and I get what he is doing. "I'd jump right in and try and stay down for as long as possible. Just sit right there at the bottom of the lake looking up at the sky from beneath the water."

"Trying to look up at girl's legs more like!" Rainbow sighs and looks away but I see a smile on her face and this time Dodge joins in with the giggling and I'm just happy to be thinking about something else.

"I'll have you know I have the utmost respect for any girl that wants to swim in the same lake as me! I'd even show her how to improve her stroke!"

"You'd stroke something alright!" It's River's turn now to laugh and it's a little too loud so we all kind of duck down and hope that the Guard hasn't heard us. Others are beginning to murmur, to talk to one another and I guess that if it's hot and thirsty work for us then maybe it's the same for the Guard's as well. Maybe they know what's up ahead for us and are letting us have a talk amongst ourselves. After all, what could the harm be?

"Have you ever kissed a girl?" Samson's voice is as childlike as he is able and for a moment it utterly disarms River who has no idea he is being teased by a ten year old. His face flushes and he straightens his back and coughs a little.

"Of course I have! Loads of times!" But no one is convinced by his words, least of all Rainbow who rolls her eyes and slaps his arm, all the while keeping an eye out for the Guards prying eyes.

"Yeh, if you count the girls I've seen you draw on your arm!" She then mimics kissing her forearm. "Oh! I'm so in love with you!" We all begin to giggle and for a few painful seconds try our hardest to suppress the laughter that needs to get out, laughter that I'm worried will reverberate around the whole of Sanctum if we let it.

River looks up at Rainbow and for a moment I feel sorry for him, his eyes are watery and he looks down at the ground as if he's had enough, as if he's about to cry. Maybe we went a little overboard? Maybe we went a little too far?

"Aaaw, River!" Rainbow looks at us and then back to her brother, "I didn't mean it! I was just…"

River looks up and grins broadly. "Gotcha!" We all giggle as Rainbow blinks for a few seconds.

"You rotten little…" But even she starts to laugh as we all hold our stomachs and try not to draw even more attention to ourselves than we have done already.

The giggles die down and we all settle back into the plodding rhythm the group has adopted since the Courthouse. It's when I look back up that I begin to see something on the horizon, blending in with the heat haze that ripples from the road as it slowly curves round to the left, a riot of colours that I couldn't make out before. I instinctively hold out my hand and Rainbow eagerly grabs it as we all hold each others hands.

"Whatever happens we stick together!"

Their voices are barely a whisper this time but the purpose is strong. "Together!"

As we continue on we start to see more banners lining the road, all seeming to say pretty much the same thing; variations on the fact that we're trying to win back our dignity and maybe even our freedom, that the Wastelanders are a scourge on the city and that each Citizen must choose who they think will survive.

It's the last part that I don't like, the idea that people are being encouraged to choose. It trivialises what we're up against, makes it into a game.

The atmosphere has dropped, as if the air itself has gotten harder to breath. I can sense everyone retreating into their own minds, their own private fears as the same question from earlier in the truck rises up again, the question of why they weren't being lined up right there to see us as soon as we arrived at the Peoples' Court, why we've been marching along an empty stretch of road for so long?

Then I realise that since the Court house, we've been going pretty much down hill, so from wherever they are we must look like a great multi coloured snake, weaving our way along the road. Building anticipation. Building frenzy.

"Can you hear the noise? Is it the people waiting for us? Is that music like in the Square?" I want to answer Samson but I can't tear my eyes away from the banners as the Lane begins to turn and a wave of murmuring rises up from those in front of us.

Up ahead in the distance seems to be some sort of platform about thirty feet up in the air that spans the width of the road, beyond that I can begin to make out people on either side of the street. The beginning of our audience.

I was right! We're now coming to the bottom of the valley, so they've been able to see us walking more or less from the Square, building anticipation, building excitement.

The noise is increasing now, voices, cries, laughter all merged together into a dull roar that seems to be getting louder and louder.

It feels like the roar of the water in the tunnels and I catch sight of Rainbow but her eyes are wide and fixed firmly ahead.

This is it.

The start of what we've all been dreading .

The Festival of the Wasteland.

"I don't like it! I don't like it!" I can feel Samson pressing against my side and I try to nod, try to calm him but the truth is I'm just as scared as my mind reminds me of the old woman's words on my first night in the compound;

"We've created him! We've given him all this power through our fear!"

Now more than ever, as we march closer to the platform, as we step ever nearer to whatever fate lies in wait for us I see what she meant. We're now no more than a hundred yards away and I can quite clearly see the bright yellow colours of the Senators standing upon the platform, music wafting along the breeze as trumpets begin to play to herald our arrival. The noise from the crowds lining each side of the road begins to increasing in response.

I don't recognise the music. It's certainly not the awful dirge that plays every time we are herded into The Square to hear Our Leader's wise words. It's cheerier than that, like a celebration and I begin to wonder just how long the Senators have been here, whipping up the crowd, creating whatever atmosphere they think is needed.

"Stay close together!" I feel my hand being squeezed by Rainbow, see the tension etched across River's face.

From somewhere up above a booming noise sounds, like cannon fire, the crowd responding, raising their voices, the noise almost deafening as coloured pieces of paper begin to shower down from the sky almost blocking out the sun.

I tense in anticipation of the order to stop but it doesn't come as we pass under the wooden platform, under the outstretched arms of the Senators standing proudly at its apex. Several more booms shake the air followed by more coloured paper floating down as I turn my head upwards before the shadow of the platform swallows us completely.

As we draw level with the first line of spectators I catch sight of a Senator for the briefest of moments. I remember his round, ruddy cheeks from the compound when he swept along the columns to speak to us and I remember how his words had that transformative effect that the old lady spoke of, that I experience when hearing the words of Our Leader.

I can see the sweat beading on his forehead and some of his robes clinging to his portly frame confirming what I already thought, that he's already been here for some time, whipping the crowd up into the frenzy we see before us.

But it's the smile on his face that I see most of all; as I disappear beneath the platform and emerge into the sunshine again and the full force of the noise from the crowd hits us. The turn of his mouth, the satisfied look on his face tells me he's done his bit, he's worked his audience.

Now it's our turn and I tense as the screeching sound I remember from the giant speakers in the Square echoes all around, the crowd instinctively hushing, obedient as always as the Senators words echo all around.

"THE MOMENT HAS COME, CITIZENS OF SANCTUM. WELCOME TO THE FESTIVAL!"

Chapter 30

What lies before us is like nothing I've ever seen before, like something out of a twisted fairytale and as we continue to march it's like everything slows down, like time itself wants me to remember absolutely every single detail.

The road that stretches out before us goes all the way to the Wall, the top of which we can see in the distance. We're not far away now and my stomach balls into an even tighter fist than I ever thought possible.

I notice that we've all become covered in the little pieces of brightly coloured paper and as we walk along they catch the sunlight and reflect it back dazzling us and the crowd as if we're walking on a thousand jewels all sparkling at once. I hear gasps and cries all around me but can't tell if it's the people I'm marching with or the people watching us.

As we walk on I turn to look at the audience before us. Barriers have been erected along the road side, a mixture of wood and metal, Guards linking arms to form a secondary ring of protection, for the both of us maybe? Arms point wildly in our direction as if people are trying to touch us and I feel the column shrink behind me, trying to avoid the outstretched hands. Are they excited by the promise of death or are they just glad it's not them?

It's difficult to tell what is etched on their faces but as we march on images flash before my eyes;

some smiling, some grimacing, shouting things at us but I can't tell what words they're using, it's all too noisy, too crazy. More cannons go off too but this time instead of coloured pieces of paper, strings fall from the sky, long, windy pieces of string like a million worms flutter down and as fast as I clear them from my face, more appear.

Looking down I see Samson who has pressed himself against my leg, this little kid who I saw with my own eyes best a Guard at least three times his size, now quaking and shivering at the sight of the crowd.

I look over my shoulder at everybody else, checking that their okay and I see a Guard pushing someone back into the column behind. I try to stand on tiptoes, to find out what's happening but we're marching too fast and I have to face front before I get trampled on; maybe it's all too much for someone and they tried to make a break for it?

The only thing I know for sure as we move on our way is that for the time being the column is the safest place to be because if anyone gets caught up in the crowd then I don't like their chances of survival.

Something's been unleashed! That's the feeling I've got as we carry on down the road past the cheering, half crazed crowd, a force that I'm not sure even Our Leader would know what to do with. I look to my left, towards River and I can tell by the way he's looking that similar ideas are going through his head.

"Have you ever seen anything like this?"

"Huh?"

I have to raise my voice above the noise of the crowd and the music. "Have you ever seen this kind of thing before?" River shakes his head in a slow, deliberate manner but doesn't say anything else. He doesn't need to I guess.

"I have."

I look down to my right at Samson who looks up at me with a mixture of fear and defiance. I see him swallow hard, choosing his words carefully.

"In the orphanage, sometimes the older boys would make alcohol with potatoes that they had hidden from sight." He grimaces to show his distaste and I instantly know what he means. "They would sneak off in the dormitory. Never let us little ones follow them but I remember the look they had in their eyes when they returned. I don't know how much they drunk of the stuff but I do know that their eyes would look different, somehow funnier."

"As if they were no longer themselves!"

"Exactly."

I look back towards the grimaces from the crowd as each section we pass greets us even more dramatically than the last and I see it in their eyes too. They look drunk, but not on alcohol, or at least if they are then that's not all it is because I saw the same look on the senator's face on the platform before. He was intoxicated alright, I could see it in his eyes and it's the exact same look I'm seeing now; the intoxication of hope and despair. The most powerful drug in the world and Our Leader has tapped into like I've never seen before.

It's why, as we continue walking, as I look behind me to check on everyone again I wonder if the Wastelanders are the only ones we need to fear.

A noise from up ahead breaks the spell and I look over to my right to see someone break from the column.

It's like it happens in slow motion because at the same time I can see one of the Guards turn and begin to unfurl his whip. I look up to where the man is trying to make for and I can see a woman by the barrier, arms outstretched.

"JESSIE! JESSIE!"

He's almost makes it to the crowd before the Guard's whip strikes him on the back and he half turns, his arms trying to protect the middle of his back. When he doesn't stop I hold my breath, we all do. Whoever the woman is she's someone worth dying for because the Guards break rank and envelope him as he tries to reach her again, and then he's gone from view and we're the ones being yelled at to carry on walking.

The energy from the crowd seems to have changed as well but I'm not sure if it's because of what just happened or for some other reason. I can see more anger on the faces that stare back at us from the barriers. And then the thought intrudes; what if I see Ellie and Doughnut behind the barriers? What on earth would I do?

The feeling makes the hairs on the back of my neck rise up as I catch sight of the Wall in the distance dominating the horizon. I've been so distracted by the crowd that I haven't even noticed the road rising and falling, the Wall creeping up on us. I don't know whether I feel relieved or more scared, knowing that whatever is out there is getting closer and closer.

I feel anger building and all of a sudden tears spill from my eyes as the injustice of the whole thing weighs me down and I take in gulps of air to calm my nerves. Why me? What did I do to deserve this?

I've lost count of the amount of times I've played the incident in the water tunnels over in my mind, turning over every second, always the same question; what were the Wastelanders doing there? How many are under our feet? Is that what this whole Festival is; a way of deflecting from the truth, a truth that the whole of Sanctum is under threat but not in the way Our Leader is telling us?

The thoughts are like words on the tip of my tongue or a sound that plays in the distance refusing to make itself known. And now the feeling of stupidity comes as if I'm turning something over in my mind that doesn't exist.

As if I have any sort of control over what's happening.

A wave of fresh noise breaks over me and I shake my head clear and look up and around. The Wall is much nearer now and if anything the crowd has multiplied, pouring in from the lanes that lead off the main road, scrambling over rooftops and shacks to get a look at us.

I immediately look up and scan around for a glimpse of Doughnut and Ellie somewhere up above, hidden amongst the corrugated iron and shards of wood that stick out at odd angles. My heart leaps as I imagine the two of them grinning down at me as they skip along, rolling and jumping, trying desperately to keep up with us as we march beneath them. And then the cloud appears again in my mind, the cloud that tells me their more likely to see me out there, facing *them*.

The column begins to slow down and I look up to see the Wall loom ahead of us, now no more than a hundred yards or so away. The crowd has swelled to almost unbelievable numbers and I can barely take in everything that's going on.

"Look at the people up there!" Rainbow's voice is to no one in particular and as I turn and follow her eyes I see what she's talking about. Usually you can't get within fifty yards of the Wall itself as it's guarded day and night but we're not just looking at a few people who have wandered beyond the boundary rope that tells us to stop and turn around.

As my eyes scan up I see a wave of people pouring like ants over some kind of enormous wooden structure, like the biggest ramp you've ever seen, allowing them to reach the top of the Wall, and as I look up even higher I can practically hear the mixture of excitement and fear in River's voice.

"There are people up there, look! They're walking on top of the Wall!"

I can't think of what else to say because it's so far removed from anything I've ever seen before.

We've all heard the stories of people who, for whatever reasons whether lack of food and water or just out of sheer, crazed frustration have tried to get to the Wall and then I guess escape the confines of Sanctum. But we've also heard what happens to them and so to see this many people able to walk up to the top is incredible.

Then there's the scale of the thing! The scaffolding must be fifty foot high at least and I begin to wonder where on earth they managed to get all the materials for it; the wood and the metal that seemed somehow fused together to make it such a solid structure.

We look at each other in turn but there's nothing much more to say as we stand there, dumbstruck at the sheer spectacle before us. Until Dodge opens his mouth and says what we're probably all thinking.

"Guess they're all expecting a pretty good show then, huh!" I turn towards him, wondering why his words have just hit me as hard as they have and then I realise it's because he's absolutely right.

It's all a show.

And we're the main attraction.

Chapter 31

That's exactly what it is, this feeling, this energy from the crowd, as if they're all going to see a show and they've all got their hopes and dreams of how it's all going to turn out.

"I'm scared!" Samson's voice is barely audible but this time no one says a thing as snatches of words from the crowd drift our way.

"…not gonna last long…"

"I'll bet on that one there'"'

"…is this all we've got?"

As we approach the Wall I start to smell fresh cooking, some kind of meat I haven't smelt for a long time and my stomach begins to do cartwheels.

"I wish we were back at the compound filling our bowls with stew!" River grins and rubs his belly but the point is true enough. None of us have eaten for a while and the march has certainly left me feeling thirsty and tired.

Looking to my right, I can see acrobats and jugglers entertaining the crowd, spinning high in the air and landing on each other's shoulders, all brightly coloured and exciting. I see the look of wonder on the faces of the little ones as they applaud and grin from ear to ear. They probably have no idea what's actually going on, what the Festival is really about.

"LEFT TURN!" The Guards up ahead all turn in unison and the rest of us take their lead and we begin to pass underneath the wooden framework that allows access to the top of the Wall. The noise of the crowd begins to fade as we are marched in-between the structure and the Wall and it feels strangely eerie to be able to still hear the muffled cries of the crowd but not be able to see them.

There's commotion from behind and I look to see more Guards launching themselves at another would be escapee but I turn back because it's no longer my concern. I can't afford to waste precious energy on those that don't mean anything to me. I'm surprised by my own lack of feeling but I know that in the long run I need every single possible advantage.

I start to think about what lies ahead for us and the anger that's never far away rises again as I picture my new friends in trouble. I try to rid myself of the feeling, try to focus on where we are, because the ground is beginning to shake beneath my feet and I feel dust and soil falling from above.

"It's from there!" I look to see where River is pointing and for the first time I get a good look at the underside of the new road that we are walking under, the network of wooden joists and beams that creak and groan under the weight of God knows how many footsteps, the thick supporting beams thrust deep into the earth.

"When the hell did they have time to do all this?" I see the others nod at Rainbow's words and I can't help but agree. It's as if the world has tipped on its axis and we're struggling to catch up with events as they unfold before us.

The ground beneath us begins to fall away into a slight decline, the level of the soil to our left rising as we descend further and further out of sight as if the ground itself is swallowing us up.

I can hear noises from behind, questions and stifled cries as the light begins to fade, the noise of the crowd, of the thousands of feet stamping now a loud, muffled noise that echoes all around. We keep walking but up ahead I can hear the Guards talking amongst themselves as if questioning what their next move is.

"Is it time?" I don't recognise the voice from behind, it's not Rainbow or Samson at least but I perfectly understand the sentiment behind the words.

"I don't think so…" I look around at the large tunnel we seem to be in, the Guards up ahead have lit some lanterns that hang from the wall and the light casts strange shadows, not enough to chase all the darkness away but it gives us a good view of where we are. There are other tunnels leading off from the one we're marching through and up ahead I can see a series of doors cut straight into the earth itself.

"Where are they taking us?"

"My guess is some kind of holding cell like in the compound. Put us in there and make us wait for our turn, or something like that!"

"I wanna get out there now, I'm sick of this walking, I'm sick of waiting like an idiot for other people to…" Samson's voice falls quiet but it doesn't matter because we all understand perfectly where he's coming from.

The Guard up ahead suddenly stops and I nearly carry on walking into the back of the person in front of me, more cries sounding from behind.

"Let us go!"

"What do you want from us?"

But the voices are weak and ineffectual and I can hear the Guard's answer in the form of loud whip cracks buzzing through the air. Hands are placed on our shoulders and then we are being pushed, hard, forced through the opening on our left. I turn to confront the Guard but another person is pushed through and then another until I'm forced back into the darkness of the room.

And then the door is slammed shut.

The screams are almost too much to bear as I hear more doors open, more people forced through them and I push myself against the wall, adrenalin pumping through my veins. The noises echo throughout the tunnels and I close my eyes tight shut as if this will help drown out the horrible noise.

"Jake! River!" I hear Rainbow's voice and as my eyes adjust to the gloom I see her in the far corner.

"I'm here...I'm here..." River's voice comes from my left as I try to filter out all the screaming and weeping that has erupted. I stride over to where she is, moving people out of the way and we embrace. I'm so glad to feel her warmth that for a split second I don't really understand River's next question.

"Where's Samson and Dodge?" And then all three of us are calling out but I can't see them in the room, Rainbow begins to bang on the door shouting their names. I can sense this is upsetting the others who are down here with us and I try to gently stop her but she won't be told and she shrugs off my hands and keeps banging as loudly as she can, before finally slumping to the ground, sobbing into her arms.

"I can't take much more of this. I can't take much more!"

Minutes pass like hours as we hunker down, some standing by the walls, some curled up in the corners. The dust is still falling like a fine rain as the booming noise of yelling and footsteps can be felt through the walls and floor. It feels like at any moment the walls are going to start moving in and I close my eyes tight shut as I imagine them moving closer and closer, pushing our bodies together until all you can hear are screams as bones begin to crack.

River and Rainbow are huddled together and I'm glad to see her eyes shut, trying as best she can to get some rest. Exhaustion seems to have overtaken pretty much everyone and I'm not surprised after the march we've just endured under the baking sun but I can't relax, I can't shut my mind off so I don't even bother.

Instead I begin to pace up and down, careful to step over the outstretched limbs that scatter the place. I know my own mind and I need to keep it active to stop it eating itself.

Samson and Dodge begin to play on my mind. Why were they separated from us? Why are we not all together as we were in the compound? We have the same colour uniforms so doesn't that mean we're all in this together?

I try and run through a few scenarios but the old ideas we had don't seem to stack up against what we've seen today. The march already feels like some kind of dream, because I can't believe the amount of people that were lining the streets and climbing the new structures, climbing up and up until they could reach the top.

But here's where my thinking get's a little confused. We've had some training, it's true, but we're hardly a well drilled unit or anything! Wouldn't it make much more sense to send the Guards out in their bright red uniforms? If they want a grand spectacle then wouldn't that be a hell of a one to beat?

And what about the weapons, the knives and the nets? Will they be out there waiting for us, or was it all another great big con to make us think that we're being given as fair a chance as possible? To stop any thoughts of revolting against the Guards?

But that's not the point is it? The Guard's are way too valuable, whereas we, the criminals and orphans, the undesirables in an over populated city are expendable and that's where I have to grudgingly admire the idea because it's a win win situation for Our Leader; kill some Wastelanders, reduce the amount of mouths to feed.

I brush the dust that's falling from my face and continue pacing but I know that I'm just leading myself to the same place as before; the dead end, the nagging feeling that there's something else going.

Irritated I shake my head and start on another thought process. This time I begin to examine the room that we are in, tracing my mind back to when we were outside and the floor started to fall away. The Wall was on our right about twenty yards away, almost close enough to touch as we began to descend into these holding cells underground.

I walk back to the door and try to remember how far we walked underground and if we went to the left or the right. Shutting my eyes I remember the lamps being turned on and the light illuminating various passageways but I'm sure we turned slightly to our right as we made our way further in and at one point we had to duck our head because there were some huge wooden beams above that were jutting out of the ceiling.

I think they were connected to the Wall, foundation beams or something to make sure that the whole thing doesn't come crashing down any time soon, and if I'm right then that means that we've already passed under the Wall, haven't we?

Stepping back from the door I look at the depth of the room and then at the ceiling which is a mixture of wooden planks and crumbling mortar. If I'm right and I haven't taken a wrong turning in my mind then we've gone at least thirty yards or so under the Wall.

"Oh my God!" My voice is nothing more than a whisper and I stretch my hand out towards the wall opposite the doorway and hold it against the cold, vibrating earth. I play the scene in my head a bunch of times again to check that I haven't made a mistake and each time I come to the same conclusion as before until I'm convinced.

Convinced that we've walked under or through the foundations of the Wall.

And if I *am* right then it means that we're already somewhere that I'd never thought I would be in my lifetime.

We're already in the Wasteland.

Chapter 32

The realisation hits me hard and I crouch by the wall keeping my thoughts to myself for a moment longer.

From what I remember of the position of the sun before we went under ground it was nearing mid afternoon, something between three and four o'clock

Which means darkness will begin to fall soon and the mist will begin to seep along the ground in around two hours time.

Two hours...

I look up at the ceiling that seems to visibly pulse beneath the weight of all those people; in two hours time the main show will begin and I can only imagine what other attractions have been laid on for the people until then. By the time we get out there they'll be whipped up into such a frenzy I'd be very surprised if they give a damn at that point about who lives and dies.

For a moment I allow myself to marvel at the way in which Our Leader has been able to join the Citizens together like I've never seen before. I'm under no illusion that if fate hadn't decreed that I should be on this side of the divide then I would be the first one on the wall along with Ellie and Doughnut pushing and scrambling our way to the best seats in the house.

I guess what *he's* done is to cement his leadership, remind everybody that although times are harsh and the promises he made of full bellies, wet throats and safety haven't materialised yet, he still has the means by which to dominate us, to make us dance to his tune. As much as I have grown to despise all that he stands for over the years, I also can't help but in a way admire his capacity for reinvention.

When I was younger I remember the stories told of the beginnings of the City and how Our Leader was right at the forefront, or so was said, of the wilderness, battling to save the lives of his family and children, seeing them brutalised by the Wastelanders, vowing to return upon them the blood that was owed. He was painted as the young warrior, avenging the wrongdoings and injustices heaped upon his family.

As I grew so the story changed and he began to morph into a political activist calling for the disparate groups that had sprung up to unite under one banner, under one leader. It was only a matter of time before his name was put forward, before he assumed total control.

And now we have the third act, the cleverest of all, the father figure watching over his children, benevolently allowing a shot at redemption for even the worst kind of Citizen, protecting us from the horrors that lie out there, in the dark.

A mythical figure.

The faces of Dodge and Samson flash before my eyes and I half turn to the door expecting them to be there. I know I've only known them for what amounts to a few days but I feel responsible somehow, as if I was down here with Ellie and Doughnut. After all, if we turn on each other, if we can't even help one another down here, when it would be so easy to lose all sense of right and wrong, then what are we even fighting for in the first place? Besides, Ellie would expect it of me!

The rattle of the door breaks the moment.

"What the…"

"Oh God no."

I instinctively move towards River and Rainbow but it's a little harder now that people are stirring themselves and getting up off the floor. The door cracks open and in an instant it's filled with red uniforms as people scatter to the back of the room out of the reach of their grasp.

For a moment nothing happens, as if both sets of people are unsure of what to do next before the light flooding in from the tunnel beyond is momentarily blocked out as one of the huge Guards from the training enters the room.

"Leave us alone…"

"Please no…please…"

And then it begins.

The Guards as if on his command lunge forward and begin dragging people out of the room. Gone is the neatness of the marching before and I guess now there's no need to keep up any pretence for the watching crowd.

"This one…and her! Grab that one there!" The huge Guard orchestrates as the others push and pull the screaming bodies out of the room and into the hall.

"Where are the others? Why are we being separated?" I'm one of the last to be pulled and I decide to save my energy because there's no point in getting injured this close to the main event. I can hear Rainbow sobbing after me and as I reach the door I'm able to twist in the vice like grip of the Guard and see her face before I disappear into the corridor.

"Stay strong and look after each other!" Then the door slams shut behind me. We're hustled along the corridor and I count at least ten people that have been taken from the room, their yells and questions falling on deaf ears as we turn down a right hand passage that leads to some crudely dug steps.

"Where are you taking us?"

"Get your hands off me!"

But still no response from the Guards as if they're all acting with one hive mind and are unable to respond unless given a direct order by the biggest of their kind.

I begin to feel a breeze on my skin as we near the top of the steps and I notice that here the walls are wooden, not earth.

We're no longer underground.

Chapter 33

The room we're pushed into is different from the first one, colder, smaller and as the door is slammed shut behind us for a moment all I hear is the ragged breathing of others as I try to get my bearings.

My heart rate's up and my senses are that bit sharper thanks to the adrenalin that's begun to flood my system; it feels like when I'm about to jump rooftops with Ellie and Doughnut, my body trying to calculate distances and angles, my mind filtering out all extraneous details.

I look around at the people I'm in here with and I count ten. The next thing I notice is that we've all got the same colour clothes which means we're either all of a similar age, or we have performed reasonably well in the training of earlier.

The one thing I don't recognise is any familiar faces and I suppose that's not entirely surprising; we were kept well apart from others at the courtyard and if this is happening all over Sanctum then there's no real telling what part these others have come from.

I had assumed, we all had, that we were to fight in our squads, with the people we had come to know a little but the more I think about it the more I realise we have no idea of what is in store for us. Just because we were fed together in the big hall, does that mean everyone was? Was everyone allowed to make friends like we have?

"Where is everyone else? Where are my friends?" The question could have come from my own head, but it doesn't, it comes from the small figure slumped over by the door. "Why have we been separated? I thought, I thought we were going to fight together. Isn't that the point of these uniforms?"

A cough comes from another area of the room, "Who the hell cares! You think they give a damn about what happens to us? You think your problems are of any CONCERN TO THEM AT ALL!" The last few words are shouted as the figure begins to pound his fists on the wooden door we came in through.

"Quiet, please! I don't want them coming in here again." The voice descends into sobbing and I feel I should do something but the fists soon stop their pounding and the room settles into an uneasy silence as each of us contemplates what's in store.

I turn back from the door and slide down the wall until I'm slumped forward, my forearms resting on my knees. The room is colder than the last one and I can feel a breeze lifting the hair on my arms.

My mind kicks in and I'm up on my feet trying to trace where the breeze is coming from. I remember that my first thoughts before the commotion were that we were outside and now my senses are kicking in for real and I look again around the room with new eyes.

There are thin beams of light escaping for the cracks in the wooden struts that form the walls of this new prison and I'm immediately up on my knees as I follow the dust the light reveals to the nearest gap I can reach. And then I see them high up on the wall, the metal bars that give us a view of the outside.

Standing on tip toe I squash my face against them and try to see what's out there but the breeze dries my eye up and I have to step away and blink rapidly.

"What are you doing?" The voice comes from the same guy who was pounding on the door and the tone is a mixture of irritable and exhausted, a tone I've grown to be familiar with over the last week or so. I rub my eyes one last time and then step back to the wall.

"We came up some stairs right!"

"So!" The voice is still irritable but now there's a note of hidden interest.

"So where do you think the beams of light are coming from?" A few seconds passes and then shuffling sounds throughout the room.

"He's right. Look!" But I'm too busy to turn around and help anyone and when my eye finally stops watering it comes into focus. I can finally see the Wasteland.

All the years of fearing what's outside these walls, all the bedtime stories of warning and fear, and here we are.

I step back from the wall and look at the ground. Wasteland soil.

"Hey! What the hell are you doing?" But I've no time for niceties as I push past some figures standing in the middle of the room.

"Look over there." I point my arm behind me at the section of the wall I was just at. "Tell me what you see." I hear them shuffle off, some able to see through the bars, others looking for any cracks in the wood.

"Is that what I think it is?"

"Let's 'ave a look!"

"Hey don't push. Oh my God, it's the Wasteland! Can you see any of *them*?"

The voices compete to be heard but I try to ignore them and focus on what I can see, what information I can gather. My legs begin to ache as I stand on my toes again looking out through the bars but eventually I start to make out the Wall itself at right angles to where we are. I can only see the very bottom section of it but it stretches off into the distance, its lines broken by a series of cages that I can only presume are like the one that we're currently in.

"What can you see out of that one?"

"I can see the Wall," I wipe my eye and refocus, "and I can see more of these cages." I rock back on my heels using my sleeve to wipe my face. The others are now standing and swapping places to see through the bars, the big guy standing back, a look of bewilderment on his face. I stand up and offer my hand.

"Name's Jake." I can't help but think back to the great dining hall and the introductions we all made and my heart tightens in my chest. I already understand that this is a completely different scenario but when he turns away I'm still taken aback.

"I don't care what your name is! I don't care who any of you are!" The emotion in his voice threatens to spill over and some of the others step away from him as he walks to the side of the room and places both hands on the wall, his head slumped beneath his shoulders. "When I'm out there, I'm fighting for myself, I don't want you in my head."

"What did you just say?" My brain's knitting together ideas faster than I can cope with and I step forward to the middle of the room, words escaping my mouth before I can really think about them.

"Huh?" He turns his head, looking at me from across his left shoulder.

"Pl...please don't fight. Not in here!" I frown and turn to the other voice puzzled as to why she thinks there's going to be a fight, and then the wind is knocked out of me as I'm flung against the metal bars, my shoulder taking the brunt of the force.

"I don't care where I fight and I don't care who it's with!" The same tone as before and I see him moving in on me as the others scatter to the sides. He's bigger than me by quite a way but I can see, even in the gloom, that his eyes are lost to passion and fury. His right arm angles down towards my face and I manage to duck out of the way just in time and scramble to my left.

"I don't want to fight you. I wasn't trying to..." he swings round and rushes me and I step to my right this time but his shoulder catches me in the chest and he forces me back against the wall. I can feel my anger beginning to rise as he backs away and comes at me again with another swinging fist. I step to the left this time as his swing misses by a matter of inches and he's momentarily off balance.

"I said I don't want to fight you!" I spin round behind him as he staggers forward and throw my arm around his neck before kicking at the back of his left knee. "I just want to know what you said before!" He grunts as his leg buckles and I push down on the top of his chest until he lands, winded in a heap on the floor, but I don't see his left arm until it's too late and he grabs at my clothes before pulling me down beside him.

"Please. STOP IT!" We both stagger to our feet but the initial anger has dissipated and we are left pacing up and down at opposite ends of the room, people in between us, arms outstretched as if to push us off each other again. An uneasy silence descends as we both take in gulps of stale, warm air.

"I *said* that when I'm out there I'm fighting for myself." His voice is breathless and as I try to calm myself down I play the phrase over in my head because I'm sure he said something else. "I don't want any of you in my head." With the last word he slumps to the floor and the pieces begin to fall into some sort of order.

I don't want any of you in my head.

The training replays in my head, the time spent on the compound, the dining room and a picture starts to emerge; a picture of friendships formed in adversity, as intense a feeling as I've ever felt. The colours that we've been forced to wear uniting us, the fact that we've all been split up again, just as we were beginning to bond, beginning to make friends.

Comradeship and loyalty.

Emotions that can be manipulated and exploited.

I stand up straight and take a step forward. A voice from my left pleads, "Please no more fighting! It's out there we've gotta fight not…"

"I think I know why they've put us in here! I think I know why we've been separated!" I hear a snort coming from the wall opposite, from the large figure still breathing heavily.

"AMAZING! You mean you worked it out all by yourself!" A couple of the others giggle but I ignore them.

"Any friends we've made, any people we know." I look around the room. No giggles now. "There gonna use that friendship."

For a moment there's silence and I play the idea over in my head again.

"I don't…I don't know what you mean!"

My opponent begins to rise, a smile on his face as he begins to nod. "You know, you might not be as dumb as you look!" He places a hand on his right knee and straightens up to his full height before looking around at the others. "What he means *children* is that they've been playing you all from the very beginning, manipulating your sad little emotions to make things more interesting for the crowd."

"Are any of you in here with anyone you know from before?" I look around as heads begin to turn this way and that before shaking from left to right. "Did you eat food in that place with a small group of others, same slashes of paint on your chests? Swap stories, even begin to think that they were your *friends*?"

I place a hand back onto the wall and look at the floor, all my energy drained and gone as the realisation hits.

A voice comes from the back of the room, a young voice, trembling, "They wanted us to make friends so they that could split us up, make us wear these stupid clothes so we feel a part of something, part of a group! They're going to make us watch our friends..." the voice descends into sobbing as we're all left with the picture in our minds of the Wastelander we saw at the compound. The teeth. The claws.

I want to scream and shout at the top of my lungs. I want to beat my fists on the door like my opponent did only moments earlier. But I can't because all I can think about is River and Rainbow, Samson and Dodge standing out there in the dust as *they* emerge from the horizon, the scent of fresh meat in their nostrils.

And then I'm filled with rage not only at the thought of their fate but at the thought that I'd do anything to help them, to protect them.

If I'm right then they're going to use us as bait, not only for the Wastelanders but for each other, to make us fight better.

If I'm right then they've been manipulating us all along, making us feel emotions for those around us.

So that we might better entertain the crowd.

Chapter 34

The room is silent as everyone contemplates the new realisation. The more I turn it over in my head the more it seems to fit in with what we've experienced so far; crowds of the magnitude we've seen, the fireworks and ticker tape, the carnival like atmosphere. No way Our Leader is going to ramp everyone's emotions up simply to have a bunch of all ready defeated victims standing around waiting for the inevitable.

Despite the obvious revulsion at the idea, I have to admit that it's a master stroke because even the thought of anyone of River and Rainbow out there, even Samson and Dodge, and I'd tear the walls down to help them.

Once the lid is off, how do you really contain that type of raw emotion? Isn't that what they are trying to tap into with us, hoping that emotion will override intellect, will override a sense of self preservation?

"What time is it?" The timid voice stirs me from my thoughts and I blink into the gloom, struggling for an answer.

"You know what time it is, we all do!" I look round at ghostly figures half hidden by shadows and then I realise what it is that's missing as I look back through the bars of the cage to the Wasteland beyond. The day is wearing on and that means only one thing.

The mist.

People begin moving towards the bars, those who can't reach searching for cracks to look through, voices talking over one another as fear intrudes.

"Oh please no! It can't be time already!"

"I think I can see the mist on the horizon, can you see any of *them*?"

"Oh my God! Oh my God!"

The sun by now has all but dropped below the horizon and far off in the distance I begin to make out a blurring above the ground as the mist begins its long, slow creep towards Sanctum, towards us.

The sound of the crowd intrudes, I guess they too have seen the mist and are baying in anticipation of the evening's coming events. The noise begins to die down but then redoubles again to an almost ear splitting level, the very wooden walls trembling at the power and I see hands reaching for ears in an attempt to block it out.

"What *is* that? What are they doing now?" I instinctively look back at the crack in the wall.

"What is it? What have you seen?"

"Open your eyes man! Look out there to our left about fifty yards!"

I strain my eyes as the noise from the crowd reaches another highpoint and then I begin to see what the fuss is about. From somewhere huge spotlights begin sweeping over the ground before the cages, illuminating faces, sending shadows elongating along the ground.

The crowd roars again as the cannons sound and coloured paper floats down again, glittering as the lights converge on the ground about fifty yards in the distance.

"Is it them? Are they out there?" The voice comes from behind me, from a girl who has barely spoken at all. I want to say something to comfort her, but there's nothing I can do except watch as part of the ground begins to disappear as if the dirt and dust is draining away.

"Are they coming up from *underneath* or something?" And then an ear splitting screech sounds that forces my hands up to my ears but I know what it is because I've heard it before in the meetings at the Square. It's the sound of the speakers warming up.

Someone's about to speak.

"WELCOME TO THE FESTIVAL OF THE WILDERNESS!"

The cheering from the crowd reaches a fever pitch, the walls of the cage threatening to cave in with the vibrations from the thousands of feet stamping up and down, but all I can stare at is the top of a group of heads emerging from beneath the ground on some kind of platform.

From this distance I can't make out who they are or what their faces look like but as the crowd redoubles its roar I can clearly see how they huddle together, the spotlight still shining brightly upon them.

"LET'S WELCOME OUR BRAVE FIGHTERS AS THEY STAND BEFORE US!"

My head feels like it's going to split apart with the noise as the crowd redoubles its efforts and roars approval. The high pitched whine from the speakers echo as the voice continues. "WHO WILL BE THE FIRST TO KILL A WASTELANDER? WHO WILL BE THE FIRST TO WIN THEIR FREEDOM?"

"I think there's about ten of them! They're all in white!" I sigh as the realisation dawns; it's not us! It's not our colour. Not yet! I turn back to the girl's voice from before but even she's now found a position to watch from and then I push away from the wall and start to count.

"Did you say there were ten of them?"

"Count for yourself if you don't believe me!"

"I'll take your word for it. It's just that…"

"Oh God, don't tell me! There are ten of us in here aren't there!"

The big guy starts to laugh as dust falls as the roof trembles under the noise from the crowd.

"They're gonna serve us up like little side dishes, aren't they!"

I look back outside to the group of people in the distance just as one of their number seems to make a break for it, running in the direction of the wall.

"Go on, that's it, don't just stand there like those other suckers, make it hard for them!" I surprise myself at the force of my own words as the spotlight follows the action, the noise from the crowd rising and falling in unison with the events unfolding in front of them.

Then just as the breakaway seems to be making progress I see something straighten in the air behind him and his head is jerked back, legs flying into the air in front before he falls to a heap in the dirt. The crowd sucks in a collective breath as if feeling the pain and I bang my fist on the wall. "They've got them tied up somehow. The scum have got them tied up!"

Looking back at the group in the middle I try to scan faces for anyone familiar but there just that bit too far away for me to be able to identify anyone with any surety.

"Does anybody know anyone out there?" I look back and see faces straining against the wood to get a better look.

"Don't think so…"

"I think I recognise the one on the left from the training but I can't be sure."

The figure has now groggily picked himself up and starts to tug at the rope or whatever it is attached to him but my eye is drawn back to the main group who seem to be pointing at something in the distance and then the crowd goes silent, as if everyone of us is holding our breath.

Spotlights shift towards the Mist that has been getting steadily closer and closer and as they sweep in a long arch from left to right, shapes begin to make themselves known, dim and formless.

Nightmares.

"BELLA!"

The cry comes from one of the cages to the right of ours and a sigh rises up from the crowd as a lone figure breaks from the main group and turns to look this way.

"BELLA. RUN!" The lone figure starts towards the cage and I can hear screams from the crowd willing her on but then stops and picks up the rope or chain, holding it in the air before hurling it to the ground. The gesture doesn't go unnoticed by the crowd who sigh and moan, all the while the dark shapes are getting closer as the mist continues to sweep across the wasteland seemingly gathering speed as it goes.

The sharp crack of metal on metal rips through the air as some kind of mechanism deep beneath our feet starts to chug and rumble. The girl to my left screams and jumps to the side; "What's happening? What's under there?"

"It's not us, it's them. Look!" I step over to the others and look through the bars to see the whole side of the next cage along beginning to sink into the ground. Heads appear in the gloom as the winching sound begins to rumble louder and louder until the whole side of the box disappears. The beam of light making the shadows even longer and darker.

Silence descends.

"The mist is almost upon them." I look to my right, to the mist that is now no more than a few hundred yards away from the people on the platform, dark shadows running along its width. I feel like I'm part of the crowd. All I can do is watch and wait for the inevitable.

Then the roar again as a figure sprints from the gloom of the box kicking up dust as he makes his way to the group in the middle.

"Is that the guy? Is that the one that shouted Bella? He's wearing the same colour! He's wearing white!"

My head keeps switching from left to right as more bodies begin to emerge from the cage, the first a huge man with scarring on his face and upper arms, or are they tattoos, either way he looks scarier than the Wastelanders and twice as big.

The next is a slender girl who falls to her knees as soon as she steps foot onto the dirt and dust. Then two more emerge from the gloom and split up, running in opposite directions towards the people in the middle as if they have some kind of plan.

More leap from the cage but I've turned back to the main group in the middle because something's caught my eye. The wooden slats of our cage begin to tremble some more but its from the fists that are pounding on them as the other captives yell and scream advice and instruction, but I keep my eyes on the middle. There's got to be something I'm missing. How are they expected to fight without weapons? Surely it's going to be a massacre?

"What's that?" I look again towards the group in the middle as something else begins to emerge from the ground, another platform and as the spotlights swing across it metal glints back at us from a table that has almost fully appeared.

"Are they…are they what I think they are?"

"Knives! They got to be knives!" I squint towards the table as the light swings away but I can't think of anything else that would have glinted quite so much.

"Maybe…maybe!"

I look back towards the mist and try and remember what we were told about the creatures back at the compound. I remember the Guard telling us that they hunt in small packs, usually no more than half a dozen at a time and there must be twenty people out there, although two of them are still hanging back by the cage either scared witless or biding their time, waiting to see which way it will go.

Claws, teeth and speed.

The noise of the crowd turns to a high pitched screaming as the first Wastelander breaks from the cover of the mist and launches on its hind quarters at the front of the group. The others scatter about like they've all been knocked over and I can see the creature slashing wildly with its arms. The mist seems to have come to a halt fifty yards or so from the group and although I can still see shapes prowling to and fro, no more burst from their hiding place.

"They're testing them! They've sent one in to see what will happen!"

"On my God. I think that one's dead!"

The Wastelander is still in the middle of the group but they have run in different directions as far as their chains or ropes will allow, although there are two bodies lying on the floor lifeless.

And then I see a movement to the right coming fast from the side of the creature.

"Look to the left!" I do and make out another figure running around the back. "It's the two from the cage, the two that sprinted away. They're trying to do a pincer movement, trying to cut the thing off!"

"Why don't they go for the knives? Why don't they go for the damn knives?"

The creature has no idea they are behind it, intent as it is on the centre of the group as it moves in on a struggling figure to its right. The figure puts its hands out in front as if to shield from the coming attack as the beast stands over it, red stains on its arms and torso.

The walls of the cage vibrate some more as the big guy's hands pound them again and again. "Do something! MOVE!"

"Grab a knife and stab the thing!"

The two running from either side have nearly caught up with each other when they seem to swoop down and grab at the ground. I shift my weight to get a better look and I can see that they have grabbed at one of the chains, or ropes that lies on the floor.

My eyes follow the line of the chain as they pull it from the dust and it seems to lead to one of the bodies on the floor, the first of the creature's victims, but it has some slack to it and as they run holding the chain in each other's hands I hold my breath because if they don't have enough space, if the chain tightens around the dead body before they reach the beast, then whatever they have planned will not work.

I look back at the struggling girl on the floor as it slashes at her arms that are now crossed over in front of her face. We're too far away and there's too much noise from the crowd to hear anything but it's not really necessary because the red pools that have gathered in the dust, the cowering forms of the others as they scrabble in the dirt, the lifeless bodies, tell us all we need to know.

And then the chain goes tight and they are yanked back twenty yards or so from the beast and I can't help but think how perfectly this is going for Our leader as I imagine the girl on the floor to be Bella and one of the heroes to be the man who screamed her voice.

It doesn't really matter if I'm right or wrong, what matters is how it appears.

What matters is the story.

A voice shouts out from somewhere to my left, "Do something!" and as if in response one of the figures reaches down and picks something up from the ground hurling it at the creature. The other follows his lead until they are pelting it with handfuls of dirt and rocks, until it turns slowly from the girl at its feet.

Then it's drops to all fours and begins its sloping gallop towards them before leaping high into the air, claws extended. The two runners from before wait until it's nearly on top of them before rolling in opposite directions as the beast lands in a cloud of dust, swiping to its left and right.

In the blink of an eye they are up, chain in hands as they take advantage of its momentary disorientation. The chain wraps around its neck as they sprint in circles around it and then they are pulling for all they are worth and the noise from the crowd is almost deafening as they see the creature fall to its knees, the life being squeezed from its body.

I can't take my eyes away from the spectacle as the Wastelander struggles and swipes at the two either side of it, but to no avail as they pull even harder on the chain.

"KILL IT! KILL IT!" It's as if something snaps within us all and we're yelling and screaming, banging against the wooden walls. My throat screams in pain as I yell myself hoarse but I don't care because the creature is on the floor and with the chain stretched taught either side of its neck it's only a matter of time.

"KILL THE DAMN THING!"

As my voice gives out I try and focus on the Wastelander, on its face, we're just that bit too far away too see its eyes. I can tell it's in agony as its arms thrash wildly around, no longer looking for anyone in particular.

Others are beginning to join in, throwing things at the body and as the noise all around reaches some king of crescendo a shudder goes through my spine like electricity.

I look around the cage at the bulging eyes and veiny necks of the others as they continue to bang on the walls and then a scream erupts from outside and I'm back looking through the bars. For a moment I can't see the Wastelander, just people standing around and then I refocus and I see the pool of blood that is seeping from the body lying on the floor.

And then the scream again from within the mist, followed by another and another, each more blood curdling than the last. A mixture of human and animal, but the creature is dead and for a moment I'm confused before I look to the mist as it starts to retreat.

I can see the dark shadows prowling.

That's where the screams are coming from.

They're screaming for their dead.

Chapter 35

"Why don't they attack, dammit?"

The noise from the crowd is almost deafening as the people in the middle stand bemused and then begin to search amongst the bodies, presumably to check if anyone is still alive.

The mist has retreated a little, perhaps a few hundred yards but it's still possible to make out the shapes as they prowl back and forth.

"Remember what the Guard said, back at the compound when we looked at that, that thing?" My mind flicks back and I can almost smell the fetid breath, the rotting meat. The figure the voice belongs to steps from the shadows, a pale girl with long, lank brown hair, a little bit older than me maybe.

"That's right, now what was it?" The big guy joins in and pretty soon we're all trying to remember words that seem a lifetime ago. "Dammit! I wish I could remember this stuff better!"

The girl steps forwards scared witless by what we've just seen, and then squats down in the dirt and most of us follow until we're all practically huddling together, a few electing to stay standing, looking out through the slats, checking for any more developments.

"What do we know about the mist?" She looks round at each of us, strips of hair clumped together with grease and dirt flicking from side to side. A few voices offer up tentative suggestions.

"*They* control it, like they control the Wasteland!"

"It comes and go as it pleases. They control the weather, hiding behind it. They're demons sent straight from hell!"

"If they wanted to I bet they could control the rain itself!"

"Rubbish!" The big guy stands and stretches his legs at the knee, "Superstitious crap!" He points in the direction of the recent fighting, "They no more control the weather than you or I do! And they're no more demons than anyone of us!"

"Then how did you explain the mist coming and going of its own free will then?" All eyes turn to him and I keep deliberately out of it because I want to know what people think and also because I want to sort out my own ideas, my own thoughts on the subject.

"Well how the hell should I know? I'm not an expert on the damn weather! All I know is that they just killed one of them with nothing more than their bare hands and some sort of rope!" He looks around at us but I can see fear in his eyes, the loud voice, the pacing up and down masking what we all feel.

"They've adapted over the years." I'm surprised by the new voice as I haven't heard it before and I look up to the figure that stands still looking through the bars. "The Guard said how they used to attack at any time of the day but soon learnt that the walls were too well defended during the day. I guess because of the numbers they were losing they decided to use the mist as a cover, make it more difficult for us to see them. I heard that they've learnt how to scale the walls and some of them have been getting in over the top."

"That's a lie! If they were getting in like that then Our Leader would tell us. He wouldn't let them just over run the place like that!"

"Well he obviously isn't is he! He's sending us out there to take the brunt of it."

I decide to join in before emotions get any higher, my heart still pounding from what we've just seen. "My dad used to tell me that the mist was a remnant of the Great Light," Reluctant face's turn to me, blood still up from the argument that is on the brink of erupting. "sort of like all the debris and dust from when the cities were destroyed, all the chemicals and poisons from the bombs left behind. He said that's what changed *them* out there, living in it, breathing it in day after day, it made them malformed. It changed them somehow."

I shift from leg to leg and stare at the floor aware of all eyes on me now. "He said that the mist is heavier than normal air on account of its different chemicals and so it just hangs there, low to the ground, never rising above a certain height. It's why it never gets into Sanctum, the walls are too high, and anyway, we're on a hill here and the mist always sinks back down into the valley below us where the wind keeps it in or sends it out."

The image of my dad's face appears in my mind, illuminated by the embers of the fire he would sit in front of as he spoke long into the night. "The mist follows the contours of the land and goes where it is sent by the breeze. In their own way they've learnt to adapt to it just as we have." I stand and press my hands against the small of my back. "We spend our time trying to repel it, trying to keep it out! They've chosen to embrace their fate and learnt to live within it."

The noise from the crowd outside intrudes as one by one people begin to move back into the shadows, to take up their positions by the wooden bars, time needed to figure out what's been said, to figure out what's to be done. Time that none of us have.

"The Guards are out there. Take a look." The voice rouses me from my thoughts and I take my place by the side of the cage, focusing my eye on the area of activity. Darkness has fallen now but enough torches are burning and spot lights roaming the ground for us to see what HE wants us to.

The mist is still far off in the distance but I'm guessing like everybody else that it's only a matter of time before it comes again, and with it the dark shadows that pace up and down. The Guards are in the process of clearing up the ground, throwing bodies into a cart that then begins its way towards the wall, towards a small opening I can see to my right.

The piercing scream of the speakers starts up again and I instinctively hold my hands over my ears.

"CITIZENS OF SANCTUM!" The crowd roars back. "WHAT WE HAVE SEEN IS A VICTORY FOR OUR WAY OF LIFE! A VICTORY FOR GOOD OVER EVIL! A VICTORY FOR OUR LEADER!"

The crowd begins to chant *victory* as I watch from the cage as the survivors of the first battle, all six of them, walk slowly behind the cart, the spotlight illuminating the procession, some helping the others, to the tumultuous applause of the crowd as lights flash overhead, lighting sections of the Wall and the people on it.

"Does this mean they've won their freedom? Is it all over?" None of us answer because I guess we don't really want to hear the truth.

"What's that one doing?" I look again and see a lone Guard in the middle of the battle area, kneeling down over the corpse of the creature. At first I think he's trying to free the chains up so they can be used in the next round, or battle or whatever it is they've got planned, but a chant starts to ring out around the crowd as the cart and the people behind it disappear into the wall and the hole closes quickly behind them.

"KILL THEM ALL! KILL THEM ALL! KILL THEM ALL!" A shiver runs down my spine as some of the people in the cage take up the chant and then the Guard outside struggles to hold something up but seems to drop it and I strain my eyes to see what he's doing as he stands up and looks about him.

The lights quickly sweep across the ground until he is bathed in brightness and then I see him take his long baton from his belt and bring it down with a great force. The crowd keeps up the chant and I begin to feel dizzy as the Guard then stands and faces the Wall, thrusting his baton into the air with both hands and all his might, holding aloft the head of the beast.

Everyone goes wild and the cage shakes and I'm slapped on the back by someone whooping and hollering in my ear but all I can do is back away from the spy hole amidst the cheering and the screaming.

As I shrink into the shadows of the cage I turn to my left and see the girl from earlier who spoke with such sense about the creatures and the mist. I see her crouched over hugging her knees, and I see tears pouring from her eyes. She's seen it too. Not the door in the wall. Not even the creature's head raised high on the stick above the Guard, illuminated by the spotlight, but the look in people's eyes as they leap about the cage chanting along with the crowd.

She's seen the insanity.

She's seen her own death.

Chapter 36

"**Do you think they've won** their freedom, the people that survived I mean?" The voice breaks the silence that has descended on the cage. Hunger and thirst have begun to stake their claim, people retreating to the shadows to gather their thoughts and reflect on what just happened.

I'm pleased that the Wastelander was killed, how could I not be? But the noise they make. If you shut your eyes and listen it sounds like a thousand voices crying out in pain.

I think back to the creature we were shown in the courtyard, the leathery skin, the talons; a beast, non-human. But then I think about its blood shot eyes and the way they swung wildly from left to right and I know deep down I could see fear in them, and if that's true then they have emotions of a type. They were once us after all.

They were once us.

Shaking my head I try to block out the image of the Guard holding the head in some kind of triumph, but more than that I try to block out the reaction of the people about me, the way they bayed for more blood, the way they chanted for its death.

"Our Leader has made a promise and he's gonna stick to it." The voice is the same as before, the boy to my left and I dare say that I would have said the same thing a few weeks ago but something's changed in me now, something about the way I look at things. "He'll protect us and make sure we're alright."

"What the hell are you talking about?" I look up as the big guy shuffles forward out of the shadow that all but encases him. "Did you not see what just happened out there?" He looks around but no one wants to meet his gaze as if they don't want to face up to the horrifying reality that we all share. "Six of them survived. SIX! Out of ten. And that was just with one of those, those things attacking! Just imagine what's going to happen when they all launch at us from the mist!"

"Our Leader will look after us. He knows what he's doing!"

I can't help but join in. "A Guard just cut the head off one of them and paraded it around like some kind of trophy! You really think that anyone has the first clue what the response is going to be from those beasts?" I don't really want to get into this, after all we need to preserve as much of our strength as possible for what's up ahead but my head is fit to explode with all the questions rolling around in it.

"Why do you keep questioning Our Leader's decisions? Won't we get in trouble if someone hears you?"

A loud snort escapes my mouth before I can stop it and I see the boy's face colour up. It's not my intention to embarrass him or anyone else but I imagine what River or Rainbow would say at such a thing and I can't help it.

"I'm sorry but look around you!" I spread my arms wide and look around the cage, "Just how much worse do you think things can get?"

The girl with the lank hair coughs and with a hand pushes the strands away from her eyes. "They're here to punish us."

"What!" The big guy, rocks to one side and snorts through his nose, "Didn't you call them demons before, Jesus! I'd rather be out there with them than stuck in here any longer with you bunch of freaks!"

The girl moves in a squatting position and bows her head so the hair falls over her face and then she starts to rotate her neck from side to side until the loose clumps are swinging in the air.

"We've grown fat and weak, we've lost sight of the second chance we were given, the chance to try again and forge a better society, a more humane and just one." She's beginning to sound like the old woman from before, from my first night in the prison.

"Yeah whatever! One where people walk around with creatures heads on a stick. Perfectly normal, right!"

"The Wastelander's have been sent to teach us a lesson. They've been sent to show us the error of our ways and if we aren't up to it," she starts to stand, her head still forward, hair still swinging, "if we have no real answer for them then they'll destroy each and every one of us."

For a moment no one dares to speak as she stands there before us, chest heaving up and down as if it took a lot of energy for her to say what she just did.

She sounds like the street preachers that stand at the corners of the Lanes or in the meeting places, until they're moved on by the Guards or by the rubbish that is thrown at them, always preaching some kind of apocalyptic nonsense, always trying to scare people. And it works too.

In recent times there have been more and more of them talking in this way about how we've brought this on ourselves, about how the lack of food and water is because we've fallen into sinful ways, producing too many children, too many mouths.

"Shut up lady! Keep it for the idiots who actually believe that crap." I turn to my right and inwardly smile at the kid who sits there defiantly, scooping up dirt in his hand and then releasing it, bit by bit. He's probably the only one of us not intimidated by the loose hair that still swings gently almost scraping the ground, the whole side of her face illuminated at times by the spotlights outside.

An awkward silence descends that is broken by the big guy standing and looking back through the slits in the cage.

"I wish they'd give us some water! Not much good to them if I'm drying from the inside out!"

"What's happening out there? Crowd seems awful quiet!" I ask the question more to break the silence and move things on, the preacher lady has moved back into the shadows but I worry about her,

I worry about all people who believe something so strongly that they can't see any other point of view.

"Nothing new. Can still see the mist but can't make out any more shadows, the lights are shining on it from the Wall. Maybe they've been put off by the show earlier!" He's joking but I can still sense an element of hope in his voice and then his head jerks to the left and I'm up quickly to look for myself as noise begins again somewhere in the distance.

"Something's happening. Prepare yourselves!" The noise from the crowd increases as a number of Guards emerge from the doorway to the right about fifty yards from our cage. It's the same doorway the survivors were led through.

"That's the two who killed the Wastelander with the chain!"

"Look over there at the ground, it's moving again, what is it? What's happening now? Will that awful voice speak out again?"

To the left the dark hole in the middle of the Wasteland appears and the crowd goes crazy, cheering and yelling as before as the spot lights swing round to illuminate the ground. I see out of the corner of my eye the kid from earlier place his hands over his ears.

"I don't like it. I don't like it!" But I'm unable to tear my eyes away as a lone figure rises from the ground. The moon is full in the sky, bright and clear but the lights from the wall shine down, illuminating the figure. The effect is amazing.

"That's the Senator from our compound isn't it?" I try to look closer, to strain every sinew in my eyes but the bright yellow robe picks up light and reflects in back upon us in a dazzling display. The Guards and the two who killed the creature are almost in the middle as well and then from somewhere I hear the same cannon noises and the same '*oooh aaah*' from the crowd. From somewhere high above colours explode in the sky as the group stand bathing in the noise from the crowd.

"Maybe their going to tell us it's all over and no one else has to fight anymore?"

"Maybe!" I say but there's no real conviction in my voice.

"MY FELLOW CTIZENS!" The Senator's voice booms around the arena as the crowd takes a few seconds to quieten down. "Today is a great day! Today we have seen that the creatures that plague our city are NOT invincible! Today we have seen that the CAN be beaten!"

The crowd roars its approval and the senator raises his arms bathed in the spot light, his great yellow robes spread out like wings, "I give to you the first to survive. The first to KILL a Wastelander. The first to be given their FREEDOM!"

The last word creates pandemonium as the whole earth feels like it's about to erupt from the noise all around and this time I can't help but lose myself in the moment.

"They're free! Oh my God it's true! Our leader is true to his word!" The big guy's voice is full of joy and relief and I look back to the centre, to the two men with their arms aloft as the tape floats down around them.

Maybe there's a way out of this after all.

"They have proved themselves worthy of citizenship. They have paid for their crimes and they now take their place as once again amongst us all as we seek to preserve all that is great about SANCTUM!"

"SANCTUM. SANCTUM. SANCTUM!"

The spotlight stays on them as they begin to slowly disappear from view, still waving, back under the ground and for once I'm annoyed at myself, annoyed at the fact that I can't join in the cheers and screams of delight that ring out. Annoyed that I can't simply enjoy the moment for what it is, that my mind has to turn over and over the events, has to try and pick at what it's seen until is starts to mistrust everything before it.

I step back from the bars and crouch in the dirt as the others hug each other and lose themselves in the hope of their own freedom being granted as they have just seen it done for those others.

"The sins of pride and arrogance are upon us." I turn and see the girl by my side, her lank hair still covering her face, voice almost drowned out by the chanting all around. She flicks the strands aside and fixes me with a stare that seems intent of breaking into my mind. "*They* can hear our cheers and our self congratulations and they will not rest until we all pay!"

Sitting back I stare ahead at the walls of the cage but in my mind I'm looking out past the senator and the Guards, beyond the lights and the coloured paper still falling from the sky, towards the mist that still lingers on the horizon.

I'm looking at the dark shadowy figures that are gathering once more.

Chapter 37

The wait seems to go on for ever. It seems like hours since the Senator spoke to us and then disappeared beneath the earth although it's probably only a matter of minutes but the air has cooled considerably and the mist is creeping forward again, slower this time but it's definitely on the move.

The huge moon is casting its glow, torches being re-lit on the sections of the wall I can see from the bars of the cage, the spotlights still roaming the ground before us, impatiently waiting for the next piece of action. The smell of burning oil from the torches is strangely comforting as if I'm back at home, staring into the fire, listening to dad's stories or curled up with Ellie and Doughnut.

Are they out there? Are they on the Wall watching this?

I'm in such a daze I don't even realise that the door to the cage is being opened until I hear a cry from the shadows and I look up to see the familiar red uniform of the Guards staring into the gloom.

"Stand up and follow me. NOW!" I look around expecting harsh words to follow but I can tell from everyone's face as they begin to emerge from the shadows of the cage that they are hungry and tired, as if the marching, the watching, everything from the last few days has finally taken its toll. It's as if none of us have the strength to react anymore, as if we've already given up.

"If you want us to fight you need to give us some food or we'll be no good to anyone." The words escape my mouth before I realise what I'm saying and I wince in anticipation of the sting of the whip or the thud of a baton. I hear a sharp crack above my head and quickly get the hint.

This is it!

We file out of the cage and back into the network of tunnels but the light's so gloomy I can barely see in front of me. Keeping my head down we pass the three Guards that are lined up immediately outside the cage door. I can hear gasps and whimpers behind me and I'm not surprised at all. None of us can contemplate what it must be like out there and God only knows what they've got in store to keep the crowd happy.

"They're demons sent to punish us!"

Surely they've got to try and increase the number of dead Wastelanders? Surely that's the point of this whole thing?

I can feel my heart rate increasing as adrenalin and nerves fight for a foothold in my body.

"They won't stop until…" The girl's words float in and out of my brain and for a moment I think I'm going to fall to my knees.

We trudge after the lead Guard down the gently sloping tunnel and I can't help but think about where the others are. Every few yards it seems that there's an opening or another tunnel leading off to somewhere. One of them must lead to more cells, more rooms where others wait like we've been forced to. Will they be made to help us out there in the middle like the others were? Are River and Rainbow being dragged to a cage to watch us fight like the others were? Are Samson and Dodge?

My mind starts whirring and I imagine somehow breaking off from this main group and making my way down the nearest corridor but how long would it be before I got caught? Minutes? Seconds? And just where the hell would I go? I have no idea where I am in relation to the others and any type of exit, I guess the best I could really hope for was a quick death at the hands of the Guards as opposed to out there being torn apart by those things.

The sound of the crowd is more muffled down here certainly than it was in the cage but even though I can no longer make out individual words or chants, the dull, low vibrating is in some ways much worse because it doesn't sound like anything I've ever heard before. It's like the earth itself is moaning and flexing, breathing like a pair of lungs that will soon expand and crush us.

I turn my head to see behind me and my eyes meet the big guys. I can tell instantly from the way his shoulders are hunched, fists pumping back and forth, that he's had the same thoughts as me, that he's pictured himself making a break for it but I imagine that because he's still behind me, marching with the rest of us, he's also seen the futility of the idea. Our eyes meet for an instant and then break and I'm left wondering whether we'll work together to at least prolong the inevitable or will it be each man and woman for themselves?

Noises up ahead stir me from my thoughts as the Guard in front turns and I feel his hand push me in the chest.

"Get back NOW! Up against the wall and don't you dare look up!" I'm too shocked to do anything other than exactly what I'm told so I back against the wall as the Guards press us into the rough surface, my head tilted forwards but my eyes darting around all over the place trying to soak up as much information as possible. A flash of red and yellow streaks by.

The Guards that are escorting us lower their heads as a Senator sweeps past the corridor suddenly alive with sound and movement. I look up to see if he's the one who spoke to us in the grounds of the prison but his face is a blur.

"…no idea they'd get out, but I can assure you we have our men on the case and it won't be too long before…"

"We're no where near ready for this for God's sake! We've only just started with the crowd. We can't even be sure the whole city's empty yet!" The conversation tapers off as they disappear down the corridor and out of sight but already I'm playing the words over and over in my head.

"No idea they'd get out…only just started with the crowd…empty"

Who's got out? Have some of us escaped from the cells? What if River and the others are…

"Who's in charge here?" The voice is strong and firm and belongs to one of the Guards that just rushed past. He returns and stands in front of us and

I assume he carries more power and responsibility than the others because they've kept their heads slightly bowed as a sign of respect. The Guard pressing down on me releases his grip and steps forward and I stretch out my chest still feeling his hand print on my ribs.

"I am sir, We're transporting the prisoners to the arena."

"Not now you're not! Get them back to the cage and then bring your men to the main holding area. MOVE!"

He turns and disappears down the corridor and the other Guard turns towards us but I see something in his face, something I've never seen in the face of a Guard before, like he's been flustered and confused by all the commotion, like he has no idea what's going on. He turns to the other three and coughs before wiping a shaky hand against his mouth.

"Okay, you heard what he said! Let's get these prisoners back to the cage!"

"What's going on?" The big guy asks the question I've been too scared to and he steps forward, only a few centimetres but enough to make the other Guards twitch and the main one takes a corresponding step back.

"Yeah! Why are we going back? Who's escaped?" The voice comes from behind me and I recognise it as the girl with the streaky hair. The big guy holds his hands out, palms upturned as if trying to make peace but he steps forward again.

"Don't come any closer!" The Guard places his hand on the top of the baton hanging from his belt but hesitates as do the other three as if they don't know what to do, as if their aura of power has suddenly diminished. Looking up at his face as the light flares from the torches lining the walls, I see his eyes and they are scared.

Whatever's happening has taken them by surprise.

"I'm not doing anything! I'm not being threatening I just want to know why you've been told to take us back, that's all!" His voice is calm and even and then it hits me and my heart practically leaps out of my chest.

He's taking his chance.

He's trying to escape.

Making his move he launches at the Guard before the others can react. I look down the corridor because I can hear other voices echoing and then my head flips back.

Spinning to his left the big guy grabs the baton from the Guard's hand and holds it up to his throat as he presses himself against the wall, the Guard in front of him breathing heavily, looks to the others and they begin to move in.

"What are you doing? You're going to get us all killed!" The girl's voice is high and tense. I hear whimpering coming from some of the others.

"We're dead anyway aren't we? AREN'T WE!" He increases the pressure on the baton and the Guard begins to choke, and then looks back at the other three, "Don't move or I'll crush his throat!"

The voices down the corridor are getting louder and as the big guy looks back down the way we've come and then directly at me I realise that he has no plan, that he acted on the spur of the moment, when the opportunity presented itself, and that he has no idea what he's going to do next. And then I see a blur from my right as the other three rush towards him as one, batons raised. He pushes the Guard towards them and then is off, sprinting down the corridor into the gloom.

"Get after him!" The voice is croaky and I can see confusion reigning amongst us all.

And then I'm running in the opposite direction, legs and arms pumping for all their worth, because it's each man and woman for themselves and because I don't know what else to do.

The last Guard calls after me. "Hey! Stop now and we'll go easy! We want the other one, not you!" But I'm not listening, I'm just running as fast as I can down the corridor as it twists and turns getting darker and darker. As I near another corner I can see two further tunnels split off, I'm sure this is the way that the Senator and the other Guards came and that I'm about to turn a corner and run straight into their open arms.

As I turn I look back over my shoulder and see just one Guard following me. I know my chances have just gone up as now I'm only being followed by one of them but I'm running blind and I'm assuming that he isn't.

Turning my head again I can tell that he's about ten feet behind me catching up fast, red robes fluttering behind him, baton in hand and I take a deep breath and begin to slow down until I can almost feel his breath on the back of my neck.

My mind flicks to the rooftops of the slums, to me, Ellie and Doughnut running for all we're worth, skipping in and out of the holes, jumping over the bigger gaps, trying as hard as we can to avoid putting our legs through any of the weaker parts of the roofs. I remember Doughnut being behind me and me trying to slow down just enough so that he could catch up a little but not think that I was doing it on purpose.

But then I remember falling down, tripping on a piece of rubble lying in the way and Doughnut tumbles over the top of me coming to rest in a heap of clothes and limbs a few yards in front.

NOW!

I keep the image of Doughnut in my mind as I skid onto my side and roll forward. The Guard tries to leap over my body but we're far too close to each other and his foot catches on my shoulder and he goes flying over the top landing against the wall and then dropping to the floor with a groan.

Ignoring the pain in my shoulder I'm up and over to him before he has time to register anything and then I'm struggling with his baton, trying to free it from his belt. He's groggy after smashing his head into the wall and I can see blood trickling from his hair line.

"Hey! Stop…what…" But he's slurring his words and I can tell that he's not going to be a problem anymore, and then another idea rushes to the front of my mind and I look at his bruised and bloodied face, and then his uniform.

"Listen, I'm sorry for this but I've got to do it! I've got no other choice!"

Chapter 38

The robes are ill fitting, hanging off me like I'm a little kid wearing his dad's shirt or something. The shoes don't fit either, far too big and I figure that it's best to leave on my sandals because if I have to run, which I am in no doubt that I will have to do, then I don't want to be tripping up after a yard or so.

I look down at myself, at the baggy red tunic that is smeared with dirt and at the baton that hangs loosely by my side, and then I look at the body by my feet, the half naked Guard who now looks so pathetic and defenceless passed out in the dust and soil.

I know I've got to work quick and do something with the body but I can't help but stare at the blood that has now begun to congeal around his face, the blood that I caused.

Looking around for a place to drag him I can't see anywhere that suits. In both directions the corridor simply seems to extend on with no small alcoves to hide him in. The best I can think to do is to place him directly underneath one of the oil lamps which I do with considerable trouble. I had no idea that a body could weigh so much when passed out and uncooperative.

Turning the lamp off will buy me some time, so at least from a distance it will be difficult to see anything at all. As if to test the theory I walk ten yards or so and then turn around, and at first glance the body seems concealed by the gloom but I know that a few seconds for the eyes to adjust and someone's seeing something.

I listen out for noise, straining to hear anything at all other than the muffled *BOOM...BOOM* of the crowd outside and then I start to run back the way I came because I can't think of anything else to do. I want to get out of here, I want to run as fast as I can with the Wall at my back until the sandals fall from my feet and I see Ellie and Doughnut again but I can't do it, I can't leave without finding the others, without trying to bring them along as well. How could I live with myself if I left now?

Besides, I've no idea how to get out of this labyrinth of corridors in any case.

As I jog along I run the words of the senator through my mind again.

"No idea how they got out...only just started with the crowd..."

The trouble is they're only snatches of conversation and I could make a convincing case for any number of interpretations but what does *got out* mean? Got out of the mist? Got out of the Wasteland itself? And who exactly is *they*?

My mind reminds me of how I got here in the first place, the water tunnels, the creature chasing me. Maybe they managed to capture some and they've escaped from somewhere? Maybe they made a break for the door the victors came from, forced their way in, started creating hell?

With so many ideas rushing through my head I don't hear the footsteps until it's almost too late and when I do I have no choice but to stop jogging and to walk as best I can like one of them.

Three Guards emerge from the corner and run on past without giving me a second look and I breathe a sigh of relief because whatever's happening means their heads are elsewhere. I know the subterfuge won't last for they're going to discover the body for sure, if he hasn't come round by now that is and raised the alarm himself.

I try to picture when we first entered this place. We marched beneath the wooden ramp and then turned a corner away from the crowds before descending down into this network of corridors and cells. I remember the ground gently sloping when we reached the door to our particular cell which gives me a little bit of hope because if I keep going up then surely I'm getting closer?

The corridor takes a sharp turn left and I'm presented with a further two to choose from. I crouch and listen as hard as I can, filtering out as much extraneous noise as possible when I hear a voice from behind and my heart momentarily stops beating in my chest.

"You there! What are you doing?"

Play it for all you're worth!

Turning round, I start to cough and splutter and the guard takes a step back, his face pulled into a grimace. "I'm sorry sir, not feeling too well!" I cough again and keep my head low while backing slowly into the gloom because I'm conscious of my sandals and I don't want them to give me away.

"Where are you supposed to be?" I can feel his eyes on me and wince in anticipation of what's to come. And then an idea forces its way to the front of my mind.

"Prisoners sir! The new ones from earlier today...I...I'm on duty but I felt sick and I had to..."

"Spare me the story boy."

His eyes dart from side to side. He looks worried. He looks sick with it.

"You're right sir!" and then I cough again only this time louder and longer, forcing phlegm into my mouth which I spit on the floor, all the while I think the loudness of my heart as it rattles my ribcage is going to give me away. He nods in the direction of the second tunnel.

"And with them getting out before they were supposed to," He wipes the sweat from his forehead with the back of a shaky hand, "wouldn't want to be the person who let that happen!" before looking up at me as if he's said too much to a subordinate, as if he'll get in trouble for having a loose tongue, "On your way now before I report you! And make yourself useful! We've got a hell of a job on our hands now, a hell of a job!"

Keeping my head bowed low I turn quickly, every foot step convincing me that he's going to see the ill fitting robes or the sandals for what they are, a pale imitation of the real thing.

As I venture further into the corridor I begin to feel the stirrings of a breeze on my face and this simple thing, this most ordinary of feelings makes my heart leap. I redouble my efforts before casting a nervous look back, but the figure is gone and I begin to jog again. I know I'm not far away now because I begin to hear voices but whose are they?

The voices are becoming louder and I realise that I'm going to have to get past the Guards that are posted outside the cell doors but I've got no time to sit and think of a plan, I've got no time at all.

Taking a deep breath I turn the corner of the corridor, but there are no Guards at all. I stand there for what seems an age as I see the doors of more cells and realise that I know where I am, because I recognise the wider corridor and the sloping floor, and the fact that we came down the far end not so long ago. I look as far as I can past the cell doors and up the corridor and feel the fresh breeze on my face again.

Breeze means fresh air. I've found the way out.

The thought galvanises me and I rush to the first cell on the left and look through the bars. "River! Rainbow! Where are you?" I see some figures rush from the back of the cell but when they get into the broken light I don't recognise the faces, just the despair and terror in their eyes.

"Please…please help us…" Fingers poke through the bars and I back off.

"I'm sorry, there's nothing I can do."

"Please don't go…please…"

I turn and check the next cell ignoring the ones behind me because although it's all so hazy I think we were led into one of these cells on the right but they've all heard me by now and more fingers appear at bars behind me as people start to call out and cry for help.

"Shhh. Please don't make noise!" I start to tremble because I was in one of these cells not so long ago and I just want to free everybody. The cries become louder and I turn both ways as if I'm going to see Guards rushing towards me.

"Don't leave us!"

"Come back…"

"I don't want to die!"

The last voice brings tears to my eyes but I force the emotion back down and look through the next set of bars.

"River? Rainbow?"

"Jake, is that you!" River's voice is unmistakable and I rush to the last cell in the row and this time I see River's face staring back at me from behind the bars.

"Where the hell are all the Guards?" And then he stops and looks me up and down. "Why are you dressed as one? How the…what are you doing here?" I look down and can't help but smile at how ridiculous I look.

"There was yelling and screaming, I thought, I thought, and then the Guards rushed away about five minutes ago." I look behind River and I see Samson's freckly face staring back at me, a smile half suffocated on his lips. "Something must be going on for them to leave us like this. What is it, Jake? What's happening?"

"Something's happened alright, something nobody was prepared for! I think that maybe they've found a way in, that maybe the Wastelanders have surprised them somehow?" I step back from the cell door and look all around trying to think of a way to get them out.

"You gotta be quick Jake!" I look around for anything lying about but the crying from the other cells has me on edge and no ideas are presenting themselves. "Jake. JAKE! Get us out of here!"

"Step back!" I look into River's eyes and I know that he can see how I'm feeling and then he disappears and I hear him telling people to move to the sides away from the door.

I back up until I'm pressed against the opposite wall and I allow all the fear and anger to flood my system, as my hands curl up into balls and then I launch myself at the side of the door, by the hinges where the earth looks at its weakest.

Before I hit, I jump up and twist to the side, my legs outstretched as the soles of my feet hit the side of the door with as much force as I can muster. Pain shoots through my body as I collapse in a heap and when I look back nothing seems to have happened at all.

Pushing myself up I rotate each foot before hobbling back to the wall to try again. The pleading from the other cells is incessant and I do my best to block it out as I launch myself at the door again, trying to aim for the exact same spot as before. This time some clumps of dirt fall to the ground from around the frame although when I stand back up I know from the intense pain shooting up my left leg that I'm going to be hard pressed to do it again with anything like the same force.

"Hey Jake, we've got some dirt falling in here! Let us try from this side!"

I limp to the grill. "We've got to hurry, someone's going to hear something real soon." But he's retreated back into the shadows and as I move to the left I see a whole group of them emerge and then a huge thud as they slam into the other side. I see the frame move and more clumps of dirt fall.

"Again River, with everything you've got!" This time I stand back, looking left and right, checking that the way is clear.

More rubble falls as they slam into the wall and then a clump drops to the floor and I can see through into the cell from a crack by the frame. "That's it! I can see in." I rush to the crack and start to pull at the earth until I see fingers from the other side doing the same thing. The soil is dry and old and held together like glue and after several minutes pulling and scraping the hole looks only slightly bigger but that doesn't stop Samson who struggles his arms through towards me.

"Pull Jake. PULL!" At first I think I'm going to pull so hard his arms are going to fly off and I can hear him yell with pain so I stop and he wriggles back into the cell.

"Kick the wall, we've got to make it bigger!" I look around expecting to see Guards rushing me, batons and whips at the ready but all I see are fingers and hands wriggling from the iron grills in the other doors. It feels wrong. The whole thing feels…

"Jake! Are you still there?" River's voice brings me back and I crouch by the hole and see his sweat and dirt streaked face looking back at me. "We're going to try again with Samson and this time we're going to push him hard from this side." He breaks off to say something and then I see Samson's face appear as he wriggles his hands and arms back through the hole. I can see that this time there's a little more give around his shoulders and placing a foot on the wall I lock my fingers with his and begin to pull.

"Come on Jake! You turned soft or something?" I feel his shoulders move and I redouble my efforts as he slides towards me.

"One last push River!" And then he's out. His legs sliding from the hole as we crash to the floor in a heap. I can hear more banging from the other side of the cell as rubble falls onto the floor and then more arms wriggling through.

"We thought you'd gone Jake!"

I grin through the exhaustion "Wasn't going to leave you guys now was I!" I turn as Samson reaches towards the hole to help River through and I can hear Dodge somewhere behind.

"Hurry up. Just 'cos I'm the smallest!" His voice is drowned out by the noise all around.

"Where are the Guard's Jake? I don't understand where they went!" I nod at Samson who stays at the hole helping Dodge through and grab River by the shoulder.

"We've got to get out of here. NOW!" Other people are beginning to climb through the hole, beginning to scatter in all directions and the noise from the other cells is getting unbearable. I can see from their faces that their scared and I turn towards the direction of the breeze. "If we go now then hopefully we can somehow blend into the crowd." and then I stop and turn around because something's missing, someone…

"I'm not going that way Jake!" I spin around and look back at the hole and then at River and the others.

There's someone missing.

"Where's Rainbow?" I move toward the cell door hoping that she'll appear at the hole with that crooked smile of hers, I assumed she was right behind them but I already know from the downcast faces of the others that something's happened.

"They came some time ago and took five people with them." His eyes drop to the floor, "I tried to…" Samson steps towards him and then looks at me, defiance blazing.

"Why didn't they take all of us Jake? I don't understand!"

"He tried to grab one of the Guard's arms, to stop them taking her but they hit him with their batons until he let go!" I look again at River, at the discolouration on the side of his face, how he is holding his right shoulder, but he's already half turned back down the corridor I've just come from, his mind made up.

I look back at the other bodies as they disappear round the corner and I know that whatever we decide to do we've got to do it now. And then I picture the cages, the Wastelander's head as it glistened in the spotlight. I'm surprised by the strength of my feelings for Rainbow as I picture first Ellie and then Doughnut and they galvanise me as I turn back to Dodge and Samson. Whatever we do we've got to be quick. "I need you two to be strong."

"I'm going with River!" Samson looks at me with fury and indignation and takes a step towards River and then River's by his side kneeling and holding his arms as Dodge keeps lookout.

"You know she'd want you to look after Dodge."

Dodge looks round sharply. "I don't need…" I shoot him a glance and he falls quiet.

"We'll be quicker, just the two of us." Samson wriggles in River's grip, his face turned to the ground but I know he understands what River's saying "Besides we need you two to scavenge food for us and any water you can find!" River looks at me his eyes pleading for a little help.

"Rainbow's going to need you guys to be out there." I point towards the direction of the breeze, "Now remember," I grab them both by the shoulders and pull them towards me, "you've got yourselves lost, right! Once you're out of here, make straight for the barriers and get into the crowd as quickly as you can. If anyone asks, you're lost and looking for your parents."

River steps towards them. "We'll need food and water when we reach you! Wait for us as near as you can to the entrance to the Square. Do you understand! Hide and wait for us!" Then he turns quickly and begins to run down the corridor.

I begin to push them gently away. I know they don't want to go but it's for the best. "Rainbow needs you to do this. We all do!" Samson opens his mouth as if to say something but it falls closed again.

"Go!" I smile and nod as they back away from my hands. "Go!"

And then Samson shakes his head clear as if making up his mind and turns to Dodge, pushing him down the corridor.

"Come on then, titch!" He turns and smiles at me and then picks up the pace. "Let's find something to eat! I'm starving!"

Chapter 39

I watch as they disappear round the corner and then turn back towards River who's at the far end of the corridor. The scene before me is one of pure fear, as the last few people from the cell stand around in a daze, the booming noise from the crowd, the screams from the other cells has caught them up in its grip and doesn't want to let go.

"River! Wait up!" He nods and as I jog towards him I'm stopped by a group still standing by the hole we made. One of them turns to me, her face streaked with dirt and tears.

"She won't come out!" She turns to the hole and then back to me. "Please! Please come out!" I want to help, I want to go back in there and get whoever it is out but I know that time is of the essence if we're going to find Rainbow. I move past and shake my head as she steps near me and grabs at my robes.

"You did this to us. You did this!" She goes to hit me and I step back as she swings and misses and then I look down at the red robes I'm covered in and then back at the broken figure, slumped before me.

"I'm sorry. I'm sorry."

"Leave her. We've got to find Rainbow!"

I take one last look at the scene before me and then turn and join River. "My guess is they've taken Rainbow to wherever they took you. I hope she's not..." He doesn't finish the sentence but I know exactly what he means. He hopes they haven't taken her to the arena. He hopes she's not out *there* fighting. I think about telling him what I saw; the Wastelander's head, the human bait, but he doesn't need any other distractions.

"Listen." He grabs my arm and stares at me, his face blank of expression. "You don't have to come you know!" He looks over my shoulder to where the others have gone, "You should go, while you still can."

I gently take his hand off my arm.

"What would you do?"

He smiles and then turns back towards the gloom.

We walk down the corridor, me in front and River at the back. The plan, if you can call it one, is for me to play the role of a Guard escorting a prisoner to the Wasteland and so I have the baton drawn and am trying to look as menacing as possible. Inside my guts are all churned up and I know it's the same for River because we've fallen into silence as we move as quickly as possible through the corridor.

I can remember pretty much where we're going and I figure that if we can get to the cages then we can see if she's in any of them. But again the same question comes up like a flashing light in my head. What are we going to do if we get there? The Guards are hardly going to let us poke about until we've found her. And what if she's out *there*?

I try to concentrate on the here and now. I can't do anything about stuff that hasn't happened yet.

"Have you noticed the sound?" River whispers from behind me and I jump at the sound of his voice. "That booming sound has changed." I strain my ears at first puzzled and then I realise that he's right. The crowd noise that was so deafening out in the cages is far more muffled down here and I suppose I've gotten so used to the intermittent sounds of cannon fire from a distance that I've all but filtered it out.

My head fills with possibilities of what's happening out there and I shiver as we turn the corner to our left.

"I hurt one of the Guards." I don't want to say anything about the noise in case I alarm River even more but I can't help from saying something. I keep my voice low but it feels almost like a confessional, "Broke a lamp to hide him in shadow but there's no way he wouldn't have either woken by now and sounded the alarm or been found." I leave the rest unspoken but the meaning is obvious.

Where the hell is everyone?

"What do you think's happened?" I shrug and keep moving because I don't want to admit what my brain's been coming up with. I don't want to let the images any further into my mind than they've already crept because the possibility is too horrible to contemplate. Even worse than facing them out in the Wasteland.

"Heard one of them saying something about letting *them* out, maybe…"

A noise makes my head snap to attention and I squint into the half light. "We're getting nearer to where I left him." And then I hear, from far off in the distance, muffled yelling and footsteps that seem to echo all around. I immediately brace myself as River steps in front of me and lowers his head, playing the role well. Grabbing him by the back of his shirt I push him along, the baton in my left hand ready to be waved menacingly in the air. I look down and am satisfied that, for a short time at least, he is covering up my sandals.

The footsteps and yelling are getting closer but I still can't make out what's being said although whatever it is sounds urgent and panicked.

"Whatever happens one of us has got to find her!" I grip onto the back of his shirt even more as the sounds rebound off the corridor walls and I begin to make out snatches of words as my brain stitches them together.

"Where has it gone? Where has it bloody gone?"

"Who let them in…"

"Blood…everywhere…"

River's shoulders tense as the footsteps sound around the next corner and then they emerge at the far end, a blur of red, arms and legs pumping. The Guard at the front has a torn tunic and I can see open wounds, like slash marks on his chest. My breathing becomes almost uncontrollable as they near us, four in all, dishevelled and panting, constantly looking back over their shoulders.

As they near us I can see can see that the others are bloodied as well, one of them bandaged across his right eye, blood seeping through into a red pool, making him look like some kind of Cyclops. The one at the front stumbles into River and grabs at my shoulders.

"For Christ's sake leave the prisoner and follow us!" There's a terror in his face that needs no words and his eyes practically bulge out of their sockets as a scream rings out from somewhere deep within the tunnel network. He begins to run as the others pass him, sprinting off into the gloom. "They've found a way in, Jesus! They've got in!" and he backs away, his mouth still moving but no words coming out before he turns and disappears round the corner.

We look at each other and then back in the direction the Guards are running as another scream erupts, nearer this time, and then abruptly stops.

"How have they got in here, Jake?" River looks back in the direction they just ran and I can see his body twitching to follow them, "What about the cages?" I know what he's thinking because I'm thinking it too and then he's off, running to the end of the corridor towards the screaming and I take off after him knowing that there will be a choice of routes in a minute and I don't want him to take the wrong one.

"Wait up River there's a…"

Turning the corner I all but run into the back of River. "Don't move!" His voice is no more than a hiss and although I've yet to see past him I know what's there because of the stench. The foul odour of rotting meat has filled the air. I've smelt it before, before the two of them dropped over the waterfall, before it devoured Angus.

It's the smell of Wastelander.
There's one up ahead of us right now.

Chapter 40

I try not to gag on the stench as I move my head around River's shoulder to get a better look. At the far end of the corridor I can see a hunched figure, its head whipping from side to side as it burrows its face down into something. The noise is horrendous as it rips and tears, blood flicking onto the wall and floor as it fights to grab hold of whatever it has in its clutches.

"Don't move a muscle!" I try to whisper as quietly as possible because the creature has its back to us but in my head it's like firing shot from a cannon, every word exploding in a mass of sound waves that can't help but reach its ears. River gives a nod but thankfully doesn't say anything in reply. Instead he stares straight ahead and waits.

Not daring to move my feet for fear of disturbing the earth beneath, I begin to rotate my head, to take in as much information as I can. We have just turned the corner so the corridor we're now in, if I'm not mistaken, leads to the cross roads, the three avenues, one of which I took before. One of which leads outside to the cages.

How long is it? Maybe fifty meters or so, maybe a little more but with the speed I've seen them move, I would give it a few seconds to eat up that distance and be on us before we've even had time to turn. I blink rapidly and look again at the lamps that line the walls casting an eerie glow that elongates shadows and makes me mistrust my own eyes.

In the water tunnels the Wastelander leapt from the top of the waterfall and was on Angus in a matter of seconds. I have to figure that on dry land it will be even faster. I can sense River tensing as the beast's head snaps back from the carcass. It starts to choke and coughs, hacking up something from deep within its guts. As it shifts a little to the left to get a better purchase on its meal I can see a leg protruding from the mince that the torso used to be. It still has some sort of material on it.

A dark red colour.

"Is that a Guard?" River turns and whispers as I look back over his shoulder, something about its body language telling me that it's getting ready to move on.

"Try to back up a little, one step at a time, as quietly as possible." I figure that if we can get round the turn we've just come from then at least we can buy a little time. I don't know what we're going to be able to do then but we've got to try something.

We move backwards until we're no more than ten yards from the corner when a shout from somewhere in the network of tunnels makes the Wastelander stop and sit bolt upright. There's something almost human about the sound.

The creature in front of us tips its head back and makes a series of sharp barking noises as if trying to communicate. River clearly has the same idea because he half turns and I can see the corner of his mouth twitch.

"What on earth! Are they talking to each other now?" I don't reply but turn my head and see the corner coming up, no more than a few yards away. I have to fight the urge, the adrenalin rush that tells me to bolt for the corner but my legs don't get the message in time and my right foot steps a little too far scraping the soil, dislodging a stone. Immediately its head whips round and River presses into me, trying to turn and get away.

"Uh oh!"

Its head whips back round to the carcass and I can tell that it's trying to decide what to do; finish the meal it has already caught or go after some fresh meat. Its decision is clear to the both of us when it begins to shuffle around. Something detaches from its food source and then, as it turns to face us, looking directly at where we are standing I see that it has part of an arm in its mouth, the fingers twitching as if they can still get away if they wriggle and squirm enough.

For a moment there is no movement. All three of us simply look at each other and then the Wastelander flicks its head to the side and the hand flies from its mouth, hitting the wall and sliding down to rest in the dirt, next to what's left of its owner.

Another scream sounds from far off but this time it doesn't respond. Instead it slowly rises on its haunches until it stands with a crooked back, leaning to one side. My mind flicks back to the two fighters in the arena, the way they strangled the beast and I know they can be killed, I guess *I've* killed one but that was different! I was in the water and I managed to hold onto a rock and *it* didn't. This isn't the same, this is a test of strength and if we don't think of something fast then it's going to be a no contest.

River's chest heaves up and down as he takes in massive gulps of air, beyond him the creature begins to move towards us in a series of lurching movements. I open my mouth to calm him down but he turns and speaks first.

"Follow me and for God's sake, don't lose that baton!" And then he's off, running full tilt at the creature. He takes me completely by surprise and I can see that the same is true for a creature that is probably used to its prey running *from* not towards it. And then I realise what he's doing, he's trying to gain an advantage, gain the upper hand so that I can deliver the killer blow. Of course he is! His sister's out there somewhere and nothing's going to stop him.

RUN.

River's about ten yards ahead of me when I put my head down and sprint after him, the blurred body of the creature beginning to lope towards us. It looks a little sluggish, nowhere near the speed of the ones I encountered in the water and I wonder if it's because it's been feeding and is struggling with a full belly.

"Get ready with that baton!" River's words redouble my efforts and I hold it in front of me as I see the two of them on a collision course. The creature starts to raise its right claw and we're that close that I can see congealed blood and lumps of flesh on its chin and torso.

River flings himself to the right as its claw swings down, catching him a glancing blow on the shoulder. He cries out and the beast replies with a series of clicking grunts before swiping again, but this time missing as River ducks and rolls, the beast crashing into the wall and howling with a mixture of frustration and pain.

Launching myself at its back it moves in on River but flicks me off easily and I land in a heap in the dust, the metallic taste of blood spreading throughout my mouth. The baton flies out of my hand on impact and comes to rest about five feet away as the creature moves in on River. The smell of its breath is almost unbearable as strips of flesh and skin waft from its teeth and River scrambles back, wincing in pain from the claw marks on his shoulder.

I yell at the top of my lungs, "CLOSE YOUR EYES!" and then pull myself to my feet, grabbing as much soil as I can in my right hand. The Wastelander's attention is disturbed and it turns in my direction as I fling the dirt and dust into its face, stones and grit hitting it square in the eyes.

It howls again and staggers back to the wall, scratching at its face, gouging at its own skin as River struggles to his feet and slams into its body with his good shoulder forcing the creature hard against the wall, making it exhale in pain. I scramble for the baton as, momentarily blinded, it lashes out wildly, catching River again on his side.

"HIT IT! BLOODY HIT THE THING!"

Grabbing the stick I turn, raising it above my head and rush the creature bringing the baton down as hard as I am able. It hits the side of its face and I hear a cracking sound as something breaks in its cheek or jaw.

"AGAIN! HIT IT AGAIN!"

The momentum of the swing crosses my arm over my chest and forces me away from the beast as it howls and lashes out with even more fury. Its eyes blink rapidly and it spits blood in a shower that spatters against my face and chest. Whatever advantage the dirt gave us has almost gone because as I try to raise the baton again it catches me with its arm, sending me into the wall.

The top of my head strikes the earth and a sharp, blinding pain shoots through my body. Suddenly everything is woozy, as if I'm under water and I try to right myself, I try to stagger back to River but my right arm gives way and I slump back to the floor. River is shouting at me but I can't make out what he's saying and I shake my head trying to clear it of the throbbing, trying to get my senses back.

Placing my right hand on the wall I get to my knees as the creature descends on River, trapping him on the floor, teeth bared, claws digging into the dirt. Blood is beginning to pool around his shoulder and with another effort I shake my head as my hearing starts to return.

Screaming reaches my ears but I'm not sure if its from River or the Wastelander and I look around desperately searching for the baton, but I can't find it, all I can see is River's face turning to me as he holds the creature off with all of his strength.

"Lamp! Get the lamp!"

For a moment I'm puzzled as my groggy head takes time to understand and then I'm up, stumbling across the corridor to the oil lamp that burns on the opposite side.

My hands are shaking but I manage to lift it from its hook and turn to see River push again with all his might and swing his feet up against the beast's chest. He lets out a roar and the creature stumbles backwards. It's only a few feet but it's all I need and I step forward and hurl the lamp with all the strength I can muster as River rolls further away.

The glass smashes on the wall behind its head showering it in oil and for a moment I think our chance is gone as I see the flame still encased in a smashed part of the lamp fall harmlessly in the dust at River's feet.

I can see from the creature's eyes that it thinks so too and as it takes a step forward it bares its teeth as if to strike when River kicks out with his foot at the remnants of the flame sending a spark towards the pool of oil.

The creature turns its head to look and for a split second nothing happens and then the oil catches and a flame shoots up from the floor greedily devouring the splashes on the wall.

The Wastelander turns back and moves forward again as the flames rise up and flicker in its dark, blood shot eyes and then it howls in pain as the flames on the floor spread igniting the oil that has splashed on its body.

As the flames begin to curl up its leg it lets out a deep throated scream and lunges forward again as I struggle to get out of its way, grabbing my left ankle as it stumbles against the wall. I kick out as hard as I can as the flames begin to encase its upper body and this time it lets go as its head is engulfed and the corridor begins to fill with smoke and flame, the creature's skin crackling under the intensity of the fire.

As I push back with my feet I see River trying to get up but at the way he rolls onto his side I can see that he's more injured than I thought and I struggle over to him as the flames get more intense.

I manage to drag him a few metres away before we both collapse into the dirt but even then he's struggling to get back on his feet.

"We've got to go that way." He nods in the direction of the Wastelander as it slams off the side of the corridor, arms waving frantically as the fire fully takes hold,

"We've got to get to her!"

"You hurt?" I point to his side and then wipe the blood from my forehead before it trickles into my eyes. He turns and looks at his shoulder before wincing as his hand explores the gash in his side.

He looks up at me and smiles, nodding in the direction of the creature.

"Not as bad as him!" And then it's my turn and I examine myself for injuries, but it's mostly cuts and bruises except for the lump on the side of my head and face that screams when I touch it.

A noise alerts my attention and I turn and watch as the beast's limbs twitch in the flames. The corridor is hot, smoky and the smell of burnt rotten flesh is so thick that although I'm gasping for air it's all I can do to force small breaths into my lungs.

Pushing away from the wall I look back at River still examining his wounds and I can see that he's badly injured. As we step to the left of the creature, more smouldering now than alight, I place the crook of my elbow over my mouth and try no to gag at the overpowering stench of charred flesh. It's lying on its front but the head is twisted onto the side, its face fixed in a rictus grin as the flesh has burnt almost entirely away from the cheek, exposing the full extent of the razor sharp teeth.

"They didn't teach us that at the compound!"

I try to smile but can't help for fear of what's round the next corner, for what's lying in wait for us.

We push on to the end of the corridor and I begin to turn over in my mind what just happened. It's obvious now that the Wastelanders have gotten inside the Wall, actually inside the tunnels and have taken the Guards by surprise. I guess I shouldn't be that amazed given that I first encountered them in the water tunnels and that was much further inside the city limits.

How many of them have gotten in? Why are the Guards so under prepared? That's the thing that keeps whirring away at the back of my mind. That's the thing bugging me, they've just left us, they've gone! All this preparation for the damn festival and they've left us alone in our cells. Gone. I don't understand it! I don't get it!

The Festival

I picture the crowds as we marched all that way to the Wall, the jugglers, the carnival atmosphere. If this is happening down here, then what the hell is going on outside? Have they gotten that far? It's reasonable to assume that if they're here then they've got to other places as well. Maybe that's it! Maybe that's why they're not here? Maybe the Guards have been rushing out to help defend the Citizens?

The thought sits well and I feel a little calmer. Of course they'd leave a bunch of prisoners to fend for themselves if the people of Sanctum were in jeopardy! That's exactly what I would expect them to do.

"Which way?"

River's voice disturbs my thoughts and I look ahead to see three tunnels and for a moment I have no idea which one we need until my arm rises instinctively and begins pointing at the one to our left.

The tunnel that most of the screams are coming from.

Chapter 41

Silence descends as we jog to the end of the corridor. Smoke is still in the air but it has thinned out and I sense that we are nearer the cages now because the ground has started to rise.

"We're close! The cages should be up ahead soon." I wipe my face and look at my hand which is a mixture of blood and dirt and then I see the red tunic half way up my arm and an anger wells up, an anger that makes me tear at the thing until I pull it completely off and throw it against the far side of the corridor. "If I'm going out, I'm going out as myself not one of those damn Guards!"

River looks me up and down and I realise I must look an absolute state in just a pair of torn shorts and sandals. He grimaces a smile and I look with concern at the blood stain on his side that has grown since I last saw it.

"Let me have a look at that!" River looks at the way ahead to the end of the tunnel and I can tell what he's thinking. "Listen! You're gonna be no damn good to her if you bleed to death now are you?" Reluctantly he agrees and lifts his arm with a wince and then the shirt that is soaking with blood and I can see three clear gashes running along his side, curling round to his back, like the ones I got in the water tunnels.

"I think I opened them up a little more when I pushed him off me!"

"No kidding! I thought you were gonna take all day!" I try to make light of it and hope that he hasn't heard the concern in my voice because the claws have cut deep in his flesh, far deeper than mine ever were, and there's nothing to stop the flow of blood.

I look around and see the tunic on the floor. "Knew there was a reason I'd been wearing the damn thing!" I pick it up and look for a tear that I can hook my fingers into and then begin to rip it into a strip.

"Lift you're arm for me!"

"Yes nurse!" River smiles but I can see from the colour of his skin that he's not doing good. And the blood that's beginning to collect around his feet.

My hands move as gently as they know how and I wrap the strip around his torso so that the gashes are covered. "This bit's gonna hurt I'm afraid." He nods and I pull both ends as tight as I can, his wincing telling me not to go any further and then I tie them together. It's not much but I hope that it stops most of the blood flow until we can get to safety.

Safety

The word seems an alien concept down here but I hold my tongue and move on until we reach the end of the corridor. When I turn the corner and stop dead in my tracks, my stomach twists in on itself as acid bile rises up my throat and into my mouth.

"What is it? Is it Rainbow, can you see her?" River pushes past me and then slumps against the wall. "Oh no! Oh dear God no!"

Up ahead, at the far end about fifty yards away there's a large door open and if I'm right then it's the one the victors from the first fight disappeared into with the cart full of the injured. I chose the right tunnel because it means that the cages are also that way.

We're almost there but that's not what we're both looking at, in fact I'm not even sure that River's looked that far ahead because his eyes are ranging over the scene in front, scanning the floor.

Looking at all the bodies.

"Help me turn them over, help me for God's sake!" River darts forward and begins to roll the nearest body into its side, then another, and another until he slumps to his knees, chest heaving up and down.

It's like nothing I've ever seen before. Bodies littering the floor. Limbs scattered. Blood streaking the walls. I know the damage one Wastelander can do but it isn't this much.

I start to help and we slowly make our way towards the doorway, heaving bodies over, trying to work out whether she's amongst them until, exhausted, I slump against the wall, blood covering my hands and arms to the elbow. I've got no energy left but River keeps going, frantically moving from one to the other. Wiping hair out of the faces, some of which look as if they've been half eaten.

"I can't see her anywhere! I can't see her!"

I push myself off the wall and look to my right, to the two other bodies that I haven't checked. One has fallen over the other or been thrown and I push against the top one until it rolls over and onto the floor.

"Oh no!" I fall back onto my hands and River turns to look this way.

"What! What is it?" The panic in his voices rises and I shake my head, gasping for breath.

"It's not her! It's not Rainbow!" My head still shaking I turn to look again at the girl who shared the cage with me. The one who spoke so forcibly in support of Our Leader and his plans, hair swinging in front of her face.

Moving over to her side I wipe the hair from her forehead. Her face hasn't a mark on it and I think for all the world she could be sleeping, ready at any moment to wake up. But then I look down her body, at the left arm that's missing, at the hole in her side and I pray to God that she went quickly without any pain.

"I can't see her in here!" I look up at River, at the blood covering his front, at the wild expression in his eye and I barely recognise him from the training compound. Laying the girl's body down as gently as I can I look around and hold out my arms, anger and sorrow fighting for supremacy.

"H…how has this happened?" I look up at River again, at the dazed expression on his face, at the far away look in his eyes. "What have they done to us?"

It's only when he steps over the body in front of us and heads towards the large doorway that I realise that I don't know who I mean by *they*.

River hesitates for a moment at the doorway and I wipe the blood from my hands as best I can on my shorts and walk towards him. I don't want to say it but I can't see how she could have survived any of this and I try not to picture the Wastelanders breaking through here, people screaming, scattering in all directions as the creatures pour through the door devouring everything in their way.

"You should turn around? I, I don't want you to…" His voice is flat and monotone and as I place a hand on his shoulder I feel cold clammy skin, shaking and sweaty.

I open my mouth to say something, anything.

But nothing comes out.

Chapter 42

The night sky seems dark and foreboding as we step out into the Wasteland and the first thing I notice is the lack of noise. What earlier had been a cauldron of shouting, screaming and dazzling light shows as the crowd bayed for action and blood has now been reduced to muffled noise far off in the distance.

Looking to the left, towards the cages, I see that on the first one at least, the wooden planks have been smashed open on the side facing the arena, although from this distance I have no way of knowing if it was people trying to get out or the Wastelander's trying to get in.

River rushes off towards it and I follow but at a slightly slower pace, scanning the area, checking for signs of life. The bodies are scattered all over, the moon's light making the pools of blood appear almost black and I wonder how it went down. How the balance was tipped in *their* favour.

Maybe some Wastelanders were already in the tunnels?

The thought makes sense and I remind myself of the two I saw underground in the water. If the creatures have been somehow planning this, if they've been digging for a long time then it's perfectly possible that those people ran into the corridor to escape whatever was happening out here only to then confront more of the same inside. It's obvious they're a damn sight cleverer than anyone's given them credit for. Maybe they've played us at our own game?

My mind fills with images of panic on people's faces as they are attacked from both sides. The last moments, knowing that they're trapped and there's no way out.

"Over there, look!"

"Huh!" I try to shake my head clear but it's becoming more difficult and I look towards River who's stopped short of the cages and is pointing towards something. Squinting into the gloomy distance, the moonlight obscured by passing clouds I can hear something and the sound sends shivers down my spine. It's movement. Someone or thing is out there.

Looking again into the darkness of the Wasteland, my eyes begin to adjust. My hand instinctively goes to my side where the baton used to be but it's not there and I mutter a curse under my breath and begin to inch slowly back towards River.

I can see that he's still standing stock still, staring into the surrounding darkness as the shuffling increases and then I begin to see a figure moving about twenty yards away and my instinct is to back right off because I can feel such fatigue in my limbs, in the very core of my body that I don't think I've got it in me to fight again.

"I think it's human!" I turn to River and then back again at the figure. "Hey! You okay?" He steps forward as the clouds part and the light from the moon makes things a little clearer.

The figure is staggering towards us, one arm outstretched. Beyond, in the distance I can see the mist rolling and gathering and I think I catch a glimpse of something moving within it but with the lack of light I can't be sure.

The figure stumbles closer and as the clouds clear away, it emerges into the moon light and I see for the first time what he is wearing.

As River takes a step towards the figure his legs give way, collapsing to the ground, and although the robe is tattered and stained, there's no mistaking the colour.

It's bright yellow.

Just like the Senator's.

"P…lease help me. I can't see! I can't see!"

"Hey, hey! Take it easy, take it easy!" River kneels by his side and lifts his head up and I can immediately see gash marks across his eyes and the bridge of his nose, the tell-tale sign of a Wastelander's claw. I scan near about; look back at the mist, at the shadows moving within it. "Are there any more of us?" River looks up at the mist and then back down at the bloodied face, "Out there?"

"I…I don't know what happened…" The Senator tries to sit up, straining to stay on his elbows before collapsing back down into the dirt. River grabs him by the shoulders and he turns his face upwards, bubbles of blood appearing at the corners of his mouth, breath laboured as if something, deep down in his chest has snapped and is rattling around.

"Did you come from the mist? Were you with anyone else?"

"Why did they attack us? They weren't supposed to!"

River shakes him hard. "Is my sister out there?"

"I...I..."

I place a hand on his shoulder. "Hey, take it easy! Look at him for God's sake! We've gotta get him away from here." I look back at where we came from when a muffled scream sounds from the direction of the mist.

"RAINBOW! RAINBOW! CAN YOU HEAR ME?"

"There are others...I don't know what's happened to them..." and then River stands and I know what he's about to do because I can tell from the look in his eye. It's the same look I saw when he bested the big guard at the compound, when he rushed the Wastelander earlier in the tunnel.

"Get him safe and then follow!" And then he runs towards the mist, towards the direction of the noise and I take a step to follow and then look round at the pitiful sight on the floor.

"Please, please help me!" The senator stretches out a hand and I turn from him to River and back again. What do I do? What do I do?

"Take my hand, I'm gonna get you inside, sir." I grab his wrists and then loop my arms under his linking my hands together around his back.

As I go to lift he screams in pain and coughs up blood, the rattling in his chest sounding worse than ever. I look over my shoulder at River as he disappears into the mist.

"I'm sorry if this hurts but I've gotta move you, NOW!" I haul him into a standing position with all my remaining strength and for a moment we stand there under the moonlight embracing before I'm able to get my shoulder under his rib cage. I try to ignore the screaming as I half walk, half run to the open door we came through but every step I take I imagine River taking two more into the mist. If I don't put him down soon I'm never going to find him again. I'm never going to find Rainbow.

I need to put him down. Now.

Turning to my left, the Senator's screams now nothing more than a low, constant groaning I see the splintered opening of a cage about twenty paces away. I try to keep my voice even and hope that he doesn't detect the fear.

"I'm going to place you down here, you'll be safe until I come back. I need to find the others and bring them to you." I grunt and lift him off my shoulder trying to be as gentle as I possibly can, trying to block out the images of River being mauled by the creatures, calling out confused as to why I'm not by his side.

As gently as I'm able I lie him in the corner of the cage where there's still enough of the wooden side to cover him from sight. The blood now flows freely from his mouth and the gash where his eyes should be and for a moment I'm unable to tear myself away from this pitiful sight, that only hours earlier was commanding a great audience, dazzling everyone with words.

MOVE!

One last look and then I'm heading for the edge of the cage as the old man breaks out into another fit of coughing. I'm know he's trying to say something but I've got to get back to River.

"They were never meant to do this." I stop at the splintered wood that now serves as the side wall as the sentence breaks off into a series of chest rattling coughs. Something catches my attention.

They

My head turns towards the mist and then back at the Senator. He raises his arm in my direction and then it falls into his lap.

"We, we thought we could control them."

What the hell is he saying? I move back over to where he lies, my chest tightening, and his head moves a little in response to my feet over the broken wood, his hand raised, flapping in the air as if beckoning me over. Kneeling next to him his hand gropes for my arm and I'm surprised by the strength he still has as he pulls me closer.

"What do you...I don't know what you're trying to say?" I can smell the stench of the Wastelanders on him as he raises his head.

"We thought we could control them! We thought they would do as we commanded," He gasps for air and I feel his hand tighten around my wrist. He's not a great Senator of Sanctum anymore, he's an old dying man, blinded, raving, and not wanting to be alone. "What else could Our Leader do? There are too many of us to feed, too little water for all the mouths, too many babies. Sanctum is dying!"

He turns to the left and spits into the dust and my mind starts making connections that I don't want it to.

Suddenly all thoughts of the mist, of River and Rainbow evaporate as the old man's dying words take on the tone of a confession, his voice even and calm like someone trying to gain absolution for their sins before the sight of God.

"More and more babies, more and more mouths to feed. More people and problems. We thought we could make it like it was, make it like it had been in the beginning! But we couldn't do it without *them*. It wouldn't have worked!"

His voice falls to no more than a whisper and I feel his grip loosen on my wrist. The life is draining away from him but I need to know what he's saying, it's like I need to hear him say the word.

He arches his back and coughs up more blood and I feel an overwhelming sense of helplessness as I kneel there in the dirt and dust, reality weighing heavy all around.

"What did you do, Senator? I hold his head as his fit passes and his body falls quiet. His looks paler than before as if the life force is leaving him. I know he hasn't got long but I need to know everything. I want to know if what I'm thinking is right.

Ignoring the voice in my head I hold his shoulder tight, bringing him up so his lips are almost touching my ear.

"I can't hear you Senator! I can't hear what you are trying to say!" His chest rattles again as he draws in a long breath and then I feel a hand on my arm as he turns his torn, bloodied face towards mine.

"We've been planning it for years, a glorious new beginning, but now they're the ones collecting *us*. God help us for what we've done. God help us."

For the moment nothing else exists, not the arena, not the danger all around us. It's just me and him, entwined in the dirt, struggling to communicate. I place my lips by his earlobe as he falls quiet again.

"What did you do Senator? What did you do?" As he exhales, his chest sinking in my arms, I see his lips move and bend my head as close as I can.

"We thought we could control them, we thought we could start again. If we got everyone together at the same time…easier to reduce the surpl…" Blood oozes from his mouth and nose as he falls into a series of convulsions. He exhales one last time and then, nothing.

For the longest moment I sit there, his body almost weightless against mine and stare at the shattered wooden walls of the cage that lie all around.

"Reduce the surplus"

The words roll around my head and I have to close my eyes tight shut to stop images from the last days spinning out of control. I have so many questions to ask, so many things that need answering.

"...everyone together at the same time..."

Does he mean the Festival? Was there another purpose to this all along?

Shaking my head clear I lie the Senator's body down in the dust and stand over his fragile corpse. And then I turn and walk amongst the ruins, not knowing which way to go, my legs weary, my soul sad. Muffled cries in the distance bring me back to reality.

I take a last look back at the Senator, at how in death even his yellow robes, the colour of authority, seem dimmed and lifeless and then my legs move before I have time to think.

"River, I'm coming. Hold on!"

Chapter 43

It's all been a lie. The whole thing. The whole damn Festival. I want to shout it at the top of my lungs. I want to tear down the great Wall with my bare hands but as I step out of the cage I'm amazed to see how close the mist has got, as if it's crept up unheard, silent, while I've been turning over the words of the Senator.

It's no more than thirty yards away and I hesitate before plunging in because every atom of my body is screaming at me, telling me not to, warning me against going anywhere near it.

But I've got to focus on River and Rainbow. I've got to get them out.

Even as I stand there I can feel tentacles of mist whipping around my ankles, trying to drag me in and although my body instinctively recoils at the sight and touch, there's nothing I can do because it's moving inexorably forward and there's no where else for me to go.

One step.

Another.

Then I'm in.

I look around at where I think I just came from but all I can see is a murky grey wall as the moonlight tries but fails to penetrate the gloom. As if the whole world has simply been wiped from existence into nothing. A noise behind me makes me spin around and I resist the urge to shout out.

Instinctively I crouch low to the ground and try to listen before raising my voice as loudly as I dare.

"River! Hey River!" There's something out there, shapes in the distance but they could be anything.

And then the smell comes. That rotting, fetid smell of wasting flesh that tells me they're close, I know they can sense me. My heart thumps in my chest and I try to swallow but I've no saliva left.

I move along the ground on all fours as if in a sprint position, but the smell is overwhelming, noise drifting in and out, screams rising and then falling silent and then my hand hits something slimy and cold and instantly recoils from whatever it has found. The smell makes me gag and I turn my head and wretch bile onto the floor behind me.

The thickness of the mist seems somehow less when I turn my head back and I can make out a body lying on the floor but even with my sight impaired in this way I can tell that it's not all there or at least that some of it is missing like the ones in the corridor. Taking a deep breath, I crawl towards it hoping that it's not River or Rainbow.

The right foot is missing, strands of skin and flesh replacing the bone that should be connected to the knee and as I look up towards the thigh I begin to make out the tell-tale grey flesh of the Wastelander and heave a sigh of relief. I quickly move on to the torso that has criss cross pattern of wounds with one large hole in the side, intestines spilt into a still steaming pile onto the floor.

Holding my nose, trying not to gag again I move round to the far side of the corpse.

Crouch.

The command is instinctive and I do exactly as my brain tells me, my body obeying before my mind has had a chance to question anything. I look up to see a shape move in the mist and then disappear and I try to squint to get a better look, to get a sense of what's out there.

As I move around the side of the dead creature I slip on something warm and my shoulder lands in a wet pile of entrails but the shape looms into view again and my hands fly up to my ears as I hear the scream and clicking of the Wastelander. This one's very much alive.

Panic begins to take hold as I slip and slide back against the fallen body as if trying to make myself one with the corpse. I don't take my eyes off the shadow, instead I follow the shape as it moves in and out of my eye line, clicking and mewing, jerky movements superimposed by the moon's light onto the mist like some twisted puppet show.

What is it doing? Why can't it smell me?

Moving back even further, pushing myself against the dead beast, my hands slip in the blood and mucus and I try not to throw up as the outline of the Wastelander disappears and then hones into view again.

Why the hell can't it smell me?

Sweat trickles from my hairline and I wipe my face, the stench from the mucus unbearable and then I look down at the rest of my body, at the slime that has smeared across my arms, at the blood from the corpse that clings to me.

Of course! All it can smell is its own! All it can smell is the Wastelander!

I wait until the creature slips back into the thicker mist before I take a deep breath and plunge my hands further into the side of the corpse beneath me. If that's all it can smell then maybe I can somehow disguise myself from the rest. Before I can stop myself I gag as I spread the mucus over my head and face, trying hard not to make too much noise, continuing the process until I'm covered, head to foot.

The creature hasn't returned, at least I can't see it, but that could be because the mist has become even thicker than before and I hesitate before taking a few tentative steps away from the safety of the corpse.

After a few moments I hear a cry come from somewhere and turn my head in the direction I think it came. It could have been River but I can't be sure as every sound is distorted out here and I daren't raise my voice in response for fear of alerting the Wastelander to my presence. Whatever advantage I've won for myself, *if* it's any advantage at all, will rapidly fall away if they hear me and get a pinpoint on my location.

The scream sounds again but I'm sure there are other noises behind it, other voices and I try to listen, try to work out of I can recognise any. I inch forward on my hands and knees trying not to breathe too hard for although the stench that is now on me is not as bad as it first was, I still can't control the gagging, the instant reaction within my body to try and wretch.

Inching forward again the mucus begins to drip into my eyes and I'm momentarily blinded as I wipe my face with my forearm.

The scream again.

This time I can definitely tell that it's more than one voice and it's in the same direction as before so I move on hands and feet in its direction. Heart pounding against my ribs.

"Don't move!" I freeze as a new voice whispers from my left and I whip my head around but can't see anything for the swirling mist. "It mimics our voice. They can sound like us."

The mist moves and thins a little and I see the outline of a body crouched on the floor.

"Is that you, River? Is that you?"

"They sound like us, luring us to our death."

I see the figure's face for the first time but don't recognise him at all, apart from the wild look in his eyes, the look of someone who has all but given up; I've seen it before enough times in the Lanes, and then a hand shoots out and grabs my wrist and I'm surprised by the strength in the skinny forearm. "Help me please. Help me!"

Instinctively I try and back off from the man but he won't let go and I look past him, down his torso, to where his legs should be, but I can only see one and then I start to panic because if they can mimic us to try and trick us into a trap then why can't they use *us* as the bait.

What if they've left this guy injured for that reason, to lure more of us in?

I try pulling again but his hand holds firm.

"Don't leave me! Please don't leave me!" Spit foams in the corners of his mouth and then I see them, in the distance more figures gathering, the clicking sound of Wastelanders moving in for a feast. Just as they planned.

Mouthing the word sorry over and over, I lie on my back with my foot high up on his shoulder and pull with all my might.

My eyes fill with tears but this time they have nothing to do with the stench of the Wastelander and as I feel his grip loosen and sobbing begin to flow from somewhere way down in his chest as he slips from my grasp and the creatures dive on his body.

One of them diverts from the group and I see it raise its face towards the moon and sniff the air, trying to find me, trying to seek me out. I can see its eyes shining, confusion on its grotesque features as I hold my breath hoping the stench on me will be enough to disguise my scent.

As the feeding frenzy continues all around me I wonder if I'm ever going to get out of here alive.

I wonder if my mind will ever let me.

Chapter 44

I don't know how long I've been inside the mist but as I crawl on my belly I begin to wonder what effect it is having on me, being out here for a prolonged period of time.

Out here beyond the Wall, the fallout from the Great Light, the radiation that we've grown up fearing. The very thing that has created the Wastelanders.

I feel my throat begin to tighten as if the very molecules in the air are beginning to fight me. Taking a deep breath I try to calm down but my head fills with images of the ripped and flaking skin of the Wastelanders, of their twisted and curved spines and elongated claws. They were human once. Is it beginning to happen to me? Am I beginning to change too?

The moon is shining brightly high in the sky, casting shadows onto the rolling mist but I think I'm beginning to understand a little of how the Wastelanders move and think.

The trap they set earlier, the mimicking of the voice tells me that they are far from the mindless animals that we've been told. It tells me that they can work together, that they are not just working on instinct, scavenging for food, killing their own if the need arises. I think back to the creature we were shown at the compound, the fearsome teeth and claws, the skin seemingly stretched to burst over the sinewy deformed muscle, eyes that suggested more than simply blind hate.

If they can think, if they can organise, then they can feel as well; pain, suffering, sadness. Compassion? My mind reminds me of moments earlier and I hear the man's screams as they leapt upon him, ripping and tearing. Maybe. Maybe.

My body moves and my mind follows as I begin to crawl forward again hoping that the friction against the ground won't rub off too much of their blood because now it's beginning to harden onto my skin and clothes I wonder if its potency is going as well.

The thought seems absurd because if the breeze switches and I catch a whiff of my own stench I immediately fight the urge to wretch but I can't help but wonder if it needs to be fresh blood, fresh mucus for them to be tricked as they were before.

I need to take my mind off things I can't control so I begin to imagine the arena that I saw from the cracks in the wooden cell wall before the night came and the mist took over; the other cells spaced out along the line of the Wall, the flat, barren wasteland stretching out to the horizon. I play images over in my head, carrying the Senator to the cage, laying him down, his words echoing in my mind.

"God help us for what we've done. We thought we could control them!"

His broken body twisted, like a rag dolls. I picture him emerging from under the ground like a yellow sun, his robes billowing about him, the roar of the crowd as his very presence seemed to dazzle us all. But there's something else nagging away at the back of my mind, some other word or image that I haven't yet recalled and frustration begins to cloud my mind as I crawls slowly through the dirt and dust. What am I looking for? What is it?

"Now they're the ones collecting us!"

The senator's voice calls at me from the back of my mind and I play the words over and over, picturing the bubbles of blood gurgling from deep down, somewhere in his broken chest.

"...collecting us..."

Slowing down I turn my head to listen to the sounds all around but there are none; no screaming, no clicking, no calling out in the darkness and gloom. I realise that there hasn't been any for a while now, not since they fed on their own trap. Where have the others gone? I turn my head from left to right as the mist undulates and wafts around me, at once obscuring my vision and then seeming to retreat, opening up ten or twenty yards all around.

I must be at least seventy yards out from the Wall by now and as the mist lifts a little I see dark pools in the dirt, pools that I take to be blood. I crawl over to the first and catch the stench of the creatures in my nostrils, from the moonlight I can see the ground all around has been churned up, great lines gouged in the soil, leading off into the distance.

Squinting again I look into the gloom, following the patches of blood and gouges until my eyes fall upon a larger dark patch about thirty yards away. As I move a little closer, all the while listening out for any other noise, I begin to see the edges of the larger hole, it looks square and for a moment I'm confused. And then the mist moves in again and I'm swallowed up by its cold embrace.

My mind replays what I've just seen, the gouges in the soil, the blood, and the square hole in the ground. The mist thins a little to my left and I look down to the ground, to the gouges that run alongside my body. There are five of them running parallel to one another, about an inch apart and I don't want to finish the connections I'm making but it's too late to stop my brain.

"...they're collecting us..."

I fall back onto my elbows gasping for air, but it's not because of the stench. It's because of what my mind's telling me.

It's telling me that the gouges in the earth are from fingers and that they're leading to the trap door the senator came up from earlier.

They've been dragging bodies this way.

Taking them down below the ground.

Collecting.

Chapter 45

No sound.

Keep low.

Move.

Shifting up onto my feet I keep as low as possible and head towards the large square hole. The mist has obscured everything down to no more than a few inches so I keep its direction in my mind's eye and follow the gouges and pools of blood on the floor.

The silence is somehow worse than before because it makes me feel like there's another trap being set for me, that any moment a light is going to shine or the mist is going to drift away revealing a pack of slathering Wastelanders honing in on my position.

To my ears each step I take sounds like an earthquake and I try to reduce my body movements down to the bare minimum, my chest hardly rising and falling at all as I move closer to where I think the hole is.

The only logical conclusion I can come to is that they're rounding up some of us for food storage, that there are more tunnels beneath my feet, and I hold onto the hope that River and Rainbow are captive somewhere beneath me. Much easier to keep us alive if they need to transport us somewhere else.

As I move forward I start to take longer strides, still careful to follow the direction of the gouges but the mist is disorienting and it's not long before I start to mistrust the way I'm going. What if I've wondered off the route and am walking further out into the Wasteland? What if they're not even down there at all?

The mist shifts a little and I see a larger dark pool to my left about ten yards away. Is that it? Is that the hole? Instinctively crouching, I listen out for any noise and think I can hear muffled noises from far off somewhere in the distance. It could be coming from below the ground if whatever trap door the Senator used was still open, and if it is then how far down does it go and how the hell am I going to get down there?

Shuffling forward I step into the pools of blood that seem more frequent as I near the hole. Sliding my fingers across the ground until they meet with the edge of the hole I can tell even before looking any further that it's man made. The edge is smooth and straight and as I look back to the dirt beneath me I can see that the gouges stop at the top, the tell tale darkness of blood all around the edge.

I don't know whether the smell is me or the creatures but as I move around the edge with my fingers, a breeze lifts the hair from my face and I put my hand over my mouth and nose until it passes.

The drifting mist gives the hole in front of me a dream like quality, shimmering before my eyes and I imagine myself to be looking into a dark pool of water, nervous about taking my first plunge. I choke back the image of a creature reaching up from the gloom and dragging me down into the abyss and stretch out onto my stomach until I'm flat against the cold earth.

Sliding my fingers over the edge I wait a moment and then let my arms drop over the side until for a horrible moment they are dangling in mid air and I picture the snapping jaws, the pointed teeth inches from where my fingers currently dangle. Shifting my body closer until my chin is almost over the side I manage to straighten my arms so that they are now hanging straight down and I can touch what I take to be the wall or sides of the hole.

It seems that whatever trap door or mechanism the Senator and the other fighters appeared from has remained at the bottom of the hole and spreading my arms out and running my hands across the bumpy surface confirms the sides as they stretch out beneath me.

Pulling my arms out I roll onto my back and contemplate my next move. I can hear almost continuous muffled noises and despite the tricks the mist plays with sound I'm pretty confident that they're coming from below but I can't make out what they are; whether they're Wastelander or human and how far away from me they are.

What good is it to drop down into the hole only to find myself plunging head first into a nest of the damn things? What good is it to River, to Rainbow, for that matter Doughnut and Ellie if I break my leg?

I need to think clearly, to take account of what I've learnt about them before I make my next move.

I have to assume that they are intelligent, or at least they have an idea about what they are doing. I've seen it with my own eyes after all. If I assume that I'm right and they've taken survivors of the initial massacre down below ground then it would make sense to have some kind of guard with them.

I need to stay in the here and now. I need to find a way down *there*.

Rolling onto my back I look up at the moon that still shines brilliantly in the sky almost directly above me and for a moment everything is peaceful, more peaceful than I can remember for I don't know how long. I can see some stars winking at me as the mist flows over and around and I let out a long breath.

Turning onto my front I look back over the hole. As I stare into the gloom I begin to see what I'm looking for and I look back up at the moon, to the mist that is beginning to move away again and then back down and this time I'm sure I can make out the platform that the Senator must have risen up on. I move as close to the edge as I dare and I pray that the mist holds off long enough for me to get a proper look.

Running my hands along the sides of the walls again like before, this time I know what I'm feeling; every foot or so is some kind of groove that seems to run straight down and I guess they're for the platform, like runners so it can move up and down easily.

As my eyes continue to adjust I can see that the platform is about twenty feet or more away and I can only really see half of it because from up here it looks like it's tilted. Maybe in all the mayhem it got stuck somehow, or the cables it runs on snapped, who knows? All I know is that it's my only chance of a way down and I've got to move fast before those creatures decide they've have enough for one day and start to return.

Standing up I walk around the hole aware that I've already spent too much time thinking and deliberating before hitching my legs over the hole facing away from it until my stomach is flat against the edge although most of my weight is still on my forearms.

I figure that the sides of the hole are rough enough to give me a few hand and foot holds until I'm near enough to jump although as I begin to lower myself until all of my weight is on my hands and I'm now flat against the inner wall, the confidence of earlier gives way to an all consuming fear.

As I dangle in mid air all I can think of is the snapping jaws of the creatures as they wait for me to lower myself into their trap. My legs begin to scrabble against the wall as my arms shake, tension making my forearms feel like lead. Why the hell did I decide to do this? What on earth was I thinking?

Rainbow

My mind pictures her laughing in the hall when we were together in the compound and I force my legs to slow down until I can feel the wall with my feet as they search for a hold or a small ledge to rest on. My right foot manages to catch onto a stone or rock that's sticking out of the side and it takes a little of the pressure off my arms but my other leg is still dangling in the air making me lopsided, throwing most of my weight onto my left arm.

With no vision to help it's up to my hands and feet to do the looking for me and I shuffle my left foot up until my knee is bent and I manage to wedge it into one of the runners for the trap door. It's awkward because the runner can't be any more than an inch wide and I have to turn my foot almost on its side to jam it in but it gives me vital seconds to rest my left arm which is throbbing with the effort.

I can feel the strength from my body beginning to wane as I try to find a place for my free hand, the pain in my arm almost unbearable.

And then I slip.

The fall is longer than I anticipated but I know that time slows in these situations and I turn my body so that the angle of the floor means my feet and ankles won't take the brunt of the impact.

My feet hit first and I feel a jarring pain shoot up into my hips. With all my strength I turn to my right so my shoulder is the next point of impact, not my back and I land with a *whooomph* as the air is forced out of my lungs. The floor wobbles beneath the impact and I begin to slide down towards the lower end still scrabbling to get onto my back, trying to use my heels as brakes.

I haven't had time yet to assess the impact on my body as I try to scramble back up the floor but the angle is too great and I continue moving towards the gloom at the end, only coming to rest when my feet hit the opposite wall, my legs and most of my backside in mid air as I strain to hold on to the floor.

For the longest moment I'm stuck in this position, my brain trying to catch up with what just happened. Worried that if I try to move my legs I'll slip into the gloom I try shifting back onto my shoulder but as I move, the pain shoots along my body and I'm scared that I've done something more than just sprain it.

My shoulder screams at me as I struggle to sit up and I start to gingerly explore what I've done to myself hoping that my groping fingers don't find any sticky blood and exposed bone. At the same time I start to rotate the shoulder, slowly and carefully, because even though I can barely see anything down here, as I hold my left hand up to what moon light there still is shining down I can tell that there's no blood which is a massive relief. Fresh blood is like a honing beacon to the creatures and I have no intention of making things any easier for them than they already are.

After a few more seconds I'm happy that it's more of a jarring or a sprain than anything worse and I can just about lift my arm out from my side until my elbow is nearly horizontal and my mind begins to settle on where I am and how the hell I'm going to get any further. I look up and around straining my neck to get as good a look as possible.

It's pretty much as I expected; four walls with a moveable floor stuck at an angle. I already know that there's a gap between the lower end of the floor and the wall because I almost went plummeting off it and I guess that's there because the angle of the floor has created it.

With a sigh I realise that it's my only real hope of a way down but with only one good arm for climbing I already fear my chances have been at least halved.

Shuffling back towards the edge of the floor I stop for a moment as it creaks a little and then continue until I'm as far as I want to go. My arms aren't long enough to let me lean over the drop and see what's down there so I turn onto my stomach, wincing as my shoulder protests and turn myself around so my chin now rests pretty much on the edge. The floor continues to creak and sway a little but with no other choice I ignore it and inch myself over until my head is exposed and looking down into the gloom.

To my great relief the drop is not as far as I feared.

Doughnut would give his right arm for this opportunity! The thought comes from nowhere and is so powerful that for a moment I expect to see him emerge from the corridor goading me on to jump down and in my mind's eye I see him spinning over the edge and landing in that graceless way of his, usual in a cloud of arms and legs but always without a scratch on him.

When the scene has played itself out I know exactly what I need to do and, extending my left arm over the edge I begin to grope around on the underside of the floor until I come to a network of piping or tubing that I guess must link to some kind of hydraulics system.

Shuffling forward again until the edge is now just above my belly button, I curl my head and neck in towards the edge and roll off the side. The piping starts to creak and moan but I know what I'm doing and as I grip onto it I unfold my legs and begin to swing backwards before letting go and landing on my feet with my good arm as support on the floor out in front.

My right shoulder continues to send pain out to all parts of my body but I'm too pleased with myself to worry about it. I can't believe I've actually made it down here, out of that damn mist.

But the feeling is short lived as I approach the door in front of me. At first it doesn't want to budge and fear whispers in my ear telling me I'm going to die down here. Telling me that I've come to then end of the road. I try my best to ignore it and press again with my shoulder resting all my weight on the door as it begins to shift a little, a crack of light shining onto the floor, much brighter than the oil lamps I'm used to.

My heart feels like a hammer against my chest but what choice do I have? Where else can I go?

Shielding my eyes against the bright light I push the door open again and step into the unknown.

Chapter 46

The door leads into a brightly lit corridor and as I inch my way in, my eyes struggling to adjust to the light, I'm immediately struck by how different everything seems, how new. Beneath the Wall the tunnels were crudely dug with wooden slats to hold up the earth and burning oil lamps to light the way. They were claustrophobic and humid.

They were totally different to the one I'm now in. Reaching out with my hand I touch the smooth white walls and although there is only a glow in the distance, it is magnified by the surface. The only other place I've ever seen like this is the Peoples' Court. I can't even really work out what material it is because all I'm used to is whatever I can scavenge. It's like I've entered another world, another reality.

What else has Our Leader been keeping from us? What else don't we know?

I picture where I am in relation to the Wall. It must be at least fifty or sixty yards away by now, maybe even more and I think back to how amazed we all were in the cell when the Senator emerged from the ground, how amazed the crowd was, the roar almost hurt it was so deafening, but *this* I can't explain at all. This is something different, and it's got me even more frightened than before.

My heart begins to race as I keep close to the wall and follow the corridor. It's not long before I come across tell tale smears of blood and mucus on the white walls and floor reminding me where I am and what has been happening, what *is* happening all about me. The streaks of red stand out as if shouting at me to stop, to turn around and go back, but I know that's not an option.

"Collecting us!"

Rainbow and River are somewhere down here. I know I'm right.

I've got to be.

As I move on through the corridor light seems to ripple from bulbs above my head, a bluish light that blinks on and off before dying away into the distance and then coming back again towards me as if something's broken, a connection that's loose. The effect is eerie, like I'm getting only snapshots of the corridor before it plunges into darkness and all I'm left with is the imprint in my mind's eye.

A noise up ahead startles me and I stop still realising that I'm completely out in the open, completely exposed to any attack coming from either the front or behind. I hear the noise again but I can't work out what it is.

There's more blood up ahead on the right hand wall and as I reach it I see that there are chunks of flesh as well but I'm no longer sure whether it's human or Wastelander and I picture what must have happened in this corridor; people running for their lives as the creatures leap and bound after them, forcing them towards the trap door. Maybe some got on the platform and it started to rise only for the creatures to drag it down, to break its mechanism.

But what *is* this place? Where the hell am I?

That noise again, but this time it's louder, somehow more urgent but the question remains; if that was the platform the Senator and fighters rose up on, then this place must be linked to the tunnels under the Wall! What must those fighters have thought when they entered this place; the moving lights that shine from nowhere, the gargled noises far off in the distance? They must have thought they were entering into some sort of dream, or nightmare.

Slipping around the corner I focus on the right hand corridor and immediately see that it's longer and straighter, the ceiling a little higher than before with what looks like a series of doors ahead of me.

As I move a few paces my foot crunches on glass that is scattered across the floor and as the light follows on from where I'm standing I'm suddenly plunged in to darkness again as it moves down the corridor lighting a section as it goes, rippling out into the distance. I daren't move for the noise of the glass underfoot giving away where I am but as the light begins its shimmering journey back I don't see any creatures lurking in the shadows.

What I do see in more detail than before are flashes of more broken glass, windows far off cracked, doors flung open, the floor scattered with various objects, and the tell tale dark pools that I know only too well. It looks like a bomb has gone off.

Stepping as carefully as I can over the debris on the floor I move towards the first door on my left.

As the light ripples back to me I try keep the picture of my immediate surroundings in my mind's eye as I'm plunged into darkness again, reaching out for the door that stands slightly open in front of me.

Deep breath.
Deep breath.
Move.

The door moves at the merest of touches before becoming more difficult and I have to put my good shoulder to it to get it open all the way. I wait for the light to return from the corridor and when it does I cast my eyes around, trying to take in as much as possible before it disappears again.

I needn't have bothered because as soon I step fully into the room I see a long tube hanging from the ceiling, flickering and throwing out shards of light as the one in the corridor starts off on its journey again, as if it's broken or has a mind of its own or something, I'm left with a stuttering imprint of the room as I'm again plunged from darkness to light every few seconds. It makes my movements seem jerky and mechanical as I move towards the table to my left.

"Is anyone in here?" I whisper as loudly as I can, trying to control my breathing because a panic attack in here is not going to do anyone any favours. "Is there anyone in here?" No response. Just the flickering of the light giving the whole room a surreal, nightmarish feel. I move my hand over the table as I walk on towards the middle of the room before a sharp pain stops me in my tracks.

I immediately bring my index finger up to my mouth, the sharp metallic taste telling me I'm bleeding from something. Waiting until the light blinks on again I look down at the table and see what on first appearance looks to be a whole series of knives of all shapes and sizes.

The flickering light makes my movements look jerky as if it's not really my arm as I bring the small knife up to eye level. I don't know if it's the one that cut me or not but I've never seen anything like it before. Its handle is a good deal thinner than any hunting knife I've ever felt and it's so light it feels like it could blow away in the breeze, nothing like the heavy wooden handled ones we trained with back at the prison.

But it's the blade itself that's got me more intrigued because it's thin and curved, about six inches in length and I don't need continuous light to know that it's just about the sharpest thing I've ever seen.

I put it back on the table and cast an eye over the other ones; some look thinner, some longer and I can see one at the far end of the table that looks as though it has teeth, like it could cut through wood. And then another image fills my mind, of the knife cutting, but this time it's not through wood.

It's through bone.

Chapter 47

I step back from the table as the image grows in my mind. What if they're for medical use? Is this some kind of hospital? My stomach tightens itself and I stagger back towards the door, the light flickering as I look around the room at the tables that have been tipped over, at the boxes that have been strewn across the floor.

Back out in the corridor I fight the urge to run back to the platform. Wincing as I rotate my right shoulder I remind myself that even if I got back there, I have exactly no chance whatsoever of getting back onto the platform and even if by some utter miracle I managed to drag myself up, what would I do then? I'd be in a worse situation than I am now!

Walking on a little further as the light ripples over head and disappears into the distance. My head is pounding and I wonder if it's more from fear than the lights. Trying the next door on my right the handle doesn't budge and I move on past the long window that has somehow remained intact to another that is hanging off a hinge at the top.

There's more blood here, pooled on the floor and I try to step over it as I lean to the left to get around the door, all the while I can't help but think, with all the blood around and the destruction, where are all the bodies? It's a reasonable question and my mind conjures up the gouge marks, the lines that led me to the trap door in the first place. If they were dragged down here then where are they now?

This time there's no flickering light, just a single strip that comes on at the far end of the room as I enter, bathing the whole place in the same bluish light that gives me just about enough to see where I'm going. The whole room is much larger than the first and seems to be split into almost two halves. On my left is a series of large tubes that look to be about as thick as my arm connecting to a series of chest high platforms or plinths. They remind me of the stone columns in the compound except they stop near enough at my height and I can see that some of them have been broken but can't really tell from this far and in this bad light what they are.

To my right is a large table that seems to have collapsed to one side, as if one of the far legs has been removed or broken off and the whole thing has lurched over but not quite fallen. I move over to get a better look and as my eyes adjust to the continuous light I can also see some lines extending from above the table to the ceiling as if something has been suspended.

"....collecting us…we thought we could control them…"

I turn as if expecting the Senator to be standing at the door, and then move back to the table before my mind can make any more connections. Raising my hand I touch one of the lines and it feels cold, like some kind of thin metal, and I trace my fingers down its length, feeding it through my other hand until I come to the end, until I feel something much heavier and curved into a tight point.

The clanging sound it makes as I drop the line and it hits against the edge of the table reverberates throughout the room and I take a step back, my fingers rubbing together, the feel of the hook still on them.

There was something else as well, something stuck on the end, a strip of something but I don't dare pick it up again, instead I turn and move towards the plinths, towards the weak blue light that shines from the corner, my head spinning with disturbing images of what might have happened here.

I look at the first plinth but it's nothing more than a thin column about waste height with broken glass and some kind of thick liquid dripping off the shards that lie all around. I look at the tubes hanging from it and my stomach tightens.

The glass crunches under foot but at this point I don't care because I'm locked in, I'm too far gone to care about noise anymore. It's as if everything has been leading to this moment, as if nothing else exists except me in this room, amongst these *objects*.

Moving along the line to the second one I can see that it's a cylindrical glass tank that stands on top of the thin stand and as I move closer I can see that it is full of the same kind of liquid but it's a little too cloudy to see if there's anything in there from this distance. The liquid inside looks blue but I guess that's from the light in the corner.

Approaching the tank I'm about six inches from its surface and can see that there's something in there but the liquid is too cloudy for me to get a proper look.

The hook

I shiver at the thought and resist the temptation to turn around and stare at the upturned table, instead concentrating on the jars in front of me. The other two to my right are also smashed so I make for the last one in the line careful not to slip on the fluid that has leaked onto the floor, because I can definitely see the outline of something.

"Oh my God!" I take a step back into the crunching glass and then look back at the table, the lines hanging from the ceiling, the weird knives and other implements in the other room.

"...we thought we could control them...they can mimic us..."

And then I look back at the container.

At the head of the Wastelander that's staring back at me.

My eyes don't move from the head as I walk slowly round the container. It looks more or less like the one I saw at the compound; that is to say a distorted version of us with its protruding jaw and teeth and the patchwork of veins that look like they want to burst out if the near translucent skin. I've never seen one up this close, at least not without fearing for my life!

The sound of the glass under my feet brings me back to something like reality and I look back to the other stands. There are four in all, including the one I'm looking at, two of which have been smashed and whatever was in them taken or moved from here. I walk back to the first one keen to look at its contents but again the thickness of the liquid prevents me from seeing it clearly.

As I move around its base, I begin to see its contents from a different angle, the blue light revealing a little more of its secrets and a roundish shape begins to emerge, dark and indistinct but recognisable. It's another head, of that I'm sure but I can't make out its features clearly enough.

My hand reaches out to the container before I have time to stop it and I nudge the side of it. Nothing moves. I tap again on the glass not really sure of what I'm trying to achieve and, taking a deep breath, begin to step back when my right heel crunches a piece of glass and slips backwards on the fluid all around. I stagger to my right and instinct takes over throwing my hands out towards the container.

But it's too late.

My left hand knocks the side of the glass jar as my leg continues to slide behind me and for a moment time stops as the jar starts to teeter on the plinth beneath it. I scrabble to stop it falling but the fluid is against me and by the time my feet have got purchase enough to enable me to move forward again the jar has toppled almost completely over.

The noise is like some kind of muffled explosion as the jar explodes on impact showering me with glass and who knows what else. For a moment all I can hear is the shattering of glass reverberating around the room. I couldn't have made more noise if I tried; a Wastelander half a mile away would have heard the commotion.

Whatever element of surprise I may have had has now entirely gone and as I brush pieces of glass from my body I look to my feet, at the contents of the jar.

I was right. It was another head. But as I turn it slowly with my foot until I can see its face I realise I was also very wrong.

Fear drives me as I rush past the table, past the hooks, my mind trying to cope with what it's just seen and as I burst out of the room and into the corridor, panic begins to take over as I try to shake the picture from my mind's eye.

The contents of the broken jar.

The human head under my foot.

Chapter 48

I run back along the dim corridor the way I came convinced that at any moment the stench of Wastelander will overcome me and claws will rip at my back before teeth bite down, hard. I'm no longer thinking, I'm just running and as I reach what looks like the turn for the trap door I slow to a halt as the light ripples the other way and I'm left in darkness, cursing myself because in my blind panic I think I've gone the wrong way. I think I've turned left instead of right.

As I stand there in the dark struggling to control my breathing I hear something in the distance but I'm not sure what it is. Turning back, readying myself to sprint as fast as I can because I don't want to find out what it is I rock back on my heels and then I'm stock still like some kind of statue, straining to hear it again.

It sounds like "Help us!" but it's deep, somehow muffled and I think back to the words of the man up above, the trap that was set for me.

"...they can mimic us..."

But I'm already running.

As I pass more doors and corridors the true size of this underground maze begins to dawn on me. What else has Our Leader held from us for I can't believe that any of *this* was allowed to go on without his knowledge at least? But then what *has* been going on? The muffled cry has fallen silent but my mind won't switch off.

How can it with all that I've just seen.

Have they been experimenting on the creatures? I think back to the human head at my feet. Does that mean they've been experimenting on us too?

When I look up I don't even know what direction I've been running in save that it's the opposite of the trap door and the only real chance of a way out. The corridors all look the same with the lights blinking on and off and I can't help but wonder how far this complex goes. Does is extend towards the Wall? Does it push on deep into the Wasteland?

Rewind a few weeks and I would have happily said to anyone with these crazed ideas that they needed some kind of medical help, but all that has gone. Everything I thought I knew, everything we've ever been told, it's all been lies, because whatever they've been doing down here, whatever they've been planning must have taken them years.

The light fizzes and blinks above me and I stare at the white bulbs that are spaced out along the length of the corridors. I've only ever seen these things in the Peoples' Court and in the water tunnels and never really thought about it before.

I know that some in the Lanes have managed to make generators from bits and pieces lying around, creating enough power for single bulbs but the voices from the speakers, Our Leader's face on the big screen in the Square, we knew that there was enough of the old technology from before The Great

Light to help with these things yet we never questioned why we didn't have access to it.

Why didn't we question more? Why did we simply accept what we were told.

"We created him…we gave him the power…"

My mind turns back to the words of the old woman that first night in the compound that now seems like a lifetime ago. Maybe she was right. Maybe this is all our fault?

I hear the muffled voices again but this time a little louder than before.

"Please help us!"

Spinning around I'm not sure if it's my mind playing tricks on me or the acoustics in this maze making things sound nearer than they actually are. Either way I'm alert to the possibility that it's another trap.

"I hear you but I don't know where you are?" Wincing at the sound of my own voice I look around, convinced *they* will hear me.

"We need help!"

And then I'm on my hands and knees in the gloom as the light continues to blink on and off, ignoring the thumping pain that has moved from the back of my head and now sits squarely behind my eyes because I know where the sound is coming from.

It's coming from the floor.

I crawl along the side of the corridor wall searching with my fingers when the light goes out, searching for an air vent, or a gap in the floor, anything that would let sound carry.

"...hear us! We're down here. They'll be back soon...please hurry..."

They'll be back soon

Adrenalin forces me on and I keep searching, keep feeling with my fingers until I think I've found what I'm looking for. When the light blinks on I stare directly at what my fingers have found so that when it falls dark I'll still have the imprint in my mind's eye.

As I'm plunged once more into gloom I close my eyes and I can still see the square piece of metal fixed between the floor and the wall. I don't know whether it's some sort of drainage or ventilation system and at this point I don't care because I can feel the slightest breeze on my face when I bend down and I can hear scrabbling around, like the rats that run around the Lanes. The rats that I've seen people fight over for food.

"Can you hear me? I don't know where you are. I can't find a way down to you!"

I feel useless and exposed as I crouch in this corridor, my shoulder screaming at me to stand up and stretch but I'm not moving until I hear someone.

"Oh thank God! It's some kind of pit. They've been putting us down here for hours. Some of us are already dead."

The last word chills me to the bone but at least I can hear the voice more strongly than before which gives me hope that they can't be that far away. Hope that River and Rainbow are somewhere down there too.

"Can you tell me anything you remember, anything that will help me get to you?"

My words are greeted by a silence that stretches out before me like one of these damn endless corridors.

"I don't know exactly. I can't..." The voice fades away and I strain to hear the next few words. "...corridor...large room...down the stairs..."

I look at the vent, or whatever it is and then further into the distance, squinting to see if there's another one.

"Stay near the vents."

Standing I check again at the vent I can see in the distance.

The voice drifts up from the floor barely audible, "...coming back...more of us..."

Jogging towards the vent looking ahead I see another and then another. When I reach the fourth one along I kneel down until my lips are almost touching the metal.

"I'm almost at the end of the corridor, where now?" But there's no response and I crouch not knowing what to do; stay and wait or get a move on. So my legs makes the decision for me and I'm up and running to the end of the corridor.

Surely if I can hear somebody then that means they can't be that far away? But I know that's not necessarily the case and I think back to Ellie and Doughnut, to the tricks we used to play on the adults; whispering down old pipes so they thought the voices were coming from somewhere near them. For all I know they could be somewhere deep below, I've no idea how far this facility extends and every footstep leads me to only one logical conclusion.

That the Wastelanders will get to me before I'm able to get to them.

I turn the corner at the end into another corridor but at least this one has continuous lighting, albeit very low, and as I continue to follow the vents, I see more and more rooms that look as though they've been ransacked like the other ones, red smears on the walls and pools of blood. But no bodies.

"…corridor…large room…down the stairs…"

But which corridor? As I continue to follow the vents I notice that the floor is sloping slightly as if I'm going down hill, further under the ground.

As I take a turn into a room on my left I see overturned filing cabinets and papers strewn across the floor. I skip over the obstacles and search the place but there's no stairs at the back and any way the room isn't really that big.

Somewhere in the distance, I hear the scream of a Wastelander and the noise freezes my blood. I can't tell how far away it is, whether it's at the trap door or further down where I'm headed.

Leaving the room I turn to my left and continue on until I come to some kind of wide landing area with a large unbroken window to my left. Two more corridors start up again across from me, one heading left and the other right and I can see that the left one heads off again downhill. But it's the large window that's got me interested.

"...large room...stairs at the back..."

It's by far the largest window I've seen. Larger than the room with the jars. With the heads.

The first thing I notice in the half light is that I can't see through it, at least the glass is darker than the other ones making it difficult to see in and as my hand moves up to touch it I'm surprised at how cold it feels.

Another cry in the distance compels me to move to the door and pushing it open I take a deep breath and step inside. The room is far larger than the others and although there's no light in here, there's enough coming from the corridor to show me that there's some kind of passageway at the far end.

I look for more vents at the side of the room but don't see any and it's only when I move through the room that I start to see my breath in front of my face. In all the rush and fear I hadn't even noticed that the temperature has dropped as I look down at my arms, at the hairs that are standing to attention. Why is it so cold?

I know I've got to move on. I know I've got to get to the end of the room, to the dark passageway and I start to weave in and out of the upturned boxes and tables, ignoring the crunching glass. Row upon row of shelves are in my way, some turned over, some still upright and as I battle my way through a series of bottles towards the back of the room in a large glass case catches my attention because it's just about the only unbroken thing I think I've seen since I set foot in this damn place.

I don't have time. I've got to move on but something pulls me back towards the bottles, a desire to find out more, as if I'm half expecting them to have things in them like the other ones but they're only small, no bigger than my hand. As I move nearer I can see from the corridor light that there's nothing in them at all apart from some sort of liquid; different colours for different bottles.

And labels.

I squint into the gloom getting as close as I can my hand trying the glass door but to no avail. The labels have writing on them but it's not handwriting like I've seen before because the lines are too neat and straight.

Batch 1243: Serum 56b

Batch 1244: Serum 56c

Batch 1245: Serum 57a

There are fifteen bottles altogether and I shiver in the cold as I stand back from the cabinet. There must be hundreds more boxes in this room scattered all over, god knows how many more bottles. Is this why the room is so cold, for whatever's in them?

I think back to the other room, the medical instruments, the large jars on the columns, the two heads. What was in the other two jars that had smashed on the floor?

Are they connected to these serums or whatever the hell they are?

Backing away from the bottles in the direction of the passageway I sense something in the air, as if it's being sucked out of the room.

Wastelander!

Holding my breath I stand as still as humanely possible as my eyes pivot as far as they are able and I scan the area for a sign of one of the creatures. Nothing. Turning quickly, before my nerves completely get the better of me, I step through into the passageway and see the stairs at the far end.

The first thing I notice is the temperature. It's even colder than the room was.

The second is the stench.

Chapter 49

As I move down the metal staircase I cover my nose and mouth with my sleeve and try not to gag, although my stomach is so empty that I can't imagine anything actually being able to come up.

The stairwell is tight and the walls have changed colour, no longer a brilliant white, more a muddy brown colour like the Lanes as it spirals to the left like a corkscrew, the light from the opening above beginning to fade.

Pushing on I begin to lose track of distance as the light grows almost pitch black so that I'm feeling my way along the moist wall, each foot tapping on the step until I reach the end and then gingerly stepping off into nothing. To fall now, to get injured is almost too much to bear.

Not now. Not this far in.

There's just enough light to know that the stairs are coming to an end because I can see a feint line of light, like a right angle down below to my left. As I hurry the next few steps I realise that it might be a door of some kind, my hands confirming this as I move off the last step, quickly tracing the outline of a metal door in the wall opposite.

I can't imagine the space I'm in to be much bigger than the arch of the door and I wonder if I'm in some kind of escape hatch or exit. My fist clenches as I make to hammer on the door and then I stop myself and look back at the winding stairwell imagining my only way out to be blocked by the contorted frame of a Wastelander.

"Hey! Is anybody there? Can anyone hear me?" The compromise is weak because I daren't raise my voice to anything louder than a whisper and I try to find the largest crack of light to speak into but this can only be a few millimetres at best.

After waiting for a response I step back to analyse the door with both eyes and hands and this time I locate some kind of wheel in the centre about a foot in diameter which has to be some kind of locking system.

"If you can hear me I'm going to try and turn the wheel. I'm going to…" The rest of the sentence trails to nothing because I have no real idea what I'm going to do and I place both hands on the cold metal deciding that clockwise is as best a way to turn it as any.

As soon as I put pressure on the wheel my right shoulder shoots pain all along my arm and down the side of my back and I try my best to ignore it as I strain against the wheel but it doesn't budge and I stop to get my breath, stretching out my hands and fingers.

Rotating my shoulder I place my hands on the wheel determined to at least budge the thing when my blood is chilled by the clicking of one of the creatures. It's feint and far off above me but I can hear it all right and if it means the same as outside then it's some kind of calling noise. It means there could be more than one and there heading towards me.

I have no way of knowing where it is because, as I've already found out, noise travels far down here, so it could be way off down the corridors.

It could also be at the top of the stairs.

Refocusing I turn my attention back to the wheel. Ignoring my shoulder I drop to my knees with the effort as I feel the wheel give a little. It's no more than a fraction of an inch but it gives me a little more hope.

Hope that evaporates when I hear the clicking of the creature again followed by something falling and crashing to the ground. I close my eyes and picture the Wastelander in the room above, papers spilling to the floor as it pushes tables and cabinets aside.

Maybe the blood has worn off and it can smell me? Maybe I've been making too much noise all along? Either way I'm back at the wheel straining as hard as my body will allow, blood rushing to my temples as if my head's about to explode with the pressure.

The noise again. Where the hell is it? Is it above me? Is it on the stairs? I strain harder on the wheel as it slowly begins to turn.

"COME ON!"

As it continues to turn it begins to creak loudly and I can't help but stop for fear of it alerting the Wastelander. The scream that is unleashed somewhere above tells me all I need to know and I try again desperate to get the lost momentum back.

The creature's talons scrape on the stairs above and I feel its presence looming over me as the wheel begins to turn again, slowly at first but then a little easier, the line of the door extending, dim light spilling into the stairwell as it begins to open. The creaking is mirrored by the creature's roar as I hear its claws scraping the sides of the wall, bounding down the stairwell.

I can feel it behind me and I lean with all my might on the wheel and then break for the door squeezing my body into the tiny gap as I feel its breath almost at my neck. My ribs cry out as I try to force myself through, my hips cracking against the edge as I instinctively lower myself and fall onto the other side, the Wastelander's claws slamming and scraping against the edge of the door.

Scrabbling onto my back I wince in anticipation of the hot, fetid breath as it descends upon me but it doesn't happen. Instead I see its arms waving wildly around the opening, swishing and scraping the air and I realise that it's too big for the gap. It can't get through.

My chest heaves up and down and I turn and push myself from the ground when its claws slip back into the gloom and for a split second I think its retreated and gone back up the stairs. The screech of the wheel tells me it hasn't and for a moment I'm powerless to do anything as I see the wheel begin to turn and the door move a few more millimetres.

Scrambling onto my feet I back up a few steps and then hit the door with all I've got. I hear the creature grunt on the other side as the door closes a little and I move back a few more paces and hit it again and again until I can't feel my body anymore, until the door has slammed shut.

Slumping to the ground I reach up with what remaining strength I have to turn the wheel the opposite way but there's too much tension on the other side for it to go far. My only chance is to move, to put some distance between myself and *it*.

Ignoring the pain and fatigue I stand unsteadily as its muffled screams galvanise me into movement and as I stumble away from the door I see for the first time where I am. The room is far larger than any of the others up above and walking on I see spaced out red bulbs lining the piping that runs above my head that seem to go on forever and that give the whole place an eerie, surreal feeling.

Steam shoots at me from various angles and I dodge it and move on as I notice that under my feet is a kind of gangplank or walkway of metal with what seems like hundreds of little holes in it; like the one in the water tunnel only far longer. The throbbing and humming of machines fills the air. It must be the engine room that powers the corridors and rooms above?

I start to jog as I need to put more distance between me and the door and as my eyes adjust to the low level light I begin to make out more and more of the room I'm in.

Room.

The word doesn't do it justice. It's more like a long wide ventilation shaft or something and as I move on I look to my left, to the edge of the walkway and beyond.

Leaning over the side to get a better look I begin to make out another section of flooring a few metres below the gangplank I'm on. I can still hear the screech of the wheel as the steam continues to jet from various pipes all around but there's definitely something below me, because I can see it moving against the holes.

The screech from the door galvanises me and I dodge the jets of steam and begin to run. The rattle from the pipes all around seems deafening as I keep one eye on the way ahead and one on the movement below. If it's more of *them* then I need to find another door and quick because I'm easy pickings in here and there's only so long the other door will hold it back.

But there's something else as well, something beneath the noise that I can't quite make it out as my footsteps reverberate off the metal walkway.

"…down here…"

The voice stops me dead and I cast an eye back towards the door. I definitely heard something that time.

And then I'm at the hand rail and looking down over the side onto the perforated flooring below except it doesn't look like that now, it looks like…

"WE'RE DOWN HERE!"

This time the voice is strong and urgent and as I climb over the rail and drop the two meters down below I can't help but call out.

"River? Rainbow? It's Jake." A feeling of excitement takes hold because the movement I saw earlier must have been human, mustn't it?

"...they can mimic us..."

I crouch down, sweat pouring off my brow. If it's a trap then I should be dead by now and as I see more movement below I look carefully through the holes in the metal to see arms moving, followed by a face.

It's Rainbow. And she's alive!

Chapter 50

"Jake! Jake! I can't believe it's you!"

I look around me and then back down to the floor because whatever joy I feel is stopped short by the sound of the door screeching at the far end of the walkway and the scream of the Wastelander.

"Listen, Rainbow, I've gotta…"

"They've been throwing us down here for hours now." Her voice is different somehow; strained and scared. "Some are dead, River's…" I can't hear her last words because some kind of commotion breaks out around her and I can hear other voices that I don't recognise.

"We can't reach it. You need to find the latch and lift from your end."

But I'm no longer listening because I can hear the Wastelander above, it's got through the door, and as I dart underneath the walkway I see something fly down from my left landing with a thud and a crunch metres from where I was standing.

It's a human body, and its face is turned towards me.

Forcing down a scream I look around me as those stuck below start to moan and weep. I've got to get out of sight but I've backed myself into a corner because if I run, it'll hear me and if I stay then there's every chance it will see me. Looking up I see how the walkway has been reinforced every few feet or so with metal rods that run its width.

Feeling above my head there's just enough space for my fingers to curl round and I swing my legs forward and up, trying to catch one of the other rods so that maybe I can hang there underneath. If it really wants to find me then it will but if it's busy with its catch then I might be okay.

The scrape of its talons on the metal above tells me that it's about to join the body down here and I swing again, this time wedging my right foot between the rod and the wall. It's not ideal as my arms are already shaking and I don't know how long my shoulder will hold out but as I search for somewhere to put my left foot I angle it horizontally and to the side and press it up against the nearer of the two rods so that at least the pressure can hold me in place for a little while longer.

The creature drops down with a grunt and I can see its deformed and elongated feet twitching on the metal as it scuttles over to the body. I'm far enough under the walkway that I can only see it from the knee down, but even that's enough, and I pull myself further up until my nose is practically touching the underside of the path.

Wiggling my fingers across the pole I find a little gap near to the side, enough that I can push my wrist through until my elbow can take more of the weight. Shifting from foot to foot I feel more confident that I can now stay up here for longer, if need be.

The problem is if it smells me!

I've got lots of the blood still on me, dried like a second skin but some of it must have come off and as I stare at its legs no more than a few meters from where I am I take a huge lungful of air, hold it in and pray.

For the longest time it just stands there sniffing the air, trying to locate me and all I can do is look into the open eyes of the body that lies beyond it, its right arm twisted beneath the stomach at right angles to how it should be as if the elbow has bent the wrong way. I don't recognise the face but I recognise the last emotions the poor man ever felt because they're etched on his lifeless face; pain and fear.

And then the body's on the move, being dragged like a lifeless doll by its foot across the metal flooring and I can hear more squeals from below as if they've been forced through this process a number of times.

From this angle I can see more of the creature now and as it huddles over the corpse. I can see the muscles in its back, sinewy and stretched like a network of veins and its bony arms with the scars of battle crisscrossed all over.

It stands and I can only see its legs again as it shudders and strains, a strange gargling noise spewing from its mouth as a large panel of the flooring starts to creak open.

And then the noise comes.

"Jesus no…"

"Please let us go…"

"Is this one alive?"

As screams and shouts leap from below. I can see the creature struggle with the corpse as it keeps one claw on the metal lid, the other scrabbling for purchase on the body.

"Keep away! KEEP AWAY!"

The voices are desperate and fearful and my arms begin to shake as I watch the Wastelander almost drop the lid on its own leg as it screams in frustration; its talons not suited for this kind of task. I can't hold on for much longer, my body stretched to breaking point.

Rush it!

The thought comes from nowhere and I freeze as the idea echoes around my mind.

Rush it! Kick it down there!

And then I hear Ellie's voice as if she's right here alongside me.

"Harness *their* fear! Let *them* deal with it!

Now it's Doughnut's and I picture all three of us huddled together on the slum rooftops of Sanctum, conjuring up some stupid scheme or other to while away the morning. Before I've had time to even decide, my legs are unfolding from the metal struts and I stifle a yell as my muscles creak and groan.

In my mind's eye I can see as clear as if they were next to me; Doughnut with that stupid, goofy grin of his and Ellie looking at me with her brow all furrowed ushering me forward with a wave of the hand as if it's my turn to start the trouble, my turn to get it all going.

As my feet touch the floor I slide my arm through and stretch it out a few times, my eyes never leaving the back of the Wastelander now balancing the metal on its knee as the corpse is dragged along side. I wait in the shadows until it lifts the lid high, arm outstretched…

GO!

In less than four strides I'm directly behind it and with whatever strength I have left I kick out at the base of its spine just as it turns. For a split second our eyes are locked and I can see brown speckles throughout the blue iris and then it lets out an almighty scream as my foot connects with its spine, snapping bone, propelling it forward into the edge of the lid.

As the creature scrabbles to retain balance I kick again because if this doesn't work, if it gets its senses back, then i'm dead and I know it. My foot barely glances its hip but it doesn't matter because momentum is now against it as it desperately scrabbles to keep hold of the lid.

I hear people scattering below screaming and shouting as the thing crashes down into the cage, my chest and lungs screaming with the effort. In my mind's eye both Doughnut and Ellie are yelling something at me but it's as if they're in slow motion and as I look back at them, at their mouths open wide I begin to understand what their saying.

It's two words and as I realise what they are I find myself shouting them out as well.

"KILL IT!

Chapter 51

I fall to my hands and knees and crawl to the edge of the drop as the creature crashes to the bottom and for a split second there's nothing, except the desperate cries of the beast as it writhes in pain as the people below part like water.

"For God's sake KILL IT!"

And then movement as first one moves alongside the writhing body fists raised, then another, then another, until all I can see is a flurry of arms and legs kicking, screaming, tearing.

A single organism bent on destruction.

On revenge.

When it's over I can't help but look back at the Wastelander, unrecognisable from the onslaught as part of its chest continues to rise in jerky, sporadic movement.

No one wants to speak. No one knows what to say but we've got to because this is our only chance to try and get out before more of them arrive as they surely will. Forcing myself into movement I lean over the side and look down into the hole at the scared and bloodied faces that look back. I can see figures slumped to the sides not moving and try not to wretch at the smell.

"Jake! Oh thank God!" I see a figure rush from the side and as it approaches the centre of the hole I make out Rainbow's long, dark hair, straggly and damp but it's hers alright and my heart lifts at the sound of her voice. I want to tell her how happy I am to see her, how much we've been through to get back here. I want to hold her but there's no time and I stretch my arm as far as it will go.

"Can you grab on to my arm? Get River to give you a push!" And then her face falters as she looks back into the gloom.

"He's hurt, Jake. Leg's broken."

"Hey, tell him I'm okay! Kick his ass if I need to!" I can barely hear River above the noise but I can tell his voice is weak as if his strength has left him. Looking to the right as hands creep over the edge of the hole I realise that others are beginning to help each other climb out.

We've got to go now. We've got to.

"Can you move him, Rainbow? Can you get him over here?"

She disappears into the gloom as the first person makes it out of the hole, wild eyed and dishevelled.

"Hey! Where do I go? Where do I go?" He looks directly at me and then at the corpse behind me as he drags himself up and over the edge. More hands emerge from the gloom struggling to hold onto the edge, crying for help.

"Help me! Pull me up...pull me up!" But the man's gone, running off into the distance and I go to shout after him when I feel a hand on my wrist pulling me down towards the hole.

"P...Please help...please..."

"Hey...hey! Don't pull me down! Let me..." But the panic in the woman's eyes tells me she's not listening and my arm starts to give out as the weight of her body nearly topples me into the hole and then she starts to lift and I can hear Rainbow below.

"Pull her up, Jake. Get her out of here!"

When she's finally out of the hole, my chest heaving, biceps pumped with the adrenalin I look back down as I begin to get jostled by other people as they emerge.

"Can you move? Can you stand?" I try to keep my voice steady, light even, but I can see from how pale River looks that something's badly wrong as he drags himself into the light, grimacing as his leg follows, twisted and broken in what looks like several places, the blood from his side wound leaking onto the floor.

He fixes his eyes on me and I can see the determination in his face as he urges his body to rise with all his strength. Rainbow hurries to his side to help him as he grimaces with pain.

"You shouldn't be doing this. We can make it!" She looks back to me for help but there's none I can give and I half turn as the scream of another Wastelander sounds far off in the distance.

"Grab her arm, Jake! Pull her up!"

"No. NO! We'll get you up first won't we Jake! Won't we?" She look at the two of us again but River's eyes are fixed firmly on mine as the sweat pours from his forehead and whatever colour there was in his face drains away until he looks little more than a ghost.

He's not going anywhere. We both know it.

"I'll get up after you." He tries to smile but only the corners of his mouth flicker. "Someone down here will give me a lift." As he speaks he shuffles Rainbow towards me until I can almost reach her and then takes her hand in his lifting it towards my outstretched arm. "Jake's got you, he's not going to let you go anywhere." He stares up into my eyes and I nod and then clear my throat as the scream sounds again somewhere in the corridor's above.

"Grab my hand Rainbow! That's it, hold on tight!" And then River grabs her around the waist and lifts her up with all his strength and I see his good leg begin to buckle, grabbing her arm just as he begins to fall.

"Get her out of here, Jake. Get her out, NOW!"

I pull until my arms burn, my shoulder crying out in pain as we collapse into a heap at the side of the hole and then she's up and at the edge, both hands over stretched towards River, tears spilling from her eyes.

"Please River. Please take my hand! Please!" The Wastelander's scream sounds a lot closer than before.

"Get her away Jake. NOW!" I place my hand on her shoulder but she shrugs it off and makes to jump down into the hole so I grab her by the arms as she spits and wriggles and begin to move her in the direction some of the others have run.

"Let me go, let me go! River. RIVER!"

"We've got to move. We've got to get out of here."

"Go with him Sis! I'll see you soon. I'll see you real soon."

I feel completely numb as I drag Rainbow away from the hole. Don't even feel her hit me on the chest, or really even hear what she's screaming at me. I just hold on and keep pulling her until I feel her arms loosen a little as she stops fighting me. I keep dragging her along until she stumbles and drops to her knees.

"We've got to go back! WE'VE GOT TO!" But there's no real strength left in her voice because she knows deep down that there was no way he was getting out of there and she looks up at me as two others run past us, her face streaked with dirt and tears.

"Please come on." I look behind her as a clicking sound fills the air and I see a hunched figure in the distance jump down and make its way towards the hole. I don't even know where we're going or whether there's even a way out of this damn place but I know we've got to put as much distance between us and the creature.

River

River's face flashes up into my mind and I have to shake it clear because if I think too much then I'm not going anywhere. I look up as Rainbow stands and looks directly at me, as if she knows what I've just seen, as if she knows what's moving towards the hole, towards her brother.

Her face is hollow and emotionless. Her eyes full of hate. I just don't know who it's aimed at; me or the creature.

"They dragged us down some stairs, some winding stairs that lead from the surface." Her voice if flat, as if she's cut off her emotions and she moves past me without looking. I follow silently because there's nothing else to say.

Because from behind me, from the direction of the hole, the screams have started.

When we reach the far end of the chamber I see an open door with the same wheel on it as the one I came through earlier and I can hear the footsteps and voices of the others as they make for a way out.

As I follow Rainbow onto the steps my mind keeps returning to River, to his eyes as they locked onto mine, to his face as he pushed her up with all his strength.

My legs begin to buckle as images rush in for everywhere, as my mind begins to give up its hold on the here and now.

The stairs spiral upwards seemingly forever as I see Rainbow's hair swish around above me, as I hear the yells and shouts of those ahead of us, the screams of those behind.

Lactic acid builds up in my calves until they feel like they're going to explode.

River

I shake my head and grip onto Rainbow as the stairs spiral round because I've got to get her out. I've got to get her to safety. I promised River and I'm not about to let him down.

As my head starts to wobble, spots swimming into my vision I think I make out something dimly up ahead in the direction we're moving, a body. And then Rainbow starts to yell.

"No! No! don't close it…don't…" I nearly run into the back of her and have to take a step back as she stretches out her arms and catches the metal lid before it's forced shut.

"They're coming up. We can't let them out. We can't let them…"

"Jake! Don't just bloody stand there! Give me a hand for Christ's sake!" For a moment I can only blink at the scene in front of me, the face of the man above disappearing as the lid continues to close, the night sky above him, stars twinkling.

"Help her Jake! Get her out of here!"

River's voice is like an electric shock and I step forward and place my hands on the cold metal, push with all my might as the lid slowly stops moving towards us.

"We, we need to shut them in!" The man's voice is at fever pitch, gripped by fear and I put my shoulder to the lid, propelling myself upwards with everything I've got until the lid starts to move the other way. Until I'm half way up the ladder, my torso out in the open air. The man has fallen onto his backside and he stares at me open mouthed.

"Th…those *things* are down there! We…we've got to shut the lid!" Rainbow pushes alongside me on the ladder, dragging herself up and out by her arms, until she rolls onto the dirt a few feet away.

"They're up here as well!"

Dragging myself up I scramble to close the lid as the Wastelander's scream echoes up the stairwell. I'm running on instinct as the smell of disease starts to pour from the hole. If I can't get it closed then we're all dead and I strain with whatever strength I have left. "Jesus! It's almost reached us!"

As the lid begins to close I feel it lift again as the creature thuds into it from underneath and it's all I can do to stop myself rolling off the damn thing. Rainbow is a few yards away but I can see that her eyes have gone, she's glazed over, lost somewhere in her own mind. "Rainbow! RAINBOW!" Her head turns a little and she looks up at me. "We've got to get this lid closed, NOW!"

As the creature hits it again I half turn onto my side and press down with all my weight. There are claw marks in the earth where its talons have broken the surface and I know that if it hits again I won't be able to hold on. "Please Rainbow! Please."

At first I don't see her and I think that it's a Wastelander coming from somewhere in the darkness, and then she's by my side and we both push down with all our might as the Wastelander screams and thrashes. "Push! PUSH!"

The talons slide from under the lid and I roll away to avoid them and then they're gone as if its fallen on the stairs trying to get a better hold. I can hear it scream again but it seems a little further away this time. "NOW!" Rainbow practically jumps on the lid and it gives way at last, slamming shut as the creature's scream is stopped dead in its tracks.

We're safe. For now.

Chapter 52

All I can do is slump onto my back, my chest heaving up and down, lungs grateful for the fresh air, pain wracking almost every inch of my body.

The mist has thinned and as I look at the sky I can see patterns in the stars that I don't think I've ever seen before. It looks for all the world as if someone has deliberately arranged them that way as they sparkle down at me.

I try to make sense of all that I've seen even though I know it's useless. As far as I'm concerned the world stopped spinning what seems like an age ago and it hasn't started up yet. I need to tell someone about the serum, about the white corridors, the rooms.

The heads.

"Rainbow!" As I turn to my left I see her standing up and staring into the distance. Ignoring the pain in my knees I push myself up alongside her looking at the side of her face, how intent she's staring and then I follow the direction she's looking. And then I'm the one staring.

The Great Wall stands perhaps five hundred metres or so in front of us, bodies littering the ground, which means that we're standing further into the Wasteland than I think anyone has ever stood, and survived. But that doesn't seem to matter now, not after all that we've been through.

"Can you see the lights?"

Rainbow's voice is low and calm as she stares ahead. I look beyond the Wall into Sanctum itself and I begin to make out orange glows of different sizes shimmering in the distance.

"I don't think they're lights, I think they're fires!"

I turn towards her but she's already striding off in the direction of the Wall and for a split second I'm all alone in the dark.

"Hey, Rainbow! Where are you going?" She stops and I see her shoulders move up and down, sobs coming from deep within.

"River." Her head bows down and I see her shoulder rise up and then she takes a deep breath and looks back at me with the fierce defiance I saw in her face the first time we met back in the compound. "My brother told me where he said for Samson and Dodge to go!"

And then she turns and strides off into the distance and I want to call after her but I don't know what to say or do as she begins to disappear into the gloom. I don't even know if she wants me with her as I start to follow. Everything's changed.

Everything.

Looking past her my eyes fix on the flickering orange lights on the Wall. If the Wastelanders are out in the open now then there's no telling what damage they've done to Sanctum and my mind turns back to River's pale face in the gloom of the cage.

I promised him I'd look after Rainbow, that we'd meet Samson and Dodge by the Peoples'

Court, and then there's Ellie and Doughnut somewhere beyond the fires, waiting for me too.

As I follow Rainbow into the darkness, the moonlight our only comfort, a simple realisation breaks over me.

That whatever has happened.

That whatever *this* is.

It's only the beginning.

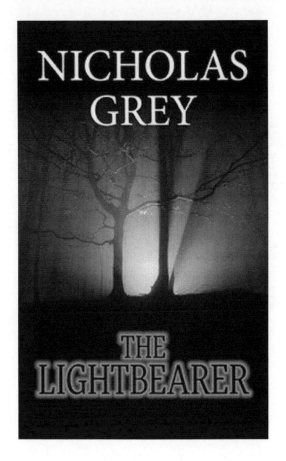

Printed in Great Britain
by Amazon